FLAME OF
THE OSAGE

FLAME OF THE OSAGE

FRED GROVE

CUTTING EDGE

ISBN-13: 978-1-962896-28-3

Published by
Cutting Edge Books
PO Box 8212
Calabasas, CA 91372
www.cuttingedgebooks.com

CHAPTER ONE

THE SIGN on the peeled red boards of the depot read TWO SANDS, which gave the place a name, if little else. At first glance it was merely two lines of frame buildings, brash yellow in places with the brightness of new planking. When you looked further toward the town's core, there was a cluster of weathered sandstone structures glowering above the crowded street. Beyond this, wooden derricks made spiderweb tracings against the late afternoon sky. An unfamiliar smell blew out of the southwest. A devil's mixture of grease and sulphur, sharpened by September heat, compounded of dust and the town's unwashed closeness.

The train—an engine, coal car and two coaches—had paused briefly, as if impatient to escape through the shaggy blackjacks and the distant, rounded hills. Like a man in a hurry, it had deposited Myles Pearce and the other passengers and left them on the windy platform. The cowman, the man with the merchandise kits, the oil scout and the gambler took off at once, going up the dusty street with a kind of hopeful expectancy.

Myles lingered a moment, because he dreaded the chore ahead of him.

He was frowning when he crossed the tracks with long-legged steps, grip in hand, shoulders tight in the unaccustomed suit coat. Following a beaten footpath, he had the sensation of a violent pulse in the air. A grumbling, clanking and snorting from the oil field, a humming racket from the busy street. The humping hills drew his attention and the sight momentarily lifted his depression. In them he read the promise of land he'd known elsewhere, anchored firmly by native grasses, cooled by winds from far-off places.

But, bringing his interest back to the town, he felt the impression fade. For no reason at all Two Sands reminded him of a smoky-eyed woman, giving and yet taking, whose invitation welled up from the same depths that also could make her cruel.

Well, he thought without enthusiasm, Frank always liked a town with the hair on.

Turning in on the boardwalk, hollow-sounding under his boots, he found himself drifting by a stream of high-wheeled automobiles, wagons and saddle horses. He smelled the kicked-up dust and the warm, earthy odors. He saw a string of six-horse teams, headed out of town, straining against sections of chattering steel oil-well casing chained on heavy wagon frames. He admired the massive animals, matched blacks and grays, and noted the circus effect of white and red rings on the stout harness rigging.

A raucous honking smote his ears. He saw a young Indian, obviously enjoying himself, steering his red roadster like a battleship through the sea of horse and wagon traffic. The outbound teamsters cursed the intrusion, but had no time to argue the right-of-way.

Soon Myles, moving under wooden awnings that shaded the walk, began noticing bright blankets. These oil-rich Osages were big Indians, heavy and broad-faced, most of the old ones still braided. Booted ranchers, their plain-faced women and restless kids, strayed in and out of the stores, the elders yarning with neighbors. Brawny drilling crews in candy-striped shirts puffed on tailor-made cigarettes and picked their teeth in front of crowded short-order cafes. Meat frying smells, strong along the street, whetted Myles' hunger.

All this made him think of the Burbank strike a couple years back, when he'd caught the boom spirit briefly and drawn his fourteen dollars a day dressing tools. Except Two Sands had an air of arrogant permanence, a going cowtown become a still more prosperous oil town.

Down the street he saw uneven lettering on a swinging tin sign, OSAGE HOTEL, ROOM & MEALS. He came to it and entered a dingy lobby, filled with tobacco smoke and groups of noisy men. Everybody seemed to be speaking at the same time or trying to.

Through the steady babel, he crossed to the combination clerk's desk and cigar counter. "Room?"

The clerk scowled. "Not much left." His brush moustache looked black against his pale, peevish face as he slid the register around. "Take twenty-four—second floor. Wouldn't have that, but they had a big lease sale in Pawhuska today."

Myles signed his name and after it added, "Flint Hills, Kansas." Picking up his room key, he asked quietly, "Know a man named Rikker—Frank Rikker?"

"I'm new here. Better see Old Man Hill. Comes on at eight. Or you might ask at the Palace Pool Hall."

"Much obliged."

Unlocking his door, Myles entered a storehouse of musty, stifling heat. The staleness drove him to the window, which he jerked high. All at once the metallic sounds of Two Sands crashed in, rising and falling. He listened several seconds, aware of a returning dejection.

With luck, he told himself, I'll be out of here tomorrow.

There was some measure of comfort in the thought Quickly, he poured tepid water from the cracked pitcher into the bowl on the dresser, scrubbed himself, shrugged into a clean shirt, and went downstairs to the cramped dining room.

It was coming on early evening when he finished his meal. Impatience carried him outside. A wind came pulsing in the early twilight, pelting fine grit against the boardwalk and the grimy hotel windows. It came on steady pressure from the wide-shouldered hills, purple now along the broken skyline. It rolled in weighted with freshness and the mystery of space, dissolving the hanging sulphur smell. He breathed it in lonesomely, for it had the tang of the hill country he'd left behind farther north.

At last, he turned down the street.

He found the Palace noticeable by its activity and reek. Men tramped in and out in a steady stream. Myles, filing through, met a thickness of layered smoke and the moist smell of sweaty bodies. Billiard balls made a constant clicking above the murmuring talk. Domino players shuffled and slapped the oblong pieces.

He stood a while, idly scanning the crowded tables, then crossed to the counter. It took a moment to catch the attention of the squat, bald-headed man behind it. "Frank Rikker around tonight?"

"Who's that?"

Myles repeated his question, though he thought he'd said it distinctly enough.

The man seemed on the verge of answering when his washed-out glance hooked upon a lounger in range clothes who'd half-turned at the name. "Not a sign," came the snapped-off reply.

Myles, without knowing why, realized he'd expected something like that. He persisted gently, "Know where he works?"

Watery eyes wavered. "Hard to keep up with everybody."

"You know him, then?"

"Heard the name's all."

Almost too casually, the ranch hand had turned so that he faced Myles, who saw yellow, quarrelsome eyes strike across him in an expression difficult to define. This man had a broad, flat nose, thick lips and a solid, compact body. His expensive high-peaked Stetson and loud checkered shirt appeared at odds with the soiled Levis, dirtier than any man's need be, and the sandy, stubbled face.

Myles recognized the breed. Not a real working puncher or a boom camp laborer. Just one of the many hardcases drifted into the Osage. Just Burbank all over again.

"Maybe," Myles asked, easy and unhurried, "you know Frank Rikker?"

"Never heard of him. Why?"

"I'm looking for him."

"That or snoopin' for whiskey peddlers?"

Myles allowed a definite bite of irritation to enter his tone. "I look like a Federal?"

"They take all shapes. Or maybe you're an oil scout?"

Myles slow-grinned. "I can't qualify there, either. The point is I haven't seen Frank Rikker in a long time."

"How long?"

"Oh, some time."

"Kin of his?"

"Could be."

The blocky body slowly stiffened. The yellow stare threw back a glint of interest. "Well, ain't you or not?"

Myles tried to rein in his annoyance, but it tore loose. "For a man who's never heard of Frank Rikker, you seem pretty interested."

His words broke on a building stillness. He became conscious of men staring, of games stopping. The man's unwarranted bad humor astonished him. Yet he'd seen killings touched off by less in Burbank. Old warning signals flashed. He waited, his arms slack.

It came sooner than he expected, savage, wholly unreasonable. "Nobody calls me a liar, Jake!"

"Don't call me Jake."

At that moment a man, cue stick in hand, stepped across. "Come on, Kutch," he broke in mildly, at the same time sizing up Myles. "You're in this next game." His dark, shrewd face loomed a full head higher than his bulkier companion. He was drawn down to the stringy meat of his bones, with a level speculation in the narrowed eyes above the Roman nose. He took Kutch's thick arm.

Kutch shrugged him off. "Go 'way, Lee." His temper seemed to harden, fanned by a moody surliness. "I said nobody calls me a liar, Jake! Y'hear?"

Myles recognized the familiar tension of a wolfish crowd, hushed for a fight. Trouble was the last thing he wanted after traveling this far, but he heard himself saying wearily, "You're calling it yourself." Once more he was waiting—a somewhat raw-boned man, seemingly indifferent.

Kutch took two quick steps, springing along the counter. His left hand shot out, clamping upon Myles' right. But he caught the old barrows maneuver. As Kutch swung a haymaker for the knockout, Myles planted his feet wide, braced. He jerked backward suddenly and felt his trapped wrist rip free as knuckles swished past his face, narrowly missing.

On instinct Myles threw a short, looping left. It slammed Kutch alongside the jaw, a whapping clout that shocked the quiet. Kutch heaved around, hurt and surprised. Myles smashed the broad nose. Blood spouted. Kutch screamed. He swayed.

Then Myles drove his right to the thick middle. The blow had all his weight behind it. Kutch sagged, buckled. He landed on his rump and kept flattening. He lay there, unable to rise.

The entire violent thing had happened in moments.

Lee just stared in disbelief. Convinced, he raised a damning glance.

"He's yours," said Myles, breathing fast. Till an instant ago he'd fought without deep feeling. Now a shaking anger rolled inside him, because Kutch had brought on a senseless brawl.

Still glowering, Lee stooped and lifted. But he couldn't handle Kutch. Two men joined him. Together they got Kutch up and outside.

"Where th' hell's Coon Pollard at?" exploded the counterman. "Been a fight here ever' night for a month!"

Men laughed. Presently, the crowd returned to the pool and domino tables and the games resumed as if nothing unusual had happened.

"What about Frank Rikker?" Myles insisted. "You same as said you knew him."

"By name, that's all." The bald-headed man continued to watch the door. Another moment and his voice dropped off, low. "Maybe you don't know it, but you picked on trouble there in Tharp Kutch."

"That so?" Myles felt resentful.

"A fact. He's rough. Funny thing happened one time. Man named Ed Yancey braced Kutch. Right in here—same as you. Few weeks later they found him in an alley—knifed. Couldn't prove a thing. Funny…"

A customer came across the conversation, and Myles, recognizing a hard wall when he ran against it, walked out. Still, he'd been warned.

Kutch and Lee weren't in sight, so he went toward the hotel. He walked slowly, in puzzled thought, at a loss to fathom Kutch's reason for picking a fight.

The lobby clock showed some ten minutes before Hill came on, and Myles decided to wait outside and savor the faint coolness. Other men bunched along the walk, talking in low tones. He was absently observing the street when up it rode an Indian on a pinto pony, followed by a flop-eared brown and white hound. Myles paid no particular attention until the horseman reined up, slid off on the Indian side, the right, and tied up to a hitching rack.

Next the Indian freed a gunny sack from behind the cantle and lumbered into a grocery store, much in the unconcerned manner of an ambling brown bear. Shortly, he returned with the sack bulging. He hoisted it behind the cantle, securely tied it with the leather skirt strings, then unwrapped a package, squatted down, and began tossing chunks of meat to the eager hound.

FRED GROVE

The Osage might have been forty years old or sixty. It was hard to tell. Time, it seemed to Myles, had marked him at some vague point in life and left him unchanged thereafter. He was hatless, his coal-black hair was in two ropy braids in which stringers of bright red cloth had been woven. His brown shirt was as shapeless as his grub sack, worn without care, open at the neck and down the first few buttons. His vast trousers hung loosely, somehow held up by the miraculous strength of a slender length of cotton rope, knotted at the ends. His feet, covered in plain, unbeaded moccasins, were broad sub-structures for the ponderous body.

He was a man of many layers of thicknesses. And this solid girth, hunkered down, made him look shorter, although he had lacked little of matching Myles' rangy height when he stood by the pony. He had a wide slab of mahogany face, a fullblood's fleshy face, eyes the color of campfire coffee; and curving down, buttressing the rough features, was a mighty stanchion of hooked nose. But the huge furrows of his grin, creasing fully now while he fed his dog, made Myles forget everything except his expression of contentment.

Boots clipped the plank walk. Myles saw a cowman step across to the Indian. "Howdy, Charlie."

The Osage glanced up, said, "How, Clark," but continued to feed the hound.

"Been wantin' to talk to you," the white man spoke amiably, lowering his voice. From the restless way he held himself there was about him a mixture of high-strung impatience and headstrong impulsiveness. He looked around thirty or more, trimmed to a rider's lankness, eyes quick and nervous, maybe a little worried.

"Jus' come in."

"I know. Been lookin' for you. It's about the lease."

Charlie stood and pitched the last piece of meat. The dog caught it and wolfed it down. Charlie let the paper flap away on the wind before he spoke. "Yeah, 'bout the lease."

"Time's about up. I want to renew it."

The Osage said nothing for a space. Myles had shifted back to check the lobby clock, but even here the voices were distinct. The men against the hotel wall were watching intently. It came to Myles that they waited for something he didn't know about.

Finally, the Osage said, "Changed m'mind."

"What!"

"Yeah."

"No call for that." There was, Myles thought, a desperation mounting in the rancher's voice. "I always paid my grass bill on time. You know that."

"Yeah. 'Cept yuh put too many cows'n pasture." And now the fullblood showed his first real hint of any emotion. "Brush grow up." He waved a plank of a hand for emphasis. "Grass mighty bad."

"Listen, can I help it if we have a long dry spell and the cows graze 'er down to the ground? Why, I been depending on your grass, Charlie. Sid Tyson's got everything covered like a blanket between here an' the Hominy country. Nothing left but yours."

"I tol' yuh 'bout too many cows, but yuh went ahead," Charlie countered stubbornly. Still, he seemed incapable of great anger.

"Mean you'll let it lay idle for a year?" Clark's tone changed to a hopeful note.

He got an abrupt shake of the broad head. "Sid gonna get lease. Sid m'friend."

Clark took a forward step. "By God," he cried passionately, "you'd do that! Lease it away from me! Why, you'll break me!"

"Sid give his word. Not too many cows." Charlie said it in a determined spacing of the words, yet with a noticeable reluctance.

Clark was beaten into silence. He stared down, and Myles could understand what the loss of a grass lease could mean. At length, he heard Clark's angry voice, "I'll remember this, Charlie. So will you!" His face firmed, settled in a bleak frame of defeat. He turned miserably away.

The Osage watched him go, the decision in the hewn face struggling against a faint bewilderment. In a moment he crawled aboard the pony, grunted to the hound, and rode off.

A man drawled close to Myles, "Oil money sure makes an Osage ride high in the saddle. But Charlie Blackhorse might be right. Clark Slater's no Sunday school teacher."

A different clerk stood behind the desk inside when Myles entered the lobby. He was a very old man, this Hill the day clerk had mentioned, but thinly erect and the shadow of better years still faintly marking him, except that a beaten caution peered out of eyes which once had been prouder and braver.

"I'm afraid I can't help you much," Hill answered after Myles put his question. "Folks come an' go fast in these oil fields." He smiled in a vague sort of way.

"Don't figure he'd be working at that. He'd be on a ranch."

Hill's smile faded. "You're sure he comes to Two Sands?"

Myles nodded. "Got a card from him postmarked Two Sands. He mentioned a ranch job. I wrote ahead before I left. Told him to meet me at the main hotel."

"This is the main hotel, all right." Hill smiled again, briefly. "The only one in town."

"He must come in here. Everybody seems to."

"Well, now, I can't say for sure." The old man hesitated, and Myles had the sudden conviction that he saw evasion in the thin wedge of face.

Myles leaned forward. "You know him or don't you?"

"Frank Rikker … well." Hill returned a straight look. It told nothing, absolutely nothing. His fingers drummed the desk top.

"We're foster brothers," Myles said. "I didn't tell you that."

Old Man Hill sighed. His eyes were at once keen, no longer evading, almost apologetic. "Any time a stranger comes in here and inquires about a man, I try to help if I figure it's right. But sometimes, even when I know, I keep my mouth shut … Yes, guess I know Frank Rikker."

Elation climbed in Myles. It shaded off when he saw the lack of response. He was almost afraid to ask, "What's the matter? Frank in trouble?"

"Didn't say he was, did I?" Hill rapped back. He'd become tight-lipped again, with the caution of a man who'd caught himself on the brink of talking too much before a stranger.

"Look," said Myles, stepping back, "all I want to know is where I can find him. What ranch."

The careful eyes narrowed. "Well, you might ask at Sid Tyson's place. Northeast of town. But you never heard it from me."

"Good enough." Curiously, Myles added, "This Tyson some bull of the big prairie?"

But Old Man Hill had turned to the key rack, his interest focused there. He'd said his piece, Myles realized. This was all.

"Much obliged."

Outside, Myles felt a growing bafflement as he walked toward the taxi stand he'd noticed earlier. He sensed that it wasn't so much what Hill had told him, but what he'd left unsaid. He was annoyed to find the taxi stand deserted. He intended to go to the Tyson ranch tonight. Waiting was suddenly intolerable. Begrudging the delay, he decided to walk around town till bed time. First thing in the morning he would hire a car and finish his errand.

He found himself strolling in the direction of the depot. Traffic had slimmed to a scattering of late-leaving wagons and automobiles. The crowd thinned. Soon he walked alone. The only noises growled distantly from the oil field beyond the town. Scores of gas flares made the scene eerie. He felt a near stillness for the first time since arriving in Two Sands.

So it was, when he stepped from the boardwalk to the path, that he picked up a rustle of sound somewhere behind him. He glanced over his shoulder and stopped, seeing nothing. A vague feeling tapped him and passed. Going on, he wondered if his reflexes were playing tricks again. In France, on night patrol in the dark, brooding forests, he'd experienced the same shadowy but sure sense many times. But this was Two Sands.

At the depot, he lingered over a cigarette and noted that blackness had already come to this end of town. While he considered the street, more lights snapped off in the shack stores and eating joints. Only establishments in the center stayed lighted.

Unhurriedly, he started retracing his way. His boots rapped the boards and he approached the rise of black buildings on his right. Walking past the first frame shack, he had no premonition of wrongness. He was thinking of Frank Rikker, of their feuding that retreated so far into the years it was hard to remember when they had not wrangled. Regret filled him and Dow Rikker's rough old voice echoed in his mind. "I'm not ordering you to bring him back, Myles. It's up to you. Except it's been a long time. A whole damned lonesome year for Sarah and me."

And here he was, because he owed a debt of long standing. He felt an upsurge of impatience, tinged with bitterness, knowing that he hadn't counted on Frank to meet him.

He went by the shack and was nearing the second, where a black gap yawned between it and the next, when an unaccountable coldness raced up his spine. It was an awareness in the silence, imperceptible and yet close upon him. It touched alive an instinct that went beyond thought.

It handed him around, facing the darkened opening. Even as he jerked, all his muscles strung wire-tight, he knew that he wasn't alone.

It happened without any warning. Out of the black opening rushed a man. Myles glimpsed the closing image of a body and one arm raised menacingly and striking downward. Splinters of pain bit through his shoulder before he could dodge. The blow staggered him. All at once he felt himself break to his knees, striving to block the rain of knuckles hammering his face and chest. He tasted blood, hot and salty. Dazed, he rolled aside and managed to brace up on tottering legs. The indistinct bulk before him crouched and bored in, threw a roundhouse right and missed. Myles backed up, still bewildered by the unexpected attack. He had the illogical thought, He's got the wrong man. He'll know in a second.

But a swinging blow rang his head. Myles wiped blood from his mouth and the recklessness of fury exploded in him. He had ceased backing. His head was clearing. He drove forward, both fists working. He felt his knuckles strike flesh and bone. He loved the violent feel.

Just for a brief interval the man gave ground, off the walk, his face blurred by the sooty darkness between the shacks. Then he lowered his head and Myles felt his belly cave in. During one sogged-out flash of agony, he had no wind, no strength. His legs buckled and his arms dropped. He caught the quick, hoarse breath, "Get outa town!"

Some involuntary sense sent Myles ducking in, arms grasping the muscled torso. He hung on, doggedly absorbing the punishing jabs, till finally he could drag in great gulps of air, till the light-shattering dizziness quit.

Heaving, grunting, Myles lurched free. He cracked his shoulder into the weaving shape and felt it spin backward. The man cried out. He was flung against a flimsy wall. Glass crashed inside, the noise sharply brittle in the night A shout came from down the street.

With swift elation, Myles leaped after him. As he moved he saw the man's body bend and spring in that crouch, heard a wild and broken noise in the hacking throat. They met solidly in the tricky dimness, blindly slugging.

Somewhere boots pounded loose planking. There came electric shouts of "Fight! Fight!"

Immediately Myles could feel a frantic desperation, a hurry, in the man. The blows rained faster. Myles waded in, seized with an overpowering hate to wreck any part of this tireless fighter. He felt no pain, just a fierce, primitive joy when he took the knuckles and landed his own. Suddenly, he yearned to finish it.

He barreled forward—and flailed only emptiness. He whirled and searched the ebony depths, alert for a ruse. He didn't understand till he caught the race of boots toward the alley, then it was too late. Sheer impulse carried him some steps onward before he hauled up.

Rough voices shouted at him from behind. He turned and sighted men huddled in the street, upon the walk. He went unsteadily toward them.

"What's goin' on in there?"

A heavy weariness pressed across Myles' shoulders. His hand, brushing his bruised mouth, came away wet, sticky. His face felt puffy. His chest and arms ached. His head throbbed. He'd taken a pretty stiff handling. Not yet had he answered the voices, for his dull mind was fixed on that white blob of his fallen hat. He found it near the walk.

"Hey, you! Speak up! Where's the other guy?"

Swaying a little, Myles scowled at them. He was not looking for sympathy, nor would he have found it. What held him was the gleaming savagery of a boom-town crowd, these men brawlers themselves, now put out because they'd missed what had sounded like one fine knockdown-dragout.

Deep in Myles a spark of still-smoldering anger flared high. "Expect him to hang around?"

A dark-skinned, agile man, made darker by his greasy clothes, whom Myles took for a rig builder, gave him an admiring appraisal. "Hell, you're the bird that cooled Tharp Kutch!"

His discovery brought them all in closer. The knot of men had grown to a good-sized crowd, gathered so fast that Myles wondered where they'd all come from. Everybody had something to say. A fat-growing Indian boy, reeking of peddler whisky, called out in mock challenge, "Fight anybody my heavy!" and was soon engaged in a half-hearted tussle by a white youth, who tickled him in the ribs. Everybody gawked and talked, elbowed and laughed, and made Myles the uncomfortable center of all this.

He was shouldering himself a clear path, when one of the bunch raised his voice in pretended relief, "We're safe now, boys. Here comes Coon Pollard." Everybody laughed once again, as if it were an old joke.

The crowd parted and two men came in, their arrival acting as a stopgate against the up-street drift that Myles had started.

The lead man stopped, working his gaze upon Myles. "What's this?" The high-pitched voice approaching uncertainty. The body was stumpy, the face round. An over-sized badge was pinned on his shirt pocket and the heavy belt and holster clung so precariously around the barrel of a stomach that they seemed in danger of sliding down.

Wasting no words, Myles told him.

"Get a good look at him?"

"Too dark."

"Don't give me much to work on." A glimmer of officiousness spread over the moon-faced features. "We got a hospital here, if you need patchin' up—"

"Let it go," answered Myles. He was suddenly weary and his temper short.

"Wait a minute, Coon."

An unexpected quiet caught the crowd, a hushed, respectful waiting.

It was the other man, Myles saw, who'd arrived with Pollard. A middle-aged man who didn't look his years. In the light from the street, his eyes were bright and black and deeply cool under the broad-brimmed cowman's hat. He was wide-shouldered and narrow through the hips, and although neither tall nor broad, he managed to look more capable physically than much bigger men about him. "Maybe that fellow's still around," the man said.

Pollard looked up, nodding.

"Perhaps we should search the alleys."

It was offered as a mere suggestion, Myles thought, toned so as not to tread on Pollard's official toes. And the man's following glance, taking in the crowd, said that every mother's son here had an equal vote in this as much as he. His voice had a weight, even here, creating the notion of a man larger and younger than he really was. It carried a blandness and also the quality of persuasion—like something maybe you'd hear in a courtroom, Myles thought.

"Was thinkin' the same thing, Sid," Pollard nodded.

"Whatever you say, Coon. You know about these matters. I'm no lawman."

Coon Pollard's round, banty shape appeared to swell taller. "You men!" he sang out. "Come on, let's take a look!"

They trooped gleefully in behind him, making a racket, and streamed between the shacks where the fight had occurred and romped toward the alley.

Watching them go, Myles was aware of a delayed reaction. He had just seen a keen mind in action, a mind coolly pulling the strings of this rough crowd and none of them realizing it. The fleeting thought passed almost the moment he had it. He wheeled, relieved that he could go at last, and saw that he was not alone. The man he'd been thinking of stood a pace beyond.

"Guess you've had a rough time tonight," he said affably. His warming chuckle was a powerful balm, healing Myles' physical hurts, making him feel better in spite of himself. He thrust out his hand. "I'm Sid Tyson."

But Myles was hesitating, jarred by the association- of the name. It banged off the walls of his mind and settled fast. He started to mention Frank Rikker then, but something checked him. Next, though not quite understanding why, he spoke only his own name and shook hands. Tyson's grip proved surprisingly strong. Myles' impression grew that everything about Sid Tyson was somehow surprising.

"Coon does the best he can," Tyson murmured, his tone apologetic. "Thankless job, town marshal. I figured it would be a good idea for him to lead the boys on a little goose chase, although your man took off for the tules long ago. Lets 'em blow off steam." He paused on a reflective note. "Having Coon look into this puts people in the frame of mind of always working with the law. Lord knows we need that in Two Sands. Too much rough stuff going on. Like that fellow. He try to hijack you?"

"Didn't get that far," Myles explained with feeling. "Broke and ran when he heard the crowd coming."

"Too bad you didn't see his face good."

Myles said nothing, wondering if it would have made any difference. Pollard did not impress him. Only now did he recall the savage words mouthed at him as he fought. They lacked sense—another thing he'd keep to himself.

They were walking slowly as they talked, and Myles noticed an erratic movement ahead. The unsteady motion of a drunk bracing himself against store fronts, pausing, and then continuing in the same aimless style. Just now, he stopped and seemed to be watching them.

Myles would have gone on, but Tyson, glancing across, spoke in warm recognition, "Bennie, boy! Why don't you go home?"

At his greeting an Indian strayed forth, weaving, "Borrow dollar, Sid?"

Tyson chuckled. "Don't tell me you're busted already? Payment was just this week."

"Borrow dollar. Damn hungry."

"Well-1—" With a show of good-natured tolerance, Tyson dug inside a pocket and produced a roll of bills. He peeled and pressed a greenback into the lifted hand. "Better get off the street, else Coon'll be locking you up."

Bennie, mumbling his thanks, was weaving off before Tyson had finished, setting a zig-zag course for an all-night cafe.

8

"Too bad." The rich voice bottomed on regret. "A good boy, too. He could buy me out twice—just eight headrights. Yet I feel sorry for him ... all these Osages. Too much money and not enough to do. They get paid every quarter, you know. Shame how some people take advantage of them." Indignation had put an edge to his tone. After a moment, Tyson was speaking again in his pleasant manner, for it seemed he could be nothing else, his voice inquiring but courteous, "Don't believe I've seen you around before."

"Just passing through."

"Looking for work?"

"No."

"Friends here?"

Despite the casual sounding question, a vague annoyance nicked Myles. He shook his head. He felt very tired.

"I see—"

They kept walking. Twice men spoke to Tyson, who answered cheerfully in return, without hesitation calling each man by his first name.

"Well, good luck." Tyson had stopped before a long touring car headed into the walk. Once more his erasing chuckle rubbed across to Myles. "I'd say be careful, but that's hardly necessary for a man who can take care of himself."

"Maybe I need that, too."

So far, Myles had been chiefly aware of the strong, compelling voice and the friendly manner. Now, in the full core of light thrusting from a pool hall window, he noticed Tyson's features in detail for the first time.

Somehow he had the curious feeling that the bland voice, in particular, might be a wall of contradiction behind which loomed a driving man's ambition. There wasn't the slightest sign of dissipation or weakness in Tyson. His jaw line was ledged, his nose broad and straight, his eyes alert and intelligent, his hands big, blunt—and competent. You almost forgot the hair, snow white at the temples.

The fleeting impression was broken when Tyson boarded the car, slammed the door and worked the starter. The motor answered with a snarl of power.

Sid Tyson waved as he drove off, leaving Myles thinking how foolish he'd look tomorrow when he inquired for Frank Rikker at Tyson's ranch.

CHAPTER TWO

T HE FEELING OF UNEASE persisted next morning when Myles Pearce left the hotel. He had slept later than he'd intended, been wearier than he'd realized. He stood slackly on the walk, content for the brassy sun to soak into sore shoulders and arms.

In the dazzling light, Two Sands revealed its slattern face. The town lay deceptively silent—a brawny young renegade sleeping late this peaceful Sunday morning after a night of brawling. Only a few heavy wagons rolled. Here and there a man stirred. Dust and paper wrappings rode on the brisk wind. The clank-clunk of cable drilling tools struck in monotonous rhythm from the oil field. His nostrils widened on the smell. He'd become so used to it, however, he hardly noticed now.

Impatient again, he walked to the taxi stand, found it empty. It was ten o'clock before a driver showed up.

He was a slight, bleary-eyed, sorrowful-featured man in his late fifties, long of face, who reluctantly accepted another fare. "It ain't that I don't appreciate the business," came the tired explanation. "Took a load to Tulsey last night an' they damn near wore me out … but hop in. Happy Adcock never turned down a man afoot."

Once aboard, Myles settled down in the front seat and was relieved to have the town fall behind. Yet, while the flivver jumped for the first line of rolling hills, he sensed an ebbing of his impatience and a growth of unwillingness. How would he say it?

A pulsating roar shattered his thinking. As he jerked instinctively to look, the nose of a blood-red roadster tore past. It had burst out of the purring quiet with all the violence of some unleashed monster, wire wheels spinning up choking, fuming dust. The roadster, a Cadillac, whipped on in weaving insolence. In those few moments, as the car drew even, Myles glimpsed an Indian woman of indeterminate age. Her broad face was turned, grinning at Adcock. She flung up a brown arm in greeting and cut around expertly, leaving them covered with dust.

Adcock slowed down, coughing and muttering.

Myles, himself choking on the acrid clouds, managed a "Who's that?"

"Sid Tyson's wife...Nellie....Drives like a bat run out of hell." Nevertheless, a grudging admiration diluted Adcock's irritation. "Come right up behind us, then opened her cut-out. She can drive—she sure can. But some day Injun meet bridge—bridge no get outa way," he predicted mournfully.

Gradually, the dust cleared and by the time they had topped the first grassy ridge and could see beyond, Nellie Tyson's roadster was a mere black bug scuttling far ahead. In a while it vanished, lost in the distance that had no end.

The flivver's lurching made Myles glance at Adcock, who braked in disgust. "She's hot again. Forgot to fill up before we left." Complacently, he leaned over the seat and came up with a gallon can. Getting out, he removed the radiator cap gingerly. A geyser of steam spewed up. The radiator gurgled and trembled.

"Gonna get me a big car one of these days," Adcock said grimly, pouring. Myles decided he liked the little man.

Soon they were traveling again. Myles let his eyes wander hungrily over these hills. Though strange, they spoke to him — the long-running ridges, an occasional gray limestone outcrop, the blue-stem grass a tufted, rich hide. This was land that called to a man. It filled his eye, his brain, and coursed through his veins like a heady tonic. His mood lifted and the focus of his thinking dwelled on Frank Rikker with a renewed determination.

Afterward, he came to sharpening attention when the fliv-ver rumbled over the pipe flooring of a cattle-guard, and, body parts shaking, sprang like a jackrabbit upon a double set of tracks sweeping cleanly through lush grass. Whitefaced cattle, sleek with fat, dotted the pasture. Myles had noted already the four strands of tight barbed wire in the fence that flanked the cross-ing. His impression of a wellrun outfit redoubled as they drove under the tall trees and approached the house.

Adcock canted his head. "Tyson's place."

It was no ordinary ranch house, framed and gray-weathered, nothing like the Rikker place and the kind Myles was used to, erected strictly for workaday utility.

Before him reared a two-story red brick structure, whose sturdy columns braced a wide, cool porch, shaded by scatter-ing cottonwoods and trimmed blackjacks. The barn drew his eye next. It was made of brown sandstone, even larger than the house, and posted off from it in lesser magnificence were newly painted sheds and stout plank corrals. Horses fiddled inside. The open barn showed more animals in stalls; the haymow looked full. The entire layout conveyed an air of unbelievable extrava-gance, strangely tempered to usefulness by an orderly mind.

"Some place, eh?" asked Adcock with the familiarity of one who came here often. "Louis Garreau built it when the oil money started comin'…Died couple years back. Last fall Nellie she ups an' marries Sid Tyson. They say he's makin' the place pay. Sid's a purty smart hombre. He knows cattle, even if he is a lawyer. Runs a big crew."

Nellie Tyson's red roadster was parked in front of the house. Adcock pulled up alongside. He gave the Cadillac a brief, wistful look before he spoke. "How long you figure we'll be?"

"Maybe not long," answered Myles, stepping out.

A metal fence enclosed the vast yard. He hesitated before the gate, then released the catch and entered, struck afresh by the overflowing lavishness of the house. He followed a stone walk to the porch and stood a moment at the screen door, hearing the rattle of dishes, the hum of voices in the rear.

He caught himself delaying again, an indecision he broke by rapping solidly on the door frame and stepping back, hat in hand. The voices ran on a space, quit, and he heard light steps crossing the house. He was not prepared for what he saw next, because he had expected an Indian woman.

Out of the room's shadow loomed a slim shape, a young woman's face. A face neither plain nor merely pretty—an unexpectedly lovely face and gray eyes that curiously met his own. She was bare-legged, dressed in some kind of bright material. Although loosely worn, it clung to her in the right places; it bared the creamy expanse of throat, outlined the high, rounded breasts.

"Good morning... Is Frank Rikker around?" Her hair, he saw, was blonde and somewhat short, wavy without being curly. A loose strand kept playing over one cheek; each time she brushed it back automatically, suggesting that she had never quite conquered the unruliness.

She had not spoken yet; her face was detached, neither friendly nor unfriendly. She was not looking at him, he realized; she was looking through him.

"I understand he works here," Myles followed up.

She had finished her inspection, it seemed, which reminded him of his bruised mouth. A slow heat began to fan his face. "This is the Tyson ranch, isn't it?"

The impersonal mask of her face slowly altered, revealing nice teeth and a full mouth. "I'm sorry... You'll probably find him in the bunkhouse."

He liked the change and guessed he did look a little roughed up from last night. In the next moment, the mask slipped back. He was where he had started—at a cool distance, fenced out—and there the eyes would keep him.

"Much obliged." He swung away, going down the steps with the unmistakable impact of the unwelcomed. Turning out of the gate toward a low-slung frame building he took for the bunk-house, he noticed that she hadn't moved. In the next step he put her from his mind.

There was a beginning eagerness hurrying him, overcoming his last trace of reluctance. On impulse he strode to the door and called, "Frank!" and waited. Excitement jerked along his muscles. Silence. He called again. Then Myles heard his brother's voice, roughly querulous, from the rear of the bunkhouse, "Come on in."

Myles went in, blinking against the dimness. At the far end of the long room a man sat on his bunk, half turned. Myles took a breath. The waiting in him got tense and brittle—and already some of the fine anticipation of moments ago had slipped away. It was all but lost when Frank Rikker stood up.

Surprise widened his eyes, froze him to a stiff-bodied silence. For a flick of time, as a tiny spark flaring and then going out, Myles thought he caught a welcome. But he couldn't be certain.

Frank Rikker's face settled.

"Howdy, Frank."

"Howdy—"

Their glances locked. Myles stuck out his hand. Frank took it. His grip was brief, quickly withdrawn. In silence they sized each other up.

Frank was another image of Dow Rikker. He had the same compact, capable body, square in the shoulders. The same tousled hair, as unruly as his restless, muscular body. The same straight nose and direct blue eyes. A handsome man, younger than Myles. From there the likeness ended, for there was a discontent in Frank's eyes, in the wide mouth that could have been generous but wasn't. He wore a day's beard. He was frowning.

Myles said slowly, "Get my letter?"

"Letter?"

"I wrote you. Asked you to meet me in Two Sands."

"Didn't get it."

"Well"—Myles shrugged it off—"I found you, anyway. The folks, send their best to you."

Frank's mouth thinned. "And you?"

"The same," answered Myles, making it sound convincing. There was a pause, till he said, "You're looking good."

He got a derisive laugh and a search of the blue eyes. "Good as you, maybe? Run into a fence post?"

"A fist. In Two Sands. Right nice little town. Strangers always welcome."

"Fix him up the way you did Buck Hoyt?"

Myles ignored him. Mention of the Hoyt fight was one thing he'd wished to avoid, if possible. "He got away in the dark."

"No woman in it this time?" Frank was faintly mocking.

"I got jumped," Myles said patiently, determined that Frank wasn't going to ruffle him.

"He didn't have a knife?"

Myles felt his tolerance crack. He pulled in a long, steadying breath. "Lucky for me he didn't. Look here, Frank. I didn't come all the way to the Osage just to argue a damn fool brawl."

"I haven't forgotten it." Frank became scoffing again. "And how're you and Laura Bailey hitting it off?"

"That's beside the point. You don't see any war hatchet on me, do you?"

"Don't have to see it," Frank replied bitterly.

Myles fought a storm of feeling, till it sank down and he knew that he controlled it. "I'm in a hurry, Frank. What's the deal here?"

"Good. I like it."

"Some setup."

"Best in the country," Frank said, firm and blunt.

They were talking in circles, Myles saw, and he wondered how he could maneuver back to delicate ground. He reached for brown papers and sack tobacco, taking his time, hoping Frank would furnish the opening. He struck a match on his thumb nail and smoked for a minute. Finally, the silence told him that it was up to him. So he began carefully, "You got a nice stake back home. More than you can make here as a hand."

"Depends." A resentment clouded Frank's eyes. "Down here in the Osage you roll your own. Whatever you're big enough to handle. I do my work and Sid Tyson lets me buy a few head to run in with his stuff."

"Not bad. Except—"

"What?" Frank demanded.

"Dow and Sarah want you back." Myles recognized that he was framing it poorly, but there was no other way. "Why'd Dow ever build up the ranch but to leave it to you?"

"And you," Frank corrected, and, sarcastically, before Myles could go on, "Hell, I'm tired of somebody telling me when to tie up! He sent you here—I know!"

"Don't blame him. This was my idea." Myles was lying, doing a fair job of it, but he sensed that Frank wasn't fooled.

There came the dragging silence again, a creaky tension. Their glances clashed. Myles tried once more. "How about it, Frank? Even for a visit?"

Frank was a moment answering. "Sure—sometime—maybe." He spaced out the words. "But I like it here."

Myles eyed him, somehow puzzled. It almost seemed that Frank was repeating something over and over to convince himself. Myles said, half bantering, "I saw one pretty good reason at the house. That blonde—"

Frank did not smile. "Savannah?"

"Blonde, big eyes—"

"That's Savannah," said Frank, and Myles could not decide how Frank might feel about her.

"Savannah how-many?"

"Tyson ... but Sid's her stepfather." Frank's mouth settled. He tilted his head, a motion that said he was out of patience. "Talk won't do it, Myles. You're wasting time. I told you I like it here. I'm staying."

"What will it take to make you change your mind?"

"Nothing now. I'm sold on it here."

It hit him again, the self-convincing note. Myles was aware of a sudden regret, of the great things he wanted to say and could not—and a vague, intangible wrongness. He heard himself asking, almost suspiciously, "Anything wrong, Frank?"

Frank looked up very fast. Myles tensed for his outburst.

"If there was, I could handle it," Frank said, instead, rolling his shoulders. For the first time today he sounded like the old Frank Rikker—spoiled, headstrong, touchy proud. He seemed amused. "Tell the folks I'll be home one of these days. That's a promise."

He's lying, thought Myles. He won't be back. Not for a long time.

A tide of resignation swept over him, an obscure bewilderment. "All right," he said bleakly, his reply as mechanical as Frank's had been. "I'll tell them."

Frank looked relieved. In a matter of moments he had dropped his mockery, his sullen attitude, and become almost congenial.

"Don't let any grass grow under that promise," Myles said. A few minutes later, after more meaningless talk, they shook hands and Myles left the bunkhouse.

Wind, rustling the cottonwoods and blackjacks, felt cool on his face. He was scowling, disgusted and angry with himself. He had not been persuasive. He had not climbed the wall between him and Frank as he'd hoped. He had accomplished nothing—beyond a vague promise. Worst of all, he had let the Rikkers down.

Happy Adcock yawned from the front seat and checked his pocket watch. "Hang around long enough and we might draw an invite to eat."

The suggestion roweled Myles. "Let's go," he said curtly, getting in. "Isn't there a north train this afternoon?"

Adcock nodded, stretched and turned to the wheel, retarded the spark lever, and got out stiffly. He was going around to crank the car when Myles heard the clanging of a cook's triangle behind the house. Hands began strolling up from the barn and corrals. He eyed them indifferently at first, then felt his attention quicken.

Tharp Kutch and the man called Lee were walking together. He saw them turn the fence corner and approach the car on their way to the front gate. Just then, the flivver's engine shivered and caught and Adcock returned hurriedly to ease the throttle. Myles took his seat. Glancing back, he ran against the straight-on stares of Kutch and Lee.

Daylight made Kutch look more formidable. Thicker and barrel-chested, his broad nose flatter, his small yellow eyes close-spaced. His partner was rail thin in contrast, stoop-shouldered, the Roman nose a hooked beak.

The bull and the hawk, Myles thought wryly. He kept looking till they passed through the gate and boldly entered the house by the front door. "Who's the tall one?" he asked Adcock, who was letting the motor idle a moment.

"Lee Wiley. Works for Sid. The other'n's Tharp Kutch."

"I know."

Adcock's eyebrows lifted. "Friendly cusses, ain't they?" He was turning the car when a man appeared on the porch and waved. It was Sid Tyson, hatless, in shirt sleeves, his hair a snow white mane lending him an almost benign appearance. Adcock stopped. Tyson left the porch, flagging them down as he crossed the yard and opened the gate.

"You boys light and eat," he said, striding up to the car. His alert eyes, pinned on Myles, lighted in instant recognition. "Myles—Myles Pearce—isn't that it?" He hadn't even hesitated over the name. "Just in time. Eat with us."

Adcock glanced hopefully at Myles. "Plenty time to make your train."

"It's always late." Tyson's chuckle offered a host's freehanded generosity.

Myles teetered on refusal. He was a stranger here, for one thing, and his mind was still anchored to the dismal knowledge of his defeat. Then, peculiarly, his mood shifted. He checked himself at the queer stab of acceptance within. He thanked Tyson and was out of the car, walking beside him, before he understood why he had accepted. He wanted to see more of this strange ranch, which could switch from cold unwelcome to warm hospitality. Where two hired hands lorded through the front door, while the others went around by the rear.

Over his shoulder, he saw Frank standing outside the bunkhouse, steadily watching. Myles walked on.

Tyson, who had noticed, asked genially, "You acquainted with Frank?"

"His folks raised me."

"Oh..." There was a glimmer of interest in the observant eyes, at once smoothed out when Myles failed to elaborate, and Tyson added, "He's a good hand."

He made a show of courtesy at the door, his manner proprietary as he held it open for his guests. Myles found himself in a large, high-ceilinged room, where the exaggerated extravagance was renewed. The heavy, overstuffed sofa and bulky chairs were upholstered in what looked like red velvet. His boots sank into a cushion of red carpet that muffled his steps. A coal oil lamp, gaudy and overdone in painted red roses, stood on a massive walnut table with claw feet. In contrast, the walls flung back a gloomy nakedness. Stairs arched upward to the vast upper story of the house.

Tyson's chuckle became a sigh. He indicated the furnishings with a condoning hand. "Never argue with a woman about her house."

An Indian woman came to the kitchen door. Myles recognized her instantly. Her shining black hair hung in long braids. Pock-marks marred the otherwise smooth coppery skin of her pleasant face. A full-blood, he judged, some years younger than Tyson. If she had any handsomeness, it was in the straight carriage of her stout Indian body, seeming larger in the dark purple dress, and in the brown, friendly eyes.

"This is Myles Pearce," Tyson murmured. "Mrs. Tyson...Myles."

Myles said, "Pleased to meet you," and saw her reaction of pleasure.

A secret amusement washed a slow-breaking smile over the broad face as she looked at Adcock. Her heavy lips moved. "See you got here all right."

Adcock matched her grin. "It's a wonder, Nellie. Somebody dang near dusted us off the road."

"I can guess who it was." Tyson spread his strong hands helplessly. "What's a man going to do with her, Happy?"

"That's easy—just stay out of her way."

Nellie Tyson's pleased laugh ran among them. "It's on the table, Sid," she said.

Moving through the door, Myles would not have noticed if he hadn't glanced around for Adcock. Turning, he saw Tyson touch his wife's shoulder. Her face underwent an abrupt change, softening. Tyson's hand stayed there just a brushing instant before dropping swiftly down. Although Myles faced about, he noticed the crowding hurt in her eyes. Almost at once she was smiling again, laughing maybe a little too much, as she spoke to the wrinkled old Indian woman in the kitchen.

After Adcock and Myles had washed up at a bench on the long, screened-in back porch, Tyson waved them to places near the head of the lengthy table. "We all take chuck together," he said. It was a casual reference. Yet to Myles it revealed the man. He was careful in his handling of his crew, eager for their good will.

Pulling out a chair, Myles spotted Wiley and Kutch along the opposite end. Kutch kept his gaze front, upon the platters of food. Frank was the last in. There was an empty place on Myles' right, and he wondered if Frank would pass it up. Frank took it without hesitation.

Across from Myles, Nellie Tyson sat at her husband's left, her dark eyes preoccupied. Tyson, a calm tolerance blanding his forcible features, presented the picture of the generous ranch host. He reached for a bowl to pass and ran his glance down the table's length. On that signal the crew started attacking the platters of fried steak, potatoes, bowls of vegetables and heaps of biscuits.

Tyson ate steadily for a while, with relish, till his eyes, wandering to the vacant chair beside his wife, mirrored a question. "Where's Savannah?"

Nellie Tyson did not answer at once. First, she seemed to gather her thoughts from some distant place. "Dressing," she said, and put her attention to the plate she had not touched. A certain soberness touched her face.

Well into his meal, Myles picked up the tread of light steps overhead, and then down the stairs, crossing the kitchen, and quickly onto the porch. The crew gazed up expectantly and Myles saw Savannah.

It struck him that she had a liveliness he'd missed before in the shadows of the room. She had changed to a man's gray cotton work shirt, open at the white throat, and blue Levi trousers and boots. Although the shirt was so large the seams fell past the rounded points of her shoulders, it cupped out over her unhampered breasts. The Levis fit her like shrunken buckskin leggings, clinging to long, graceful legs. Her waist was slim, her hips boyish. Her sleeves, rolled up to elbows, revealed tanned arms and strong-looking hands for a girl. Her hair wasn't as blonde as he'd thought. More gold and reddish. In fact, a strawberry blonde.

He saw Frank look up once, swiftly, then return to his eating.

Her vibrant "Hello!" took them all in as she reached for the chair next to Nellie Tyson. The crew beamed sunburned, red-faced smiles of masculine appreciation.

Seated, Savannah glanced up. Myles saw a quick recognition, soon controlled, as Frank mumbled an introduction. She smiled back, but the full force of it came to rest upon Frank, who bent his eyes away. Myles noticed this. Now, she took a man's helping from the platters. The crew relaxed.

Tyson stared with new interest at Savannah. "You're rigged out for work on Sunday?"

"I promised Jeannette I'd help her this afternoon. She's short-handed."

Tyson turned questioningly to his wife. "When did Jeannette run shy of hands? I've told her she can always call on us. Guess I'll have to remind her again."

"You know how Jeannette is." Nellie Tyson's words were a blend of defense and apology. "She's kinda independent."

"Which is a good thing," Tyson nodded in approval. "Too bad more Osages don't put their money in cattle." His affability had returned, despite a shade of annoyance. "You know, Nellie, I hoped she'd come over today and visit, it being Sunday. Been a month, I believe, since Jeannette had dinner with us."

Nellie Tyson nodded. Her Indian face expressed regret and perhaps a guardedness. She made no reply and an awkward stillness now dominated the long table, silencing even the crew.

It took Savannah's voice, swinging like a warm wind between the Tysons, to break the hush. "Jeannette has a big spread to run, Sid. I'd be worried sick if I had that responsibility. I'm no cowgirl."

"You'll do." It was Nellie Tyson, smiling now. A fondness came into her voice, gently teasing. "That's what these young men want. Some poor girl to do all the chores, so they can loaf in town."

Savannah laughed. "Then I'll never be married. Last time I roped a calf, Frank had to rescue me."

The crew grinned. Frank flushed, looking uncomfortable. "Why, I was worried about the horse. Afraid he'd get rope burns." He took refuge behind a cup of coffee.

"Don't let him get away with that," Nellie Tyson bantered. "Just an excuse. He likes girls."

Savannah's eyes thanked her. There was a close feeling between these two women, Myles decided, an understanding.

"Seems Frank should be the one riding over to Jeannette's," Tyson said mildly. "Not Savannah."

Frank Rikker's head came up. "If Savannah can stand me, I'll tag along. Never know. She might try bein' a roper again—maybe get lost in the blackjacks."

She flung him an airy rebuke. "Oh, I don't know. But I'll bet you know the way—you go enough."

Tyson's gaze, split between Frank and Savannah, lifted then. He seemed pleased. The meal was finished. He stood and next the crew stood and began filing out.

Drifting through the gloomy vastness of the house, Myles found Savannah beside him, the others ahead. She murmured, "I wasn't very nice, was I? If I'd known you were Frank's brother ..."

"Well, I didn't speak up."

"I'll know you next time."

"A long time, likely."

"You're leaving?"

He nodded.

Her eyes searched his face. "It sounds queer to say, here ... but I wish you wouldn't."

Happy Adcock's call, "Better ride if we make that train," cut short their conversation, and Myles, nodding, turned to go. When the Tysons had been thanked, he left the house.

Frank sided Myles and Adcock to the car. There Myles turned slowly. "Think it over, Frank."

"Meaning I should go?"

"You should. You owe it." There was an edge to Myles' voice.

"Up to me, I think."

"Just don't make it too long. People get older every day."

Frank Rikker said nothing, his face stony. He kept his right hand stiffly to his side. Adcock had the flivver running, so Myles swung to the seat. His mind was not clear as they passed under the trees. The road left the shade and bent toward the high, clean prairie. He turned his head for a final look, troubled and baffled.

The house stood dark and brooding, out of place against the backdrop of wild blackjack ridges. He didn't know why, but it did.

CHAPTER THREE

IS MOOD HELD ON WHEN Adcock flourished up to the hotel and anounced. "Twenty minutes to spare! How's that, son?"

Myles had to grin. "On the money. In a minute you can unload me at the depot."

Upstairs, in his dingy room, he started jamming things into his grip. But even as he snapped the lock, uncertainty overtook him. His mind wrenched backward. To a certain land and a certain time, long ago, yet so burned into memory that he could see everything—

He was still shocked into streaks of silence and fear by the absence of home's familiar faces and voices, when he first saw this great man and the giant black horse.

They came out of hills that seemed another world, out of the mystery of cow country and a boy's sprung-eyed fantasy. A steady interest kindled in the rider's blue eyes as he dippered himself a drink from the cedar bucket on the porch and visited with the nester.

Pieces of the nester's low talk drifted across the yard to Myles. " ... fever got his folk ... No kin we know of ... "

Afterward, the man left the way he rode in. But Myles followed the pair, in mind, long after they had dropped from sight in a fold of the shaggy, mysterious hills. For the last flicker of distant movement left him tight with fear again.

But to his surprise the man was back in a few days, saddling in on the black. Except there was one difference. This time a bright bay pony jerked on a lead rope. Myles and the other children gathered around.

Stepping down, the man scanned the young bunch and Myles felt the eyes singling him out. Unhurriedly, the man clumped forward, his silver spurs making a jingling. He spoke to Myles, "How'd you like to ride that bay pony, son?" Myles nodded before he thought.

With one swoop of a thick arm, Myles was hoisted to the pony's back, so easy-like he might have been an empty feed sack. The man was laughing as he did it, pleased it seemed, and Myles could feel the strength and solid refuge in this man who laughed more than he talked.

In spite of that, the ground seemed far away from his high perch aboard the pony. Next the reins were in his hands. He looked at the still faces of the long-haired kids bunched there in the yard.

A squashy feeling began in Myles. It blubbered up from his drawn-in stomach, suddenly clutched at his throat, snapped a misty curtain across his eyes. With everything in him he fought to force it down.

All at once he wanted to stay here with these folks, if for no other reason than he knew the faces. Them and the dirty, littered, chicken-dropped yard, which had taken on the wonderful blessedness of familiarity.

The nester kept looking down. He was saying, "You're gonna live with Mister Dow Rikker, here, Myles."

Myles swallowed. Why, this was like before, when they'd taken him off in the wagon from the silent home place.

"I'll come back for his things," Dow Rikker said and mounted. "Butcherin' time, Bill, there'll be half a beef for you. Been a bad year, I know." And turning to the kids, he said, "One of these days Myles will be back to play with you."

They rode at a walk out of the yard, with Myles afraid to look back. He had learned this much: it only made it harder and he didn't want to bawl. But once beyond the yard, he could not resist the desire to turn and wave.

It was a mistake. At once the mist filled his eyes and there rose a lump big as a turkey egg in his throat that he could not swallow.

But long before Myles sighted the frame house under the green cottonwoods, or saw the scattered sheds and corrals and heard the clanking windmill, he knew that he belonged. Maybe it was how Dow Rikker, never talking much, settled his glance on you now and then, and grinned when you happened to catch him doing it. Just something told you, a feeling all through telling you it was true. The realization made Myles sit the pony extra straight, as he figured an old *hand might*. He hoped Dow Rikker noticed.

It wasn't very long till Myles saw a tall woman running from the house, long skirts flying. She was already waiting outside the picket-fenced yard when they rode up and halted. Even as Myles followed Dow Rikker's move and came sliding down, her arms were reaching.

She hugged him till his thin ribs protested, and there was no breath left inside him, and she held him at arm's length and sort of measured him, up and down, with her warm, hungry glance. Her sun-browned face seemed almost plain, but the features were softly turned and mighty pleasant, and she had brown eyes that made him think of a face he'd never see again.

"Sarah ... this is Myles Pearce." Dow Rikker's voice made it sound important.

"You come right in!" She said it in a way that told Myles she already knew who he was. Then she fixed her husband with a severe look. "Dow Rikker! That long ride and I'll bet this boy's had nothing to eat! I know you—you'd ride all day!"

Dow Rikker's laugh was wind in the trees. He said in a gentling humor, "Now, Sarah, give a man time to put up his horse before you start stuffin' the holy daylights out of him. Anyhow,

Myles here couldn't eat more'n a panful of biscuits and a jar of plum butter. Now, could you, Myles?"

He winked big as he spoke, and awkwardness rose in Myles because they were making over him. Remembering his obligation to the bay pony, he looked in doubt from Sarah to Dow.

"I call him Redskin," Dow Rikker said. "But you can change his name if you want to."

Myles could not speak for a moment. He was struggling against an unexpected surge of feeling, almost a choking. Did he mean—? Between bites on his trembling lower lip, he tried to hold his voice steady and certain, for even then he was hoping that he could be like Dow Rikker. "Redskin? Why—that's a good name." But still he hesitated, unsure of what he should do.

"Then take him," Dow Rikker said fast, a light in the blue glance. "He's yours."

Moving on wooden legs through a sheet of blinky haze as he fought back the swelling in his throat, Myles took the pony's reins. Afterward, in a floating triumph he had never experienced before, he tramped to the barn with the Rikkers. He unsaddled and fed the pony. At that moment, he was the richest boy on earth.

That first evening, so chuck-full of supper that Dow Rikker roared his approval and Sarah beamed when Myles let his belt out a notch, Myles began to understand more about the Rikkers.

No children ran whooping through the shaded yard. Myles missed the nester kids and the noisy fun. Only here it was the discovery of something he'd thought lost, a place without strangeness, and close to what he'd known before the sickness came. When he got up of a morning he'd know what to expect and it would be there, the same people and the same things around him.

Soon he realized what Dow Rikker had in mind, though never speaking of it. He and Sarah had no son—Myles was here to fill that gap in their lives.

Then Myles began riding Redskin to the wearisome school, impatient till afternoon, when he could hit a high lope for the ranch. He could remember Sarah's patience in overcoming his suspicion of that school, its rules and the time he figured was wasted inside.

On other days he and Dow Rikker were real partners. Sometimes in summer the sky seemed a great ball of fire, and the searing wind the devil's breath, and the grass lay curled and browned and Dow Rikker fretted over water. Sometimes they rode in cold so intense that the crying wind, hurtling across the ridge tops, pressed icy fingers through Myles' thick mackinaw. Sometimes he watched this great man hack water holes in the frozen creeks with his hand ax.

Myles listened, too. Always, their talk circled from cows and horses to water and grass, saddles and ropes and spurs, and back once more to cows and horses. And none of it ever got old, even when told over.

There were days when Dow Rikker called attention to the keen spring smells, sweet off the grass, and the different sounds you could make out about whippoorwill time, which was just before dark.

Later, under the warm quilt in his room, Myles heard coyotes howling from the high places in the hills. But he didn't shiver as he had at the nester's, bedded down with the other boys. Because coyotes made a music that soon put a man to sleep, just like Dow Rikker said.

Late the next spring, the Kelsey woman from the place west of them came to stay a spell with the Rikkers. Not that Sarah really needed any help that Myles could see. About that time, though, he felt an air around the house and noticed that Dow and Sarah talked low sometimes, like they had a secret. Pretty soon she seldom turned her hand and, when she did, Dow would scold her.

When the baby was born, Dow Rikker named him Frank, after an old hand he'd known in the Cherokee Strip. "Give a boy a good name and let him grow up to it." That was what Dow said, while telling everybody that he was the luckiest man alive drawing this second son he and Sarah never figured they could have. It made a man feel he was being blessed for taking in an orphan.

Dow Rikker worked hard not to favor Frank as the boys grew older. Except it didn't come about as he planned, even-Stephen between them. Instead, Frank seemed to resent the impartial treatment, until it seemed that Myles, drawn closer to Dow by their old understanding, was the real son and Frank the taken-in boy.

It was the senseless Buck Hoyt fight that touched everything off. Myles tried to shut it out now, but could not. There it was again, accusing, the details marching through his mind, nagging, taunting, reminding—

Hoyt, a quarrelsome, chunky-shouldered man with a knifer's reputation, stood in the doorway of the lighted school house. A swagger to him, a mounting insolence. He was just drunk enough to be meaner than he was ordinarily.

Perhaps, it never would have happened if Frank hadn't been dancing with the sultry Bailey girl, whom both brothers were courting. Hoyt, spotting her, shouldered through the dancers and took her arm.

Frank muttered something, but did not step aside.

Hoyt's eyes darkened angrily.

Laura Bailey, sensing trouble, put in placatingly, "It's all right, Frank. I don't mind." Her eyes, teasing, rejected neither man.

Frank seemed not to hear. His face colored. When Hoyt's grip tightened upon her arm, Frank shoved him.

The fiddlers stopped playing.

Jolted backward, Hoyt regained his footing and came stomping in. Frank met him. The impact of their hard bodies thudded in the quiet room. Frank was quicker than Hoyt. He smashed Hoyt's face, his middle. Hoyt was knocked to the slick floor.

As he reared up, the Bailey girl screamed—and Myles saw Hoyt make a streaky motion toward his pocket. All this time Myles had stood like a spectator, hands knotted, half striking when Frank struck.

He was not aware of movement, of lunging across. He batted down Hoyt's arm before Hoyt could bring it up. He crashed into Hoyt and carried him to the wall. Through a red haze he saw Hoyt try to dodge.

An overpowering violence drove Myles. A savagery he did not know that he had. He grabbed the arm and bent and twisted it...back, back. Hoyt cried out, the cry lifting on and up till something snapped. The cry shrilled to a scream, then merely a sucking of breath, and Buck Hoyt lay writhing upon the floor, his arm broken.

Myles glared down, the furious fire in him burning out. A revolting nausea smashed his insides as he went out the room.

He was standing by the saddle horses, building a smoke with unsteady fingers, when Frank found him.

"Hoyt had it comin'," Frank began, his voice sounding strange, all wrong. "So I guess you think I ought to thank you?"

"He had a knife," Myles said. "He was going for it."

Frank Rikker's mouth twisted. "What if he was?"

"He'd a-cut you up good."

"Hoyt was my business." Frank's voice changed to a whiplike quality, quirting his wounded pride at Myles. "But you couldn't see that. You had to step in—so Laura could see what a man you are!"

For a moment Myles couldn't speak, and by the time he could, Frank was going for his horse.

The following day Frank rode south, in the direction of the booming Osage country...

The squawking of an automobile horn penetrated Myles' consciousness. He was still standing, his hand on the grip. He'd been there some time, he supposed, deep in thought. The noise drew him to the window and he glanced out

Happy Adcock's flivver was parked below. Its horn kept on, squalling insistently.

Lifting his grip, Myles went slowly down stairs, paid his bill, and walked to the car. He felt a queer hesitation in himself as Adcock said, "That train might just fool us an' be on time for once."

Thoughtfully, Myles tossed his grip into the back seat. As yet he'd made no move to get in.

Adcock looked at him. "Forget somethin'?"

And then Myles heard his own voice, as some detached part of himself speaking, "I'm not taking the train, Happy. Not today … You know the road to Jeannette Garreau's?"

CHAPTER FOUR

A T LAST the great house was quiet.

Nellie Tyson, alone in the gloomy cavern of the high-ceilinged living room, sat woodenly on the red divan, feeling the stillness, listening to the metallic rustling of the wind through the cottonwood and blackjack leaves.

A few minutes ago she had gone to the kitchen where the good old Oto woman washed the dishes. "Grandmother," said Nellie in Osage, "you work too hard. I will finish this. Go on."

The old woman bared her toothless gums in a grin. "You pay me money," she answered, keeping to the Indian talk," ... I work."

There was no telling her age, but it mounted up to many winters. She was all brown wrinkles and sagging breasts and thin gray hair which hung like straggling rope ends. Her black eyes were twin coals, banked and dimly glowing in the caves under the bony ledges of her eyebrows. Her skinny arms kept working up and down, sloshing the soapy rag vigorously.

Without another word, Nellie crossed to her and gently untied the apron strings. The old woman's hands dropped. She faced Nellie, her dark eyes grateful and humoring, reached for a towel and dried her veined hands. Of a sudden she was chattering, almost gaily, an opportunity she found only when Nellie was around.

A wonderment stirred her. Her moccasins made a scuffing shuffle. "You Osages funny," she said, near scolding. "Never worry 'bout tomorrow."

But she was very much pleased. And when Nellie added a five-dollar bill to her generosity, the old woman grinned. Eyes sparkling, she cached the money in a small paper sack which she kept in the pocket of her flowered calico dress.

It made Nellie smile—that sack for a pocketbook. She was still smiling after the old Oto woman had scuffed out to her quarters behind the house. Nellie washed and dried the dishes, the platters and pots, scrubbed a rag over the black face of the wood-burning stove. That the house was not piped for gas had never bothered her. In fact, she liked wood better; it made better bread and she liked the good smell. It was a Way long familiar to her, and she clung to the familiar now with a tenacity that often worried her.

So then it was, inevitably, as she returned to the empty front room and had sat a few moments, listening, that her mind fled to Louis Garreau. She had forgotten the others soon as they'd gone. Happy Adcock and that quiet young man with the bruised face, Frank's brother; Sid and the boys, who had saddled off to Clark Slater's ranch for an afternoon of calf roping.

Louis Garreau was never far from the surface of her thoughts, never completely missing. His image hovered there in the mist of her memory, the one good thing that would never change or disappoint her. At first, when alone, she would think of him with a rush of fierce contentment which no one else could share, unless it was Jeannette. Then, swiftly, that feeling would give ground to a grieving desperateness, a loneness, and she always found herself lost in a drowning sea of unhappiness, brooding, relieved only through violent activity.

She could feel it rising around her at this very moment; and, fighting it, she forced herself to stand. The feeling became an insistent pressure against her brain, drawing her face taut, tensing her muscles, making her afraid.

Two years, she thought. Louis has been gone two years. No, about two years and a half now. It seemed forever.

She was struggling within herself and she walked heavily to the foot of the stairs, the weight of her solid body creaking the floor. Her breath came with difficulty. She held on to the banister for support.

Finally, ashamed of her weakness, she took the stairs. Deliberately shunning the banister, she climbed steadily to the landing and reached the second floor. Here the broad hall opened on spacious rooms. As she came to Savannah's room, a pleasing scent reached her. Nellie paused. A good girl, she thought. Like another daughter.

Going on, she passed what had been Jeannette's room. It was empty now, a mocking guest room, seldom used. And Jeannette, on the few occasions she visited, never stayed over night.

Heavy-footed, Nellie approached the bedroom that she had shared with Louis. Then she glanced at Sid's across the hall.

A kind of gratitude filled her. Sid understood. He had from the start about Louis. Wasn't he a pallbearer for Louis? True, because he was Louis' friend. Sid understood Indians. She had tried to make it up to him—and failed. After a few weeks, he had suggested that he move across the hall, though he had put it in such a way that did not hurt her, saying in that chuckling laugh of his that he was hard to sleep with.

Except he seldom crossed the hall to her room. Now and again she wondered, lying alone in the darkness, if she had failed him as she had Louis, when she let him ride alone that time in the storm and something told her it was bad.

Nellie Tyson, sighing heavily, entered her bedroom. As her gaze automatically sought Louis Garreau's picture on the walnut bureau, an avalanche of memories came crashing down upon her.

For a moment she saw the features quite clearly—the dark eyes, half smiling and amused; the high, proud forehead and nose; the strong chin and mouth and the coppery Indian coloring, shaded off to a lighter bronze by the heavy mixture of

French blood, a blood that people said made a man laugh a lot. One reason, she knew without consciously admitting it, why she had married Sid. He laughed a lot, like Louis.

Without any warning, the image changed, clouded over. She blinked rapidly, unable to see the face. Almost blindly, she felt her way to the window and plumped down in an old cane-bottom rocker, long ago expanded to fit the lines of her ample body. After a while, the wetness left her eyes and the haze had gone. Sitting here, she had a view that seldom failed to comfort her, to drive away her dark moods. The wild prairie and the blackjack hills and ridges.

Many times she had watched from this same place, under the treees in the small frame house, before the great one was built. Watched for Louis to ride down the farthest ridge, for him to jog along its base and out upon the prairie and up to the single log barn. But the sight wasn't good today. It raked up too much.

The realization of a dead end terrified her. She discovered that she was clenching and unclenching her hands. Close to panic, she stood and her whirling thoughts spun in another direction—to the only escape left her.

Striding over, jerking open a bureau drawer, searching amid the orderly layers of sachet-smelling clothing, she found the cool neck of the bottle she had hidden there after the flying trip to Stoke's Place just outside Two Sands. Yet she still delayed, a reluctance staying her hand. She even let her grip relax and for an instant she thought she'd won. Then some deep, violent force took hold of her, and she was dragging forth the bottle and uncorking it and gulping the raw corn whisky.

It burned her throat, fired her chest, exploded in her stomach. She gagged, coughed, swallowed, aware of a fiery heat flushing her body, her cheeks. She had another drink; it did not burn so much as the first. Feel better already, she thought.

There was a restless reaction all through her now, and a certain thankful uplift. Staring at the oily beads inside the shaken-up bottle, she sensed a returning confidence. Firmly, she replaced the cork in the bottle and tapped it hard with the heel of her palm. With a disdainful demonstration of restraint, she stuck the bottle under the clothing, closed the drawer, and quickly left the room. A decision formed in her mind. No longer would she stick in this brooding house. She would not let it get her down. She would not give in to whiteman whisky.

Her exhilaration continued as she went walking under the cool arms of the trees, around the house, down to the barn and back again. She drifted eastward from the house. She was well past it, out of the timber and feeling the bright sun on her bare arms and neck, before the beginning comprehension of where she was going crystallized.

She stopped stone-still. The dark, brooding wave caught up with her as she did so, engulfing her. She became panicky again, staring around her, because only now did she know where her blind steps had intuitively pointed her.

She saw her destination through a shimmering haze, through a glimmering of dancing, flickering heat-devils. A low grassy knoll rose out of the plain sweeping away from the frowning ridges. She saw the high iron fence enclosure. The American flag, tattered and faded by weather, whipping in the wind. She saw the spire of up-reaching stone that marked where Louis lay. Out here. All alone. Suddenly, overpoweringly, she longed to be with him.

The sky spun. She was running, sometimes stumbling, but running. She had no clear thoughts, no breath in her tortured body, not feeling the prickly weeds and burrs and the thick, high tufts of grass that lashed her legs. She did not remember swinging open the stubborn, hinge-rusted iron gate and falling upon her knees across the gray mound.

She heard a woman crying somewhere, as in a twisted dream, and was startled to find that the crying came from her. It was a mourner's voice, part wail, part cry, throattom, savage.

Something welling up from long-ago time, the primitive anguish of a full-blood woman keening for her man dead.

It took time for an awareness to touch her. When it did register, dully, it was like returning from unreality. The sounds in her throat strangled off, though still sobbing. She was exhausted, her entire body as deadwood. She felt no perception of time.

It entered slowly that she had not given in this way since the afternoon they brought Louis here. On that day, with the wind hot, she had stood by the dark hole in the prairie and lifted her contorted face to the cloudless Osage sky and wailed from her heart; wailed and cried while Charlie held her as he would a frightened child. She had felt no shame then and she wasn't ashamed now. Instead, all the stored-up turmoil inside her had been released. She felt better again.

She was able, finally, to summon up a sort of shaky control. Standing, her knees wobbly, she rubbed her hand over the smooth, shining surface of the black marble monument. The Two Sands undertaker End assured her it was indeed a fitting memorial for a loved one, and the price only four thousand dollars.

Gently, her fingers traced out the chiseled lettering:

AN ANGEL CALLED HIM
LOUIS GARREAU
BELOVED HUSBAND, FATHER
Born Dec. 2, 1878, Died Mar. 7, 1920

Her hand shook as she touched the oval likeness of smiling Louis Garreau, a picture imaged upon porcelain so it would last forever. Now she thought angrily of the storm, of her passiveness for anything that Louis had wished. How he had ridden into the driving rain to look for a strayed saddle horse, laughing off her Indian fear of the crashing elements. How one of the hired hands had discovered his slickertangled body, drowned in swollen Yellow Dog creek. Louis, who could swim like a fish; because all Indian boys learned to swim early in the clear, rock-bottomed creeks of the Osage country.

She could not bring him back. She knew that … but how she wished she might! Just for one minute, one second!

The sobbing crept back in her dry throat. Somehow she managed to stifle it, an unexpected strength bolstering her at the moment before it broke on the awful wailing. She forced her attention away from the black stone and took notice of the weeds and grass crowding the plot.

A sudden notion seized her. She'd come here early tomorrow with a sharp hoe and clean this place good! It wasn't right to let weeds grow up around Louis' grave!

Regarding the unseemly growth, she felt a bowed-down sense of guilt for permitting such a thing to happen. She told herself that she ought to come here more. Not that she hadn't wanted to. Except it was always a struggle for her; besides, she did not have to be here to think of Louis. But she never forgot Decoration Day. Osages didn't forget. A white man might allow weeds to choke his dead, but an Indian didn't.

She grew erect, somewhat proudly. One thing she drew the line on, though. She would not put bananas and oranges on the grave, as many of the old full-bloods did. That was silly; like old days. When they killed a dead warrior's horse by his resting place in the rocks on a hill or under the scaffold…. Modern days now. She and Louis had attended the government school in Pawhuska; always kept up, been modern.

Only once had she gone back on her white man's training. That first Decoration Day after Louis died, she had draped a red silk scarf over his grave. Returning, in a few days, she'd discovered it missing. She guessed some coyote had dragged it off…. But it was worse in the cemeteries. People stole things off the graves, broke the fine porcelain pictures. Some graves had been blown open; robbers looking for jewelry, people said.

Nellie shook her head fiercely. That was why she had put Louis out here, away from town, in the country. Nobody would bother him here. Nobody—

Once more her throat constricted, tight as a vise. It frightened her, knowing that she was powerless to help herself, alternately rising and sinking under the torrent of hopeless grief.

In frantic haste, she bent down and started yanking up weeds and grass. The work went faster and easier on the still-soft mound, which she partially cleared in her frenzy. But where the fallow earth had never been turned, she succeeded merely in breaking off the tops of the stubborn roots. She labored until her heart pounded and her back ached. After some minutes, she gave up. Her dress was sweat-streaked and her hands sticky and hurting and stained with weed juice.

Sadly surveying her pitiful efforts, she admitted failure. She knew also that she had stayed too long. Slowly, with a lingering backward glance, she wandered to the gate. Over its creaking protests, she forced it shut and stood back. It gave her some satisfaction to know that stock could not get in now.

She was not even crying as she let her feet loosely adjust to the gentle incline of the knoll. For nothing lay inside her, just a dead slackness. Not until she thought of the coming night in the great house did her mind function. A crawling dread took form and she was trembling again.

A drumming along the ground shocked her into reality. The unexpected beat of horses trotting. She turned and looked. In from the east rode Sid and Tharp Kutch, almost upon her.

It flashed over her how miserable and grieving she looked. They'd surprised her, walking head down, her grief naked for them to see. Suddenly, she wanted to run, to hide. A last jerk of pride held her fast, made her greet them first. "You're back early." Her voice on the wind mocked her with its hollow, unnatural strangeness.

Sid Tyson's eyes were sharply upon her as he reined up. But he looked away as he spoke and she was thankful, "Just our bunch showed up. No fun if you can't bet a little."

"Yeah," she agreed tonelessly, fervently wishing they'd move on.

He chuckled. "Maybe Clark's out lease hunting."

She attempted a smile, and failed, realizing it was some joke she didn't know about.

Tharp Kutch, whose yellow gaze had never left her, said, "Sid's just too handy with a rope, is all. Scared Clark off. He's been gettin' his plow cleaned."

Nellie grew sensitive under Kutch's stare. It angered her unreasonably that he continued to size her up. More than once she had trapped his undressing glance upon Savannah, for instance, causing her to wonder why Sid kept him around. No way to look at a woman. Why did Sid permit it?

Furthermore, Kutch represented the one question in Nellie's mind about Sid's judgment. Tharp was too rough. She had never liked the man, which was unusual for her, since she liked most people. When she had suggested firing him, Sid had promptly defended him.

"He's a good hand, Nellie. Does his work. I'll admit he's cut a little on the rough side. But sometimes you need a man like him."

"He's just a damned potlicker," she'd argued. "Hangs around. I don't like him."

Sid was unimpressed, undisturbed. "You're imagining things, Nellie. He'll never bother you."

She could see that further argument was useless. Sid's mind was made up. So she never mentioned the subject again, but she felt no easier around Tharp Kutch. Their dislike, she knew, was mutual.

She experienced the unease now. Although there was no exact expression defined in the yellow eyes, they seemed to mock her somehow because she was an Indian, maybe; to degrade her

for harboring so weak a thing as sorrow, to expose all her intimate emotions. She felt dirty under his attention. She could bear
it no more and she began walking gradually toward the house,
keeping herself under a rigid control.

Her motion drew them after her. In a moment they rode past,
Sid saying, "We'll water and mosey over to Charlie's place. Be late
when we get in."

Her relief mounted as she watched them ride to the windmill; however, she was still angered by Kutch. Well, at least she
could thank Sid for never intruding on her poor secrets, the feel-
ings she could not hide. He understood her and she was humbly
grateful.

She'd known him some years. Distantly, when he was a lawyer in Two Sands, handling legal affairs for Louis; as a neighbor
after Sid bought an adjoining ranch, before his white wife of a few
years died and left him with Savannah, a gangling daughter by
her previous marriage. Later, he was the one familiar person to
whom she could turn when her world died. Sid was sympathetic.
He had advised her on ranch matters, about which she had scant
knowledge and no interest with Louis gone. He never made her
feel low and cheap and ignorant, as some squaw men treated the
Indian wives they'd married for money, while they kept a white
woman elsewhere.

So she had married him. Looking back at her decision in the
sober light of reflection, she decided that she had done so because
of a sense of obligation to Sid. Yet an obligation wasn't love, no
matter how hard you tried. Also, she realized, because of her
utter loneliness.

Despite that, she had remained lonely and lost, frequently
unhappy when Jeannette kept so long to herself and did not come
over to visit. It was too bad that Jeannette resented Sid, though
Nellie understood that, too. No man could take Louis' place.

Now, drifting under the trees, in the quiet shade and toward
the dark, homeless house, she knew that she would finish the

bottle. It would ease her for a while. And when it failed her, as it always did in the end, she would go off in her car and drive and drive on the lonely, wind-swept roads, through the grumbling stands of oil derricks, anywhere; drive till she could find some degree of relief and thankful exhaustion.

Nellie Tyson quickened her gait, driven by a compulsion over which she had no control. Somehow she didn't care. Once again her mind swung unerringly to Louis Garreau.

CHAPTER FIVE

WHEN HAPPY ADCOCK stopped the flivver, Myles Pearce climbed out stiffly. It was late afternoon, the blackjacks shadows thickening. September heat massed in the still timber. Big hands on hips, he stood by the running board and watched without speaking.

Although he thought he'd known what to expect after the Tyson place, he still wasn't prepared. This remote house commanded the long wooded rise; it heaved up wide and high and gave the impression that its owner sought the far view of broken prairie and ragged hills. Its inevitable red brick hulk loomed even larger than the Tyson headquarters, much newer. It was the Tyson ranch house—rather Louis Garreau's, he corrected himself upon recalling Adcock's story —on a grander scale. He could not miss the comparison, the sameness. It seemed that Jeannette Garreau, lavishing on a memory, had striven to duplicate the house of her father.

He thought, one girl and that great big house.

He turned to Adcock. "You know Miss Garreau, don't you?"

"Ever since she was born."

"Mind coming with me? It'll help me break the ice."

There was a question mark in Adcock's reaction, but he said, "Not a-tall," and obliged at once.

Approaching the silent house, Myles noted the telephone wire slanting in from the string of poles that paralleled the road to town; the double brick garage housing a purple Cadillac roadster.

The front door was closed. There was no answer to his series of knocks and he faced Adcock, tempted to tell him to turn tail for town. As yet he could not pin the exact compulsion that had brought him here; more impulse, he judged, than anything else. He had no desire to stay. But he said doggedly, "Let's look around back, Happy."

Adcock suppressed a yawn, nodding.

Late sunlight bathed the yard. A breath of hot wind rubbed off the undulating prairie floor. Myles savored it as he tramped to the corral of stubby creosoted cedar posts and thick connecting planks. His eyes went to a stocking-legged sorrel fiddling inside, to the new windmill and its shining, slow-moving blades pumping water into a stone trough. Before him rose the barn, a mountain of brown sandstone, a mail-order likeness of the one Louis Garreau had built.

All this made him wonder what Jeannette Garreau would be like. The picture of a large young Indian woman came to his mind.

Adcock leaned his skinny frame against the corral, yawned, tipped back his hat, and mopped a red bandana over his mournful face. "Hot, ain't it? Y'know, think I'll just help myself to a drink of that windmill water. Stayin' up all hours, drivin' to Tulsey, sure does take the spark out of a man my age. Not like it was when I drove night stage. Course, I'se younger then." He was moving as he talked. "Better come along. Have a look-see at Jeannette's new barn. Few humans bunk this good."

Myles was curious, but he followed slowly, held in bounds by a cowman's ingrained reluctance to prowl another man's horse barn. Adcock slid free the gate bar. Coming to the runway entrance of the barn, Myles paused and Adcock went on to the watering trough. Myles saw him hesitate and turn his head before bending to drink from the trickling pipe.

"Say, you might see if Jeannette's saddle is there in the barn? Big silver horn; fancy leather work."

"That sorrel hasn't run a lick this afternoon," Myles said. "No marks on him. My guess is she's still out with Frank and Savannah Tyson. Remember?"

"Prob'ly so. But the way they say she's had to work lately, short-handed an' all, could be she's a-restin' in the house. Maybe didn't hear us."

"Well," Myles said indulgently, "it won't hurt to look." He entered the barn and blinked a moment, till his eyes adjusted to the gloom. He could make out the slatted framework of the first high stall, the usual straw-littered floor. The familiar ammoniac smell filled his nostrils.

It occurred to him that the barn was darker than ordinary. The blurred outline of a saddle slung atop the second stall partition caught his eye. He stepped toward it, peering, hand reaching.

But he never touched the saddle. There was no warning. His head simply exploded in a blaze of splintered light. He was reeling, his boots wobbling platforms upon which he swayed. Then there was no bottom whatever under him, nothing, and he was falling off into a black whirlpool....

He was a swimmer straggling below the shadowy surface of murky, silted water. He was trying desperately to gain the faint light he saw high above. Long afterward, his lungs near bursting, he broke the surface, floundering. Even here, a crazy haze covered everything.

It dawned on him with a distant, tortuous perception that faces shimmered before him. Faces near, now far. He groaned. His eyes refused to focus no matter how hard he tried. He gave up; then, suddenly, the faces cleared.

Happy Adcock's worried features became focused in his vision. And another face—a young woman's. He was, Myles saw, flattened out upon the stable runway. As he stirred, a throbbing pain forced shut his eyes. He sank back, groaning.

"Somebody," said Adcock, concerned and puzzled, "knocked you out—cold. I was at the windmill. First thing I knew somebody hot-footed it around the barn."

"You saw him?" It was the girl, tense, wide-eyed.

"Just got a look at his back. Happened too fast to tell who. But I found this." Adcock, smiling grimly, held up a singletree. "He whammed you with this, Myles."

"Never saw him...." Pain hammered. Myles stopped short, feeling nausea flood his stomach, his mouth. He fought the sickness, drawing gulps of air.

"Take it easy," Adcock warned, and studied Myles closely. "You been out two-three minutes, I reckon. Jeannette an' me ... well, we didn't know if you was comin' to or not."

"I remember now"—Jeannette Garreau's voice held a note of blended anger and careful concentration—"I heard a horse, running hard, when I came up to the barn." Anxiety enriched the husky tone. "I think we'd better take you to the house."

They helped him to his feet. For a blackish interval, before he stood rocking on his boot heels, Myles almost slumped down. Swaying there, he felt a soft shoulder slip quickly under his, and he caught the faint scent of violets. He felt foolishly weak as she put a slim, firm arm around his waist, but he didn't mind. He saw that she came barely to his shoulders. Together the three of them weaved into the sunlight.

Myles' head was swimming. He realized he'd taken a savage clout. Tentative fingers located a high swelling on the long ridge of bone behind his right ear. His futile anger, loaded with disgust, fanned up. By the time they were out-side the corral, he was moving unsteadily under his own power. Jeannette Garreau led off to the house, inside to a lofty kitchen.

There she seated Myles and insisted, over his protests, on a cool, wet cloth for his pounding head. That done, she punched shavings and wood chunks into the black stove. While the fire snapped, she filled the coffee pot and set cups and saucers on the red-checkered table cloth. Adcock took a chair across from him.

It was pleasant and soothing there in the kitchen as her small boots tapped back and forth. Not till now did Myles notice her in particular. Despite the afternoon shadows, he could see the smoothness of her striking olive-bronzed face. Her cheekbones rose high and proud, and she had the greatest dark eyes he'd ever seen. Her slim figure had the fullness of a young woman who had matured early, yet a completeness without heaviness. It tapered up from long legs, encased in tight-fitting riding trousers, tucked in narrowly at her waist, and lifted to the half bells of her breasts under the maroon-colored silk shirt. She was vivid, feminine and competent, about Savannah Tyson's age. He smiled wryly at his oversize misconception of her.

Not until the coffee was ready did she take off her cowman's gray hat—so much a part of her, it seemed, that only now was she aware of it. Her straight black hair was really blue-black, he decided, and she wore it knotted on her neck.

The coffee had strength; after a second cup, Myles rolled a cigarette.

She pulled up a chair next to Adcock. "How you feel, Myles?"

"Better." He looked at her inquiringly as he heard his name.

Jeannette Garreau flashed him an apologetic smile. "Happy told me."

"Just who you are," Adcock explained, making a point of it, and Myles said, "That's all right, Happy. Saved me the trouble."

Her gaze rambled over him with obvious interest. "Here I've known Frank all this time and he never said anything about a brother."

"No reason to, don't s'ppose."

"Oh, I don't know." She regarded him frankly, curiously. "If I had a brother or sister, believe I would."

"—if, say, you were on speaking terms."

Her brow knitted. "Oh—"

"Forget it," he said, annoyed with himself.

"What I mean is. I would, I think, to the person I was going to marry."

Myles blinked. "Frank—you—and Frank?" She nodded and he said through his surprise, "Congratulations. When's the big day?"

"We're—not that far along," she answered. There was a pause. She seemed to want to switch the line of talk. She measured him worriedly. "We should be talking about you, not me. Why, you could have been killed! I don't understand! Who'd do that?"

"Nobody knew I was headed here." He removed the cloth gingerly, waved off another. "What about your crew?"

"Quit," she snapped. "Last week."

"I mean any argument before They pulled out?" It was incredible to him that any man would want to smash this slim, part-Indian girl. On the other hand, a lone woman in boom country invited trouble. Particularly a pretty one.

She shrugged away the question. He found his interest unconsciously on her full, sensitive lips. "Not a word," she said. "They just quit one morning. Said they could make more money in the oil fields. I didn't offer to raise wages, because I'm already payin' the top." A bitterness suffused the dark pools of her eyes; they flashed. "Not all Osages are born suckers."

He felt a mild deflation. "So you're by yourself?"

"Except when Savannah Tyson comes over—or Frank. They did today." Her laughter tinkled. "Oh, I'm not worried. Some rider'll get hungry enough to work for me by shipping time."

"Don't see why you can't get help," he said, frowning. "Sid Tyson said as much today. We had dinner at your mother's place."

Some ancient flame of feeling flared in her. "I'm glad you said her place." She pursed her lips in a thoughtful manner. "I don't mean Sid's a pauper—far from it. He did pretty well, in town, playin' guardian for Osages."

Myles skirted the edge of that implication when he spoke. "Savannah said you were short, and Tyson—"

"Exactly what did he say?" Jeannette demanded.

"That you could call on him any time you needed men."

The full lips cast a tight, crisp smile. "He did, huh?"

He kept quiet. His head ached and he guessed he'd stirred up something. He wanted to hear more.

"Go on," Jeannette told him, cold and inquiring.

"Tyson made the offer. In fact, he acted hurt because you hadn't called on him."

Her eyes were bright. "I never have—I never will."

"Getting married will settle that, won't it?"

Her face changed, then back as before. So imperceptibly that he doubted he'd really seen it—the hint of inner struggle.

Suddenly, Happy Adcock stood up. He peered at his watch. "Have to go." His hurrying glance sought Myles.

"Wait a minute, Happy." Jeannette's eyes widened on Myles, however, her gaze never wavering as she asked, "Tell me something. Why'd you come out here?"

Voiceless, he looked her full in the face, while an awareness raced through him that he could go with Adcock and step out of this. But the words were out of his mouth before it occurred to him, "You need a man and I'm out of a job." A swaying dizziness returned as he pulled erect in his chair, just now knowing his intention.

Into Jeannette's eyes leaped a surge of pleased astonishment. "You serious?"

He nodded.

"Kind of sudden, isn't it?" she asked suspiciously.

"I told you ... I need the job."

It was apparent that she didn't believe him, though her suspicion had mellowed to more of a bewilderment. Her voice bridged between them, soft and disarming, and then it rose, cool and demanding. "Sure it's got nothing to do with Frank?"

"I didn't say that."

She was plainly provoked. "You're beating around the bush."

"Look at it this way," countered Myles. "Your crew just quit and I'm available. I'm even hungry." His attempt at a grin, he saw, was wasted on her.

She made a sudden, rejecting shake of her dark head. "How do I know you're on the level?"

"You don't. I could be the biggest horse thief in Oklahoma. Maybe I am."

"I'm not worried about that."

She was driving at something beyond him, and he groped for her meaning. "Then what's bothering you?"

"I was asking you," she evaded. "Now you're asking me."

Myles lifted a weary hand. "Yeah. Where'd we start?"

"Listen, folks." Adcock divided his slightly puzzled aggravation between them. "This pow-wow could go on all night." He looked toward the door.

Jeannette was silent, watchful, her face a mirror of nothing.

Myles threw her a look and got to his feet, thinking that she'd turned him down. He shrugged and said, "Well—" and was reaching for his hat on the table, when she said in mock surprise, "Quitting already?"

He wheeled on her, so suddenly the dizzy pain flashed anew. "Didn't know I was hired." He waited. But he saw no assent. Just an expressionless face, pretty and unreadable, wiser than he'd figured. He said to Adcock, "You savvy Osage? Maybe you can find out. I can't."

Jeannette's laughter spilled over the room, somewhat pleased and teasing. "Go in town for his things, Happy. He's hired."

Myles felt the rush of exultation in his throat, sobered by an uncomfortable realization. He said awkwardly, "My grip's in the car."

Suspicion caught her at once. "Oh…you knew you'd be hired?"

"I always travel light," he parried.

Her gaze drew level. "Might as well tell you something—now. I'm not hiring you for the reason you think."

She left it there, a puzzle for him to ponder, and he reasoned that it could wait.

When Adcock started for the kitchen door, Myles followed. At the door a thought seemed to check Adcock. He murmured, "Call on ol' Happy any time, Jeannette. Don't forget it!" And cheerfully to Myles, "Been around these Osages so long I feel like a full-blood. Maybe they'll adopt me into the tribe some day, give me a headright... Why, I knew Jeannette, here, when she was papoose size. Knew Nellie and Louis 'fore they got married... 'fore he—" Hastily Adcock retreated from what he was on the border of finishing and looked in regret at Jeannette.

She said gratefully, "Thanks, Happy... I know that," but her voice seemed to stick in her throat, lodged on some hidden emotion.

He shouldered out with the abruptness of a man who had said too much. Outside, he said to Myles, "Damn me! I get to talkin' about old times an' say the wrong thing. See, she's touchy about Louis. Even when you mention his name. The whole family was mighty close. Louis he raised her like a boy when she wasn't in Catholic school. She can do a man's work, too. Don't think she can't!" Adcock reminded proudly.

They were striding to the car when Myles asked curiously, "You said Louis Garreau died? How?"

"Not natural. Drownded. Found him in Yellow Dog crick. Well— I'd better high-tail it in." Myles paid him. and took out his grip.

Adcock set the spark and cranked the engine. Once behind the jiggling wheel, he resembled a wise old tree owl. "Kinda figured you'd stay. But watch out for singletrees... An' when you decide to take in Tulsey town, ol' Happy's ready."

Myles grinned. "I'm hired up now. No time for foolishness."

Adcock winked broadly. "You're just plain lucky. If I'se thirty years younger, you wouldn't have this job, son." He put the flivver in reverse, brought it to a lurching, flourishing, spraddle-wheeled stop, waved a hand and rattled off for Two Sands.

Preoccupied, Myles strolled to the house, listening to the occasional backfiring of the flivver slamming the quiet hills. Walking on, he remembered Jeannette Garreau there in the dim kitchen, slim-legged and dark, her bronzed face unable to mask at times a wistful, small-girl loneliness. Another step and he was struck by a thought: Frank's girl. His head ached again.

About daybreak the timepiece fixed by long habit in Myles' mind awakened him in the bunkhouse. His head still banged when he sat up and the lump felt huge under his exploring fingers. But once dressed and outside in the early morning coolness, he thought hungrily of breakfast A light shone in the kitchen of the proud, towering house. He stepped to the door and knocked.

"Come in!"

She was sticking a pan of biscuits inside the hot stove when he entered. Her face was flushed as she straightened, and it seemed to him that the oven's heat heightened her vivid coloring.

"Morning, Miss Garreau."

"Make it Jeannette. And you don't have to knock at mealtime." She gave him a studying look. "How's the noggin?"

"Sound as rock."

"Well, rock can break if you hit it hard enough. Have a chair."

He sat, recognizing the sociability of a ranch-reared woman accustomed to the company of hungry riding men at her table. There also existed, he thought, a defined limit of familiarity. She wore a sky-blue silk shirt. Her dove-gray trousers were snug at the waist and tucked inside small, black-vamped boots, scuffed and worn where her spurs rode, thus leaving the impression of personal indulgence up to the hand-tooled, white steer-head tops stitched in red. Her neat black hair glistened in the yellow coal-oil light.

A comparison popped into his mind: the shining blackness of a crow's wing, the sun striking it and a man glimpsing it as he rode from shaded timber into dazzling brightness.

Soon he was helping himself to fried eggs, ham, redeye gravy, biscuits, potatoes, molasses and coffee. He ate hungrily, talking little, conscious of an intimacy in the comfortable kitchen. She finished first and drew brown papers and sack tobacco from a shirt pocket and deftly twirled a two-handed cigarette. She inhaled deeply, expelling the smoke like a man.

"Just after meals," she said, smiling self-consciously across at him. "Can't seem to manage in the wind." After that she fell silent, quietly observing him, until he finished.

She laughed in a husky, throaty embarrassment when Myles, looking up, caught her eyes. "Was just thinkin' it's good to have a man around the ranch again," she said.

"Lonesome here for a woman," he said, his nod taking in the vast house.

"Oh, I don't mind. I wouldn't live in town."

"I can understand why. Great country."

His appreciation made her beam. "Glad you like it." Her glance became curious. "You're Frank's brother, but that's all I know about you. Mind if I ask a few questions?"

"Such as—"

"What about yourself? Before you came to the Osage?"

"From the Flint Hills," he said. "Same as Frank. Overseas…infantry…didn't like French wine. Came home and decided to make a pile of money. Worked your Burbank boom for a while. Found out I didn't want to get rich digging holes in the prairie. That I liked tailin' cows better. So "—he spread his big hands—" back to the Flints."

"After that?"

"Here I am, in your hire."

She seemed disappointed. "You don't talk much. Frank either."

"Guess he spoke up at the right time, though, didn't he?" Myles said, grinning.

"Oh, that—" The dark depths of her eyes told him the sum total of nothing, unless the fleeting expression betrayed her again. For he judged by now that it edged into her features when she might be unsure or on the defensive.

He changed the subject by pushing back from the table. "I'm ready to start."

"All right." White teeth pulled reflectively on full, sensitive lips. "First thing, I better tell you what's around us, so you'll know where you are. Mama's ranch—that's taking in Dad's old allotment, too —is north of us. Uncle Charlie's is northeast. Above him is Clark Slater. His ranch is small. He depends mostly on what he can lease for grass. Uncle Charlie's range is best, especially the west half of his valley." Her eyes grew humoring. "But he'd rather hunt and fish."

"Uncle Charlie?"

"Yes, Charlie Blackhorse—mama's brother. Way it worked out, when they allotted the reservation years ago, all the family's land touches. Then Dad bought up more." The momentary bitterness he'd noticed before swept to her mouth, sobering it. "He had a dream. He wanted to see all this in one big working spread. Least he lived to see it that way a while. Different now."

She was herself again in a moment, her pleasant, throaty voice outlining what needed doing. The fence lines were two weeks unridden. Might be some screw-worm cases on the south side, where the pasture ran heavily to brush and timber. First chore called for the fence check. She'd catch up with Myles later.

"What's your brand?" he asked.

"Chain Seven—Dad's old brand—three sevens in a line with the bar under."

Moving to the corral, he felt a deepening eagerness. A blood-red bay ranged inside with the stocking-legged sorrel. He chose the sorrel and was tossing a stock saddle aboard, when he heard the sliding rasp of the gate bar.

Jeannette Garreau, hatted and booted, came jingling across the horse lot. His eyes stayed on her. "Changed my mind," she announced. "Going with you."

"Company's welcome. I'll saddle up for you."

"Never mind. Skeeter's no trouble."

Before he could move, she was easing up to the bay, bridle in hand. The gelding took the bit and she led him to the barn, brush-rubbed the short back, slapped on a blanket and started saddling. She was swift and practiced.

Myles, cinched up by then, had trouble keeping his gaze off her. Foolishness, he thought, and deliberately took the sorrel outside and waited. Moments later, he saw her step to the stirrup and swing up a slim leg.

Wind, wandering across the stony ridge, scattered a coolness and the pungency of sweet grass, dry as it was this September. It was a wind of many murmuring, joyous voices, pulsing under a sky both blue and white, hung with soft, shaggy clouds.

Myles felt fine. His head ached only when the sorrel jarred him, which wasn't often. A relief, he thought, to know where your horse tracks headed, even if you might not be around long.

First off, Jeannette had led him to the western fence line, then south and east through patches of blackjacks, past scattered bunches of Chain Seven whitefaces. Each time they looked them over, one by one. Satisfied, they worked on and gradually straightened out north. The sun sat hot and high. Near noon.

She said, "We'll go on to Uncle Charlie's."

They rode steadily, dropping into rocky draws and climbing between tumbling hills. A wagon road, appearing seldom traveled, curved in from the west. It drew them through a wire gate.

"Uncle Charlie's country now," she told him.

To the northwest, their tops showing bold above the roll of the pitching land, oil rigs formed a bristling forest of cross-hatched spires. Here and there storage tanks glistened like silver mushrooms, fat and round upon the rich prairie. Grazing cattle were small brown toys. He felt a little awed in all this upland space that had no limit.

Jeannette Garreau reined up, her attention distant, fixed. Her face gathered tautly. He saw a tiny jaw muscle quiver. "Your mother's range?" he asked.

"Was," she said and dismissed the subject by jogging on.

She was a hard woman to ignore, he discovered. Once, dismounting to tighten his cinch, he could feel her steady interest. When he turned, she was gazing off again.

They quit the hills and presently followed the road, which descended a high bluff into a shallow, spread-out valley. The road quickly became a trail, rutted by rains over the years, narrow and tricky. Below, brush and rock clad the steep limestone face.

He rode the outside. There was barely enough room for a wagon. Their horses touched flanks. His leg brushed hers for a two count. It was like an electric shock.

She pulled away instantly, as did he. But the feeling was there, whether he admitted it or not. He set his eyes straight ahead, not liking what he'd learned about himself.

Across the north-south creek, which Jeannette identified as Yellow Dog, stood a craggy ridge looking down upon its lesser neighbors. By habit, Myles cached it as a landmark to remember. This side the ridge, farther south, a wooden rig jutted above creek timber. Its pumping unit throbbed steadily as a heart beat.

As Myles' sorrel footed out upon smoother traveling, the earth seemed to drowse in an unbroken spell. It was a different sensation entirely from higher up, where the black derricks brought a feeling of intrusion and cattle moved in the distance.

He saw not a single cow. Mourning doves made lonesome, plaintive calls. Rabbits scurried in the thick grass. The horses' passage flushed a quail. It whirred off and sent back a sharp warning whistle; another bobwhite answered...Somewhere a dog barked. Two gunshots boomed. The sounds were not repeated and Myles dismissed them when Jeannette said knowingly, "We'll eat squirrel or quail."

He let the gelding laze alongside hers, feeling the solitude, the air of undisturbed nature. The road ambled on for a mile or more, siding the timber-fringed creek.

Then, abruptly, the creek twisted away and Myles saw a house. After the immense Tyson and Garreau ranch houses, this one took him by surprise. It was a single-story building of weather-stained wood, with a porch flanking its length like a sagging appendage. It was long paintless, battered and grayed-out, as if it had hunkered there in unconcern for many years. Toward the creek slumped a low barn and pole corral, both bearing the same stamp of undetermined age. Close by was a rusty looking water well pump. A pipe, held up by baling wire, ran from pump mouth to a wooden trough. Off from the house he saw an ancient spring wagon. The corral held a pinto pony.

As they crossed the yard to the watering trough, Myles eyed the shrunken house. It reminded him of a line camp, seldom used, left alone save when a rider passed.

Jeannette's voice turned him. "Not much of a place...but Uncle Charlie likes it this way. Sometimes," she said wistfully, "I think he's smart."

They dismounted and watered the horses. While he worked the pump handle, she cupped her hand under the pipe end and drank. Straightening, she swiped a sleeve boyishly across her wet mouth and took her turn pumping. She said, "HI cook us something if he doesn't show up pretty soon," and was feminine and gracious again.

"No hurry." He put his eyes to traveling the prairie in this silent valley. In the distance, far northeast, the top of a solitary derrick peeked above the creek timber. He pondered it a moment. "How'd that well pan out?"

"Dry hole wildcat. Clark Slater made a kind of line camp there last year."

She swept off her hat and touched her hair. He got the faint, heady scent of her all at once. That damn violet smell, he thought. Her face, he saw, was more oval than he'd realized. The features more finely moulded. The skin like burnished copper. He meant only to admire, but he could not ignore his quickening disturbance.

He backed off a step and spoke, his covering voice blunt, "Slater wouldn't be sore at you, would he?"

Her eyes sprang wide. "Why—no. We're neighbors."

"No trouble with him … say … over leases."

"I don't lease to anybody."

"Can you take a little advice?"

Her eyebrows rose. "If it's good, yes," she said, her face smoothing.

"I think it is…. Don't ride alone. Hire a woman to stay with you at the ranch. Hire another hand or two."

She appeared startled. "I know—you're thinking about that man!"

"Point is," he said, "I just stumbled in—flushed him."

He felt guilty, in a way, bringing it up. Beyond this morning's brief conversation, at breakfast, the knockout had been shelved. He guessed now that they both had wanted to avoid it.

"I didn't say so," she answered, scoffing, "but maybe he came to prowl the house."

"He could've ransacked it before we drove up."

She understood, nodding slowly, and he saw a fear darken her eyes, tighten her cheeks. He felt a sudden regret.

"I'm not trying to scare you. lust seems like a good idea."

She stared at him, uncertain, her mouth parted. He saw the little-girl look.

He hadn't intended to place his hand on her shoulder. But there it was, the stirring feel of her making his heart pump. And suddenly he was very unsure of himself.

"But ... "

She never finished and he never came near an answer. There wasn't time. For the crackle of brush was a sound cleaving between them. He snapped his hand down and turned.

He saw two men. He recognized Sid Tyson astride a horse and Charlie Blackhorse, who was tramping up, bear-like, from the creek. They'd seen. He knew that. Myles felt an awkward, embarrassed stiffness.

Blackhorse carried a shotgun over one shoulder. Two squirrels dangled from his other hand. The brown and white hound of Two Sands, ranging in advance, raised a deepchested challenge. A grunt from the Osage quieted him.

Myles saw Tyson's stare take them in. He saw Jeannette, beside him, slowly stiffen. Yet, when Blackhorse lumbered up, she introduced Myles without hesitation. Blackhorse grunted a "How," plopped down the game and grunted a warning for the dog, leaned the shotgun against an old log and extended a ponderous slab of hand. The broad platter of flesh enveloped Myles' hand. It was an Indian's shake—relaxed, brief, ceremonious.

"Ah, yes," spoke Tyson from the saddle. "We've met."

Myles inclined his head. "Howdy."

"He's riding for me," Jeannette said. Her voice was casual, yet cool, undercut with a suggestion of challenge.

Tyson's jaw dropped a notch. Then he was smiling, friendly and interested. "I see.... " To Myles he added, "Figured you'd be long gone by now."

"Nice country. Decided to stick around."

"You got a good eye."

That, Myles considered, could be taken two ways.

Tyson, lifting his reins to go, swerved his horse and nodded to Jeannette. "Ride over and see us. Bring your new hand. Frank will be glad to see him, too.... So long, Charlie."

He rode off, heading northwest.

As Jeannette watched him, her lips thinned.

Charlie Blackhorse hadn't noticed the byplay. He was intent on Myles' sorrel, admiring him as he drank from the trough. Blackhorse said amiably, "Good waters here," and gestured big. "Anywheres this valley good waters.... Up there"—he traced a thick finger to indicate the western base of the hill—"two springs. Natur'l." Next he wheeled and gestured emphatically. "That crick..." And, swinging back, pointing at the pump "Plenty water—jus' thirty foot down. Good, ain't it?"

When he then lowered his face into the trough water to drink, Jeannette, who'd been absently listening, said in affectionate amusement, "Uncle Charlie says if it's good enough for horses, it's just right for him."

Blackhorse drank in unbroken, thirsty gulps. He was long moments filling up. When he came erect, his dripping mahogany face glistened. He said, grinning, "Anybody hungry?"

"Who ever saw a hungry Eendian?" Jeannette asked. "I know—you want me to cook."

"Tell yuh whut," Blackhorse said, a gleam of bribery in his muddy eyes. "This Eendian'll git yuh some quail t'take home. Mighty good, huh?"

"When?"

"After we eat."

"But you'll be all afternoon." She was still teasing him.

"Won' take long," Blackhorse promised. "Big covey—jus' waitin'." He gestured south, in direction of the landmark ridge.

"A deal," said Jeannette in humoring surrender. "But no skinny birds. Better all be fat." She informed Myles, "That's all he does, is hunt and fish," and swung off toward the house.

Blackhorse gazed after her, his affection awkward. Catching the hound nosing the squirrels, he grunted him back, at the same time approving, "Dog—yuh hungry, huh?"

After that, he placed the squirrels atop a corral post for safe-keeping, and, in his lumbering gait, went to the barn and showed Myles where to stable the horses. As Myles slipped on the rope halters, the Osage dug canfuls of oats from the storage bin and forked down hay from the loft.

Myles watched the fast, fluid movements of the ponderous brown body. Big, he thought, like the old-time Osages. They were the biggest and broadest Injuns in the world, so Dow had once said, and if a boy wasn't on his buttons, why they might just slip a blan-ket over him and take him along. Impressed then, Myles was now.

Shortly, returning to the pump, Myles was the spectator as Blackhorse expertly skinned and cleaned the squirrels and pitched the leavings to "Dog," which seemed to be the only name the Osage had for the hound. That chore done, the full-blood took up the shotgun, lightly as a boy might a stick, and they walked to the house.

It was almost bare by white man's standards, closed off except for the kitchen and one large connecting room. Nothing on the walls or the plank floors. A rocker sidled up to the pot-bellied wood stove in the off room. Snuggled against a wall stood a single iron bed, covered with blankets. Dust layered the floor.

"Uncle Charlie had a hired man once, but he got lonesome and quit," Jeannette filled in for Myles during the meal. "Charlie just goes in for groceries and shells," she teased.

"An' guv'mint check," Charlie Blackhorse added. His paw-size hands lowered the bowl from which he took his black coffee. "Purty lonesome. No squaw, no kids." His drumming laugh filled the room. Dinner finished, he carried leftover meat and biscuits to the door and called sharply, "Dog! Dog!"

Outside there came a swift pattering and expectant whin-ing. Blackhorse did not move. The whining rose to a series of short, insistent barks. Still, Blackhorse hadn't moved. The barking deepened, louder, pleading, demanding.

All at once, Blackhorse pushed open the screen door and tossed the food, a piece at a time. Myles heard the snap of closing jaws, the gulping. When everything was gone, Blackhorse scuffed back. He looked pleased, contented.

"Some dog," he said as much to himself.

Later, they loafed on the porch a while, soaking up the warm sun, feeling the wind meandering across the valley. Charlie Blackhorse sat relishing his pipe, smoking with a certain ceremony. Slowly drawing in the smoke and slowly puffing it out, to scatter and ride the breeze.

Once Dow had told Myles another story. Of an old Indian smoking the sacred red pipe, the fragrant kinnikinnick tobacco making a white man's mouth juices run fast. The old Indian making an offering to the sky, then to Grandmother Earth and the four great directions.

Dog hovered around Blackhorse or ranged far beyond the yard, always to patter back and hunker in close, the liquid hunter's eyes hopefully on Blackhorse... Mebbe this afternoon, huh?

As though Dog reminded him of his promise, Blackhorse nodded his head at the creek, down it to the distant high ridge, rimmed black with timber. "Good place. 'Long that crick—big covey." He got up then.

"Go ahead," Jeannette excused herself. "This place needs cleaning up."

They prowled quietly along the creek, working through the scattered brush and thick grass. Dog roved ahead, every once in a while pausing to look back. Good, huh? And Blackhorse would motion left or right or onward; then Dog, his brown and white coat sleek in the sun, would go searching again.

Charlie Blackhorse took his time, looking and listening. Now and then he'd stop and grin across at Myles, and nod, and they'd scout on. The ridge rose on Myles' left. He could see the stubby brush giving way to the grassy slope.

Suddenly, Blackhorse motioned Dog across. Dog cut over at once, moving rapidly at first, then slowing. The spotted head turned once, inquiringly on Blackhorse, who waved him forward. Dog stalked. He kept going so long that Myles feared the slope empty.

At that moment Dog froze. Myles, at the same instant, heard a startled whirring. Quail boiled up in a brown cloud. Blackhorse's gun was banging, even as Myles threw up his own and emptied it.

It was over in a breath. The powder smell hung strong and acrid as Myles turned to see Blackhorse, grinning hugely, hold up two fingers. They both looked off where the flight had settled. One second Myles saw Charlie Blackhorse's face as a furrowed copper image in the sun. Dog nosing in the grass for the fallen birds.

Then a bullet whined and Myles heard the distant crack of a rifle.

CHAPTER SIX

OLD REFLEXES had moved Myles. He found that he was down in the tall grass, with no memory of flattening out. He kept telling himself it was a stray shot, likely a coyote hunter's, even while a stubborn reasoning said he was wrong. He had a cornered sensation. His thoughts spun to Charlie Blackhorse and the nearby brush thickets. Inching up cautiously, he took a quick look.

What he saw made him draw in a deep breath, made the fear knot within, tight and brittle. The Indian still stood. He looked broader than ever, an inviting target, broad as daylight. He seemed posted there in seeming indifference. And before Myles could shout him down, the hornet sound whirred again, very close, and on its heels the clapping report.

Blackhorse dropped at once. So fast Myles thought he'd been hit, though the Osage hadn't cried out. Myles risked another look. Blackhorse lay with all the concealment of a submerged log, floating in the grassy sea.

"Charlie—you hurt?"

Heat built up inside Myles' green wall. He waited. The stillness so keen he could hear the fine humming of insects as a throbbing pulse upon the earth. The pressure built up, kept climbing, till he could delay no longer. He rolled to one side, calling low, "I'm coming over."

"Stay there." The voice, muffled through the grass thickness, sounded surprisingly calm.

Myles relaxed. "You all right?"

"Yeah. Jus' lookin'."

"Where y' figure he is?"

"That ridge. In them rocks."

"We'll have to crawl out."

"Go 'head."

"Keep your hind end down, Charlie. Belly over to that brush nearest you...toward the creek. We can make the creek from there."

On stomach and knees and elbows, Myles began crawling, shoving the shotgun ahead of him. He snaked on as the naked feeling hackled high along his neck and back. One thing he'd learned fast in France: a man aiming down a steep slope tended to overshoot—at first. But he could soon adjust, if he knew his rifle.

He crawled faster. He fought off the desire to run for it. A drilled-in discipline, dormant these past few years, took over. He crawled slower, forced himself to hold a steady, crabbing gait, thankful for the tall grass. He was sweating heavily when he reached the thicket, his arm and shoulder muscles twitchy. He scrabbled a few feet more for good meaure, then swiveled his head, watching the weaving grass that marked Blackhorse's wake. There was a smaller stirring alongside the Osage, where brown ears and a spotted head bobbed. A slab of hewn face, shining with sweat, appeared in the parted grass.

"Keep your rear down. Come on," Myles told him, relieved.

Grunting, Blackhorse rolled in beside Myles, Dog joined them. His first act was to swipe a wet tongue across the Indian's moist face. Blackhorse made him hunker down, muttering, "Poor shootin'."

"Close enough." There'd been no time for anger till now. A hot outrage began boiling in Myles.

"Ruined th' huntin'."

The lack of concern astonished Myles. He ground a harsh conviction into his voice, "No accident, Charlie. This guy means it. He wants your hide or mine. Bad enough to try in daylight."

"Nobody shoot Charlie."

There it was again—the persisting disbelief, the naive puzzlement of a mild man who's never faced killing violence. Myles glared. "Nobody shoot, hell!" he exploded. "Somebody just did! And I'm thinkin' he's still up there."

His words drove some of the good-natured doubt from the brown face, but not quite all. Myles turned front again. He felt sorry for Charlie Blackhorse and afraid.

By parting the brush, he could see the ridge thrusting up to his left. From this distance it revealed nothing that he could discover in the shadowed timber and tumbled rock, up-ended and strewn in slabs and boulders. He tracked his glance on the opening that beckoned some twenty yards between them and the creek, along the dark tree line to a point west of the height. There, in thick cover, shoulder-high brush and runty blackjacks bristled from stream to the ridge's beginning. Farther south was the derrick he'd noticed when he and Jeannette entered the valley.

He turned back to the ridge, studied it a full minute. It was entirely too quiet up there. Right now he had a feeling he didn't like. His lips flattened. He faced Blackhorse, realizing he hadn't felt this way in five years. "Charlie, we're gonna see if that gent's up there. We're going to the creek. Only I go first."

"This Eendian can go first."

"Don't worry. You'll get your chance."

Myles fastened his gaze another time on the ridge. It simmered in the same secretive silence, the overshadowing dominance. He started crawling and pushing the shotgun and came to the edge of the brush. He looked at Blackhorse and sucked in a great gulp of wind.

Then he heaved to his feet in a run, flinging himself across the bare gap. Bent low. Boots pounding and swishing the steamy grass. The nakedness all through him again. For a lifetime the dark safety of the timber seemed far away, no nearer despite the furious pumping of his legs.

He tensed for the gun crack. But it did not come. And then he was throwing himself behind the first cottonwood, striving to handle the shotgun gently as the leafy mould came leaping up at him.

Twisting around, hacking for breath, he faced the open space not at all as confident as he had been, for a swift certainty told him that the Osage was the rifleman's intended target.

Pitching his voice low, Myles called, "Hold up a minute, Charlie. Give me time to work up the creek a piece. When you hear my shotgun, break for the creek. The blast'll make him look a second. Give you that much."

Keeping to the timber, Myles went some twenty yards and halted. Blackhorse was now hugging the ground, ready. Myles reloaded the shotgun and pulled the trigger, aiming for the ridge for effect.

As the boom dinned in his ears, he saw Blackhorse jump up and plunge forward. A mass of hurtling, massive man and trailing dog.

He was in full motion when Myles heard the rifle crack. He flinched for Blackhorse, teeth set. In fascination, he waited for the Osage to break stride and come crashing down.

The rifle spat again, quickly. Blackhorse seemed to stagger slightly, but he kept running, swiftly for his bulk. Another bullet spanged. By then Blackhorse was in, a brown bear rolling under the trees.

A heady triumph surged in Myles as he hurried to him. They did not stir for an interval, content just to lie there in the blessed damp coolness behind the tree screen and feel the wind fanning off that tall grass.

Turning, Myles noticed Blackhorse's shoulder. He scowled at the dark, spreading splotch. "You been hit."

"Don' hurt."

"Peel off that shirt. Let's have a look."

Blackhorse complied reluctantly. After a close look, Myles felt easier. The slug had torn a scarlet furrow, high along the fleshy forepart in front. It was bleeding, but not badly. Not deep.

The frustrating anger had never left Myles; now it deepened. A remembering part of him took charge. His thought of the sniper became hard and hating, no longer impersonal, his outrage that of a pinned-down man in cold, endless rain and stinking muck. His mind whipped to the covering brush farther up the creek. That was enough to jerk him up, crouching. "I'm going up that ridge, roundabout. You head for the house. Let Jeannette fix you up."

"Gonna be dead man, huh?"

"There's cover most the way." Myles was visualizing it in his mind's eye as he spoke, convinced that he could do it. "A man can cross over through the brush. Go up the ridge. It'll have to be fast. He knows he's lost us now. Maybe he's already pulled out."

It penetrated that he had unconsciously left Blackhorse out of his planning. "You're no shape to go, Charlie." And Dog, he saw, presented a second excuse. "Besides, the hound might give us away."

"Charlie okay." Unconvinced, Blackhorse flexed his bloody shoulder to prove it. "Dog he stick close."

Myles shook his head. Yet, Charlie's wound wasn't bad; he was a crack shot. Myles' unwillingness had become complex, something akin to taking a green boy on patrol for the first time.

"Dog okay," insisted Blackhorse, getting to his feet. "Two men better'n one. Whut happens yuh git shot?"

"Wasn't counting on that," Myles said ruefully.

"Both go." The Osage, nodding firmly, reached for his shotgun. His movement was decisive and final, resolved, Myles saw, by an offended pride. The Osage scanned the ridge. Now, finally, a dull anger glittered in the coffee-colored eyes.

Seeing that argument was useless, Myles said, "Let's go," and turned up the creek. The timber hid them. Dog traveled obediently at Blackhorse's heels, close in. Some of Myles' doubts dissolved.

But when he came to the brush that grew up the slope, his mouth clamped tight. It didn't look so good up close. Cover was thick, but not as high as he'd guessed from a distance. They'd have to crawl part way.

Impatience welled up. He punched in a fresh load and ducked into the thickets. Underfoot the ground gradually tilted. Soon he was rising, forcing his way carefully through the green, slashing tangles. An awareness of lateness drove him. A hard-rock anger. Sweat cracked his forehead. He went at a stalking crouch, his attention split forward and behind to Blackhorse; his shoulders humped, head canting to the ridge and the ledge that capped it.

Rock litter grated under his boots. He had reached the foot of the ridge. From here the brush thinned rapidly in places, giving way to slabs of sandstone and scattered blackjack saplings.

An unease checked him. He held up, the shotgun slippery in sweaty hands, till his ears relayed Blackhorse's presence behind him. He measured the climb, the steepness, the open stretches.

His heart was beating high in his chest as he stepped from cover. But an alarmed grunt chained him.

It happened before he could turn, without any inkling. Unless it was the whirring flutter, drumming up and away from his left and behind.

Dog! He'd flushed a bunch!

Myles wheeled and glimpsed Dog in the open, in the tall grass. Myles smothered a yell as a warning instinct wrenched him back, his eyes rivetted to the ridge top.

Too late, he saw the spurt of flame. He heard Dog's stricken howl mingling with the blast. Somewhere hoofs clattered across rock. Hoofs going fast.

He was plunging up the slope, though he never remembered leaving the brush... Motion under the trees. Just a flicker. He felt the shotgun kick his shoulder. A futile shot He'd only scare a man at this distance. He ducked behind a rock slab, reloaded.

In that pause, he heard hoofs clack distantly and fade. So he'd lost his man. But the full steam of his anger kept him roused and bulling up the slant. Warily, he legged it over the ledge into the hanging quiet.

Dust layered the mottled shadows of the scrubby blackjacks. With a slow-footed caution, he prowled over to the back side of the ridge. His scouring eyes took in the broken hills, the hiding timber. He was late, but he wanted to be certain.

Nothing so much as stirred far as the eye could strain. His shoulders dropped and he hounded back. A stamped-out place brought him to his knees, searching the ground. Here a tied horse had pawed restlessly.

His eyes tracked wider. Something glinted. He picked up an empty .30-30 cartridge, and a picture flashed. "Fired that last one from the saddle," he said aloud. "Then got the hell out."

He looked up, the belated feeling coming afresh. A new interest took him to a high, flat rock on the rim. Pulling atop it, he understood many things.

Posted here, a man could see the Blackhorse ranch house and beyond. Some two-hundred yards, he estimated, was the brushy place on the long slope where he and Blackhorse had first flattened out. Pulling his gaze in around him, he saw then a little heap of brown-paper cigarette butts.

That was all, and Myles was forced to revise somewhat his estimate of the sharpshooter. This man had been careful enough to carry off all cartridges spent from the rock. All but the last one, fired hurriedly aboard the horse. Likely he'd flung one last look down the ridge, preparatory to leaving, when Dog burst into view to set up on the covey.

Myles shook off the second-guessing. None of it helped. Nothing he'd found. Almost every rancher had a .30-30 for coyotes. If he tried to follow the horse prints, they'd peter out to nothingness in the trackless rock clutter.

Frustration gripped him as he eased down and slowly retraced his steps. He came to the rim, all at once reluctant to look down. When he did, there was Charlie Blackhorse bent over in the grass, over Dog and Dog too still.

Myles' regret was a crowding thing. In long, loose-legged strides he reached the bottom and crossed over, trying to think of something he might say. A moment ago words were ready on his tongue. Just now they lay lodged in the thickness of his throat. He moved in close on heavy feet.

Dog looked pretty messy and he was dead. Blackhorse had cradled the spotted head in his platter-like hands. Somehow Myles got the impression that Dog, with the last of his ebbing energy, maybe had licked those hands.

Moved, Myles coughed and said, "The bastard got away. Waited some time, way it looked."

Blackhorse did not seem to hear. He just hunkered there, in daze, in crushed thought. He just stared with eyes that gazed into emptiness, without focus.

"Didn't have a chance, did he?" Myles said, his regret swelling. "Sorry as hell, Charlie. Damn fine dog."

Blackhorse made a slow, nodding turn, his eyes grasping at the tribute. There shone in them something that far out-distanced mere thanks.

"Guess I was too eager," Myles said.

"No—yuh tol' me." The Osage's voice cast no blame. It was gently condoning, and proud. "Dog he jus' like t'hunt them birds. Couldn't pass 'em up. Broke away 'fore I knew it." He gave a slow, acknowledging nod. "Some dog."

In silence, they tramped back, crossed the creek below the house and came to the yard. Blackhorse carried Dog's stiff shape in his arms, Myles the shotguns.

Jeannette met them. Her eyes raked them questioningly. Myles told her before she could ask.

"Ohh—no!" She ran up to Blackhorse, her fingers explor-ing the wounded shoulder gingerly.

Blackhorse moved on, shrugging her off.

"He's all right," Myles said. "But we better fix him up some."

Blackhorse did not pause. There, in the meager shade of the porch, he laid Dog down. Stony-faced, he trudged heavily to the barn and returned with a spade. Without voice, walking past them, he took Dog in his thick arms and bent toward the uncropped emptiness of the valley floor.

Something unspoken kept Myles in the yard, kept Jeannette there, too. He watched Blackhorse grow smaller in the weaving grass, as a man striding deliberately into surf and the water slowly rising around him. Much farther on, till he resembled a brown stump left in a field of early autumn dullness, Blackhorse stopped. He inspected the ground, as if choosing a particular site, and commenced digging. He dug methodically, powerfully, and, finished, Myles saw him stoop and lift and bend downward, fill the hole and stoop again, this time tamping it gently so as to round and shape the top. He lingered a short time before returning, his pace slow.

"Think hard, Jeannette," said Myles as Blackhorse approached. "Who'd take a shot at Charlie?"

She shook her head in distress. "Nobody, I can think of."

"It happened. They'll try again."

His harsh words stirred her. "But—but what can we do?"

"One thing for sure. Charlie better not stay here. And we should report this. County sheriff's office—the Osage agency. Guess the agency has special officers?"

She nodded, gripped in a troubled silence. Myles let it go for the time, while he pictured again for himself each tiny, violent detail of what had happened on the ridge. It was still hard to believe.

Blackhorse wandered in, disconsolate. He dropped the shovel and sat upon the porch, lost in his own muteness. He held a leather collar.

Watching him, Myles thought of Dow Rikker. How he'd kept an old set of shoes or a bridle bit as a reminder of every really fine cow pony he'd ever owned in the past.

It required considerable urging by Jeannette before Blackhorse would go to the kitchen. Myles, following, saw her tear a cloth into strips and wash and bandage and force another shirt upon her uncle. "There," she said, inspecting him critically, "you'll be good as new tomorrow. It's just a deep crease." Then, firmly, "Uncle Charlie, you're going home with me!"

Unmoved, he regarded her in stony unconcern. Myles felt a wordless protest as Blackhorse muttered, "Nobody gonna run me off."

"We know how you feel," Myles threw in. "But stay here and you'll be a dead Injun. Do what Jeannette says. Stick at her place till this blows over. I'll help you all I can." He checked up, realizing that he had automatically counted himself in on whatever might happen. Whether he wanted it or not, he was being drawn into a situation remote from the Rikkers.

Jeannette sent him a swift look of thanks, and to assure Blackhorse she said, "I'm calling the sheriff, too."

"Off'cers won' find nothin'," Blackhorse snorted. "No tracks."

Myles though a space, tilted his head sidewise. "Slater—Clark Slater—he's sore about that grass lease. Think he'd bushwhack you?"

"Yuh know 'bout th' lease?"

"Couldn't help it." Myles was apologetic. "I was outside the hotel when Slater told the world. He threatened you, I remember that."

"Yeah. But he don' scare me." A secret knowledge appeared to please Blackhorse. "Sid got that lease. Signed up papers t'day. Sid m'friend."

A gasp of indignation escaped Jeannette. "You leased—to him!"

Blackhorse didn't seem to understand. "Yeah."

She whipped away, stung, fighting a feeling. But when she faced her uncle a moment later, there was a sympathy and pity in her, and resignation. "Well—it's done. And this is a poor time to talk business. Let's go."

Blackhorse made no move. "Gonna stay here," he said, proud and thick of voice. "Nobody—"

"Stay!" Myles repeated, very harsh, as Jeannette flung up a despairing hand. "Hell, this is attemped murder, Charlie! We know you're not afraid to stay—you don't have to prove it. Tell you what. If it'll make you feel any better, I can ride over every few days. Keep an eye on things for you. Pretty soon you'll be back, once this straightens out." He lowered his voice. "You don't want to worry Jeannette or Mrs. Tyson. Think of them."

Charlie Blackhorse said nothing. He sat lumped in his chair, like stone, his humorless, furrowed face bent at the floor. Half a minute passed. He shifted his heavy body and stood up. "Okay," he said reluctantly.

Later, mounted upon the saddle pinto pony in the yard, he turned his head. His brooding gaze sought the old house, the disreputable barn and corral, the black-timbered creek and the prairie that rolled like a restless sea.

There was, thought Myles, an indescribable pain and regret in the hewn features. Somehow you thought of a man looking sadly upon familar land and objects for the last time.

After supper, Myles could hear the teasing chatter of Jeannette's voice while she showed her uncle where to sleep. He heard her boots come down the stairs, cross the living room and go to the front door, where she rattled the lock.

She was frowning when she entered the lighted kitchen, her hands twisting at the apron she had donned over her riding trousers. She looked young and troubled. Myles regarded her, in that moment deeply admiring. "Anyway," she concluded, appraising the stack of unwashed dishes, "I feel better with him in the house."

She poured hot water from the tea kettle into a dishpan, her round brown arms bare to the elbows. She dropped in a bar of white soap and began stacking in dishes. She washed thoughtfully for a time. "Now what?" she asked.

Myles took up a towel and began drying dishes. "You could put in those calls."

"Uh-huh. Agency's closed this late. But I can call the sheriff's office, have them tell the agency first thing tomorrow." Of a sudden she faced him, the dark arches of her eyebrows drawing down. "What can they do? We don't have anything to go on."

"Something will turn up."

She was doubtful. "I can't see Clark Slater in this."

"He threatened Charlie."

Jeannette scrubbed in an absent way before she replied. "Lots of bluff in Clark. I don't believe he'd try anything like murder. Oh, he's ambitious. Wants to be a sport and make folks think he's a big cowman. All that ... Flies off the handle and talks tough—if he thinks enough people can hear him. No, he never will be a big man." She stared uncertainly at Myles. "Nothing makes sense, does it? What else can we do?"

"Keep Charlie in close, that's certain. Don't let him go home. Be a job, I know, restless as he'll be." A thrusting, reminding caution slammed through Myles. "Let's keep it quiet where Charlie is. I mean, not tell it around. There's a chance"—he was, he learned, already searching the possibility—"we might find out something."

"He hates to be inside, cooped up. Hunts or fishes every day."

"You'll have to do it," Myles said.

"Well, I will. I will if I have to hogtie him."

"Another thing." He studied her a second. "I'll be gone most times. Riding Charlie's country some. I aim to get nosey.

Meanwhile, there's work to do. We could use another man. What do you think?"

She nodded. "We're one short the way it is. Go in town. Find Old Man Hill at the hotel. If there's a loose hand in town, he'll know it."

Myles, hanging up his towel, said quickly, "Tonight—I'll see him tonight."

She looked relieved, her doubts vanished. "Take my car. I'll get the keys," she said, drying her hands as she talked. She hurried out and up the stairs and was back shortly, handing him the keys. His attention, catching her smoky eyes, found a sudden gratefulness.

It embarrassed him, a reaction that pointed him hurriedly toward the door. Before he could take a second step, her throaty voice stalled him, "Myles . .

He turned, not speaking.

"I—I want to thank you." One slim brown hand tucked at his shirt front. "You've—well, I—I want to thank you—that's all."

He said, rougher than he intended, "Me? I haven't done a thing but get Charlie's dog killed. A wonder he wasn't."

"Yes—if you hadn't been with him."

"Lucky," he answered. "Plain lucky. And you can't always depend on that."

He knew that he ought to be on his way. Something told him. And yet, knowing it, he drew in the elusive perfume of her hair, the compelling scent of her cloying up from the open throat of her shirt. It all combined to hold him there.

She leaned forward suddenly. In the same unexpected motion, she rose on her toes. As in a blur he saw her halfclosed eyes, her rising mouth parted. She kissed him warmly, impulsively, on the lips.

The kiss was meant to be quick. Without thought, an instinctive, natural act, unguarded.

But, at the last instant, it changed.

Sensation kicked through him. He felt his reserve go. His hands became rough. He took her shoulders, pulling her in close. Under his grip she was trembling. He bent his head; her lips were there. For a moment she responded, warm and sweet, the length of her supple body pressed against his. For a brief time that was all he knew. There was no other awareness.

Then his arms broke downward. As swiftly, she was stepping back, coloring.

"You…you didn't expect that, did you?" She hurried on, in confusion. "Well…I didn't know I was going to do it, either."

He was slow answering, still shaken. "And I didn't figure to be inside another man's fence line—and liking it."

His mouth compressed. He turned and cut through the door, seized with a vast and sudden disgust for himself.

Jeannette's purple Cadillac roadster spun Myles through the night. Within an hour he was leaving the hotel, bound for the Palace Pool Hall across from the trading store.

Old Man Hill had thawed immediately when Myles stated Jeanette's needs. There was, now, if he hadn't pulled out of town, a puncher from the Foraker country, up north. "Name's Caldwell. Prob'ly find him at the Palace 'bout now. Been here since yesterday, just scoutin' around."

Myles stepped into the smoky, crowded room, into the soursweet earthiness of sweat and unwashed work clothes and the clicking, slapping gaming. The squab man behind the counter recognized him wryly. "Caldwell. Lemme see…" He eyed the crowd. "That's him. Over there. In that calf-skin vest."

Myles wedged through. He found a restless, taciturn man, drifter stamped all over him. Despite some misgivings, Myles hired him on the spot. Caldwell agreed to collect his gear and ride out early the next morning.

As Caldwell drifted off into the pack, the banter of a familiar voice reached Myles. He glanced across.

Sid Tyson, pushed-back hat revealing his mane of straight snow-white hair, chuckled as he sank a red snooker ball. Waiting their turns were Tharp Kutch and Frank Rikker. Lolling stringily against the wall, his shrewd eyes intent, stood Lee Wiley. Just then Tyson drilled a numbered ball and called, "School's out. Afraid you boys will have to draw on next month's pay."

Kutch rolled his yellow eyes at Frank, who made a grimace.

Tyson, obviously a cool shot, ran out the table and the game ended. "You fellows still feel lucky?" he challenged, chalking up.

Frank shrugged. "I'm cleaned out. So's Lee."

"Hell, he can't Win forever," Kutch mocked. "I'll take him on."

Myles considered the group. From an observer's detachment it seemed that Kutch, never quite able to conceal his unpolished crudity, his quarrelsome tendencies, somehow presented an awkward imitation of Tyson. When Tyson chuckled, he uttered a growl of amusement. Then Tyson smiled, he grinned crookedly. When Tyson said something out of the rut of ordinary talk, Kutch tried to match it and fell wide of the mark. Thus, he remained only a surly, thickchested watchdog, permitted certain liberties, perhaps because of his tenacious loyalty.

When Frank stacked his stick, Tyson suggested, "Let's keep it three-handed. Come on! Anybody!" His eyes circled the standing watchers, lodged, and he invited, "How about you, Clark?"

"Hell, yes!" Kutch chimed in humorlessly. "Get in, Clark. Sid's just lucky."

Now Clark Slater watched Tyson, who had moved to the end of the table, and Myles saw Slater shake his head. "No, thanks, Sid," he said coldly. "I know when I'm foxed."

Instantly, Tyson's chin tilted up. His eyes narrowed. In the next moment he was smiling, his smile a curtain of amiability. "Not sore about that lease, are you? If you are, remember I've lost my share. Part of the game."

"Your game."

The words fell like an ax in the long, crowded room, chopping apart the murmuring talk, stilling it.

"How's that?" Tyson was peering fixedly at the tip of his cue stick.

"I said"—the muscles along Slater's lean jaw jumped—"your game. I can't beat it. Nobody can."

"What are you trying to say, Clark?"

"Yeah?" Kutch put in and Tyson swung on him in annoyed swiftness. "Stay out of this." Tyson had not raised his voice, but Kutch drew in like a rebuked mastiff.

The crowd had edged away from Slater till he stood alone, in the center of things. Myles saw him take in his position, his eyes sort of wild and goaded. "You know what I mean," he said in an unsteady voice. "That Blackhorse lease."

"Paid for it, Clark. Paid for it."

Slater appeared to nerve himself, to draw on the crowd's presence for courage. He took a deep pull of wind. His jaws pressed. "Stole it!" he echoed. "Stole it! My lease for years ... tryin' to break me ... offered Blackhorse skyhigh money I couldn't touch.... "

He spluttered to silence and a tardy knowledge seemed to strike him warningly of what he had just said. His eyes hooked upon Tyson, as if he expected the cowman to climb the table after him. He waited uncertainly.

Tyson, imperturable, greatly amused, allowed the tension to mount. He said not a word. Instead, he uttered a low, humbling laugh, which said everything. He stared long at Slater, and kept staring, his glance a battering ram hammering down the thin shield of Clark Slater's courage.

For a while Slater managed to hold that stare. Just for a while. Slowly, by fractions, his glance crumbled. His shoulders jerked and fell. He looked right and left, caged. He muttered jerkily, "Well ... there it is, Sid," and was no longer hesitating. He made a turning movement toward the door, too rapid for an effect of casualness, and walked through the parting crowd.

The screen door slammed like a gunshot, marking Slater's exit, and Myles sensed the concentration of the crowd upon Tyson. He was smiling and blowing gently at the tip of his cue. A tiny puff of chalk dust floated off. Very distinctly, in a voice that everyone could hear, he said, "When a man makes a brag, and won't stay to back it up—" He let the significance of that sink home, chuckling, and the men around him laughed. His point scored, Tyson waved his cue, "Who wants to play?"

In the shifting of the crowd, making room for Slater, Myles had been left on the edge near the tables. Now he saw Tyson look past him, pause, and bring his eyes back. Through a mild surprise, Tyson said, "Grab a stick."

Refusal rose in Myles. But he found himself strolling to the rack. He chose a stick and, facing around, ran hard into Frank's disapproving eyes close by. "Sid said you were still in the country," Frank said. "But I told him I'd have to see you to believe it. You're really ridin' for Jeannette?"

"You heard right," Myles replied, reaching for a square of chalk.

"Five bucks a game." It was Tyson, eager to start. "Winner breaks. New man shoots last."

A house man racked the balls. His capable hands balanced and sure on the green cloth, Tyson drew bead and shot. His striking ball was a thunderclap shattering the formation. He scored a long run before missing. While he tallied up his score on a smudged blackboard, Kutch shot and missed. He stood back, his attention wandering.

Myles could feel the bright, jaundiced glare. It aroused in him an acute annoyance. He took his turn and shot poorly, without interest. By the next time around Tyson had cleared the table.

"Looks like I'm a shade rusty," Myles drawled, paying up.

"Another game?"

"I'll watch the slaughter this time."

Tyson smiled blandly. "You're at a disadvantage. We get plenty of practice." His eyes stayed upon Myles, his mouth framing a question. But a grinning Indian youth sidled up, cue in hand, and Tyson, sighting new game, called for the house man to rack the balls. Myles retreated to the wall near Frank.

"Changed your plans mighty sudden," Frank said at his ear.

Myles watched the Indian boy, long, slender fingers sensitive as a woman's, sink a side-pocket shot before he turned. Some twist of perverseness made him answer, "I'm sold on the Osage."

"The country ... or the woman?"

"Didn't think you'd take to the idea."

"Expect me to? You, around Jeannette!"

Myles beat off an old weariness, only to have a twinge of guilt gall him. He said softly, "Frank, let's get out of here. Where we can talk."

"If you got anything to say, spill it here."

Myles hesitated, roving his eyes around. "I have ... somebody tried to murder Charlie Blackhorse this afternoon."

Frank's head snapped up. "Th' hell you say!" He stared. His reaction, to Myles, was one of honest surprise, and he wondered why he'd even question Frank. Speaking low, he filled in the other details.

Frank continued to listen, his body taut. Finished, Myles waited for him to say something.

There was no response. Frank rubbed his hands against his thighs. He rolled his square shoulders. His face looked alien, odd. He wet his lips. Unexpectedly, his brawling voice slammed Myles like a blow, "I told you to stay 'way from her!"

Unprepared, Myles could only gape after the irrelevant words.

Frank made a short, violent motion with his hand. Till this moment the hum of a hundred voices and the continuous clacking of the pool balls had merged into a steady racket that subdued their talk. Frank's voice raged through this layer of sound, overly loud, shrill, "Think I'm blind! I know why you took that job! Marry yourself a rich Osage!" He spat out an obscenity. "By God, you got it comin'!"

"You crazy?" Myles breathed across his astonishment.

His hands were still hanging low. He had them coming up when Frank hit him. He felt a dull pain explode in his head, and he was banged against the wall. He floundered along it, trying to take Frank's blows upon his arms and shoulders.

It was suddenly intolerable that he fight Frank. But the bruising blows kept landing. Instinct made him throw a fist high to Frank's face. But he couldn't follow up, stayed by the sick, stunned unwillingness. Somehow a thought took hold: It's not Jeannette. He was merely fending off the flailing arms. Distantly, he heard a shouting and yelling.

He realized his mistake as Frank tore through his guard. Except the punches broke his lethargy, summoned him in time. He was slugging back now, his laggard reluctance whipped to a headlong anger. As Frank swept in close, Myles connected in the belly. Crying out, Frank stumbled.

For a second Frank's jaw presented a swaying target. Myles sledged his fist for the opening. Frank hit the floor. He did not try to rise and Myles stood over him, his breathing ragged. A dull bewilderment throbbed in his humming head: That punch—just one—wasn't—

A short, trunky shape was hurtling at him from the side, knocking him sidewise as Sid Tyson's unmistakable voice yelled, "No, Kutch—no!"

Myles tripped and fell, rolled up, and the body atop him sprawled beyond. Lurching up, Myles glared into Kutch's snarling face.

"No tricks this time, Jake!" Kutch was scrabbling to his feet and tearing in as he mouthed the words. Myles caught him along the temple, but Kutch came on, punching powerfully, wildly. Around them Myles glimpsed bright, greasy eyes, expectant. A wolves' circle.

He felt himself knocked against a pool table. Billiard balls fled clicking. Next he was being bent backward. He sensed the thrust of a knee toward his groin, and he plunged to his right, tore loose. He swung, slamming Kutch's ear. Pain pumped through his knuckles. He saw Kutch stagger and shake his head like a dazed bull and heave forward.

Feinting in, Myles drew the windmill fists. He stepped right, then left, throwing his body behind the punch. He felt his hand blast Kutch's ear again, saw him hurled half across the table. Kutch sprawled among the clutter. He cursed and pawed at the balls; his hand clamped upon one. Instantly, he reared and threw.

Myles ducked low. The ball smashed against the wall behind him. Men scattered like quail. Wild-eyed murder in his eyes, Kutch grabbed again. His arm whipped forward. Myles bobbed down as the ball rocked past his ear. Frantic now, Kutch scrambled for more ammunition.

In that brief space, Myles heaved up and closed the gap. He saw Kutch spring, ready as a cat. They swapped punches. The man's hard body was like hammering a flour barrel, his ribs oaken staves.

Better the head again. Myles braced and feinted, just as his boot turned on a ball. It sent his foot spinning from under. He fell awkwardly, off balance, without defense.

It was then that he noticed Frank. He saw Frank hesitate and start forward as if to help ... and hold up as Kutch came springing in. Kutch's bootheels left the floor to stomp, to grind. One striking point jolted Myles' shoulder. He rolled and spun up. Frank's act was a bile in his throat, choking him.

An impossible fury hurled Myles into Kutch. His abrupt charge drove the man backward. Kutch lowered his head and butted. Methodically, savagely, Myles smashed it with lefts and rights. Kutch gave ground.

A space opened and spread. For the moment both men were too weary to close it.

Through a red-eyed haze Myles saw Tyson move between. His voice was a rope that snubbed Kutch fast, "Show some sense!" Kutch, in bewilderment, turned his stubbled face and held up.

Myles, gulping for wind, voiced his contempt. "Run outa cannon balls?"

Kutch lurched, would have rushed in, if Tyson had not blocked him and said as he grinned, loud enough for the crowd to hear, "Think I want to pay your fine after winning your money?"

A man laughed. Others joined in. The tension was broken.

Grumbling, Kutch slouched over and picked up his hat. He threw Myles his sullen, remembering hate, muttered, "Next time, Jake," and stalked toward the door.

His departure left Myles with a sharp lack of satisfaction. Nothing had been resolved. This wasn't finished. It would fester and spread as long as he stayed in the Osage. The sense of strangeness returned, the vague unease.

He searched the faces for Frank, failed to see him. As he retrieved his hat and stood and reshaped the crown, he became aware of Tyson's steady appraisal. "You're right handy," the cowman said.

"Too bad you spoiled the fun."

"Figured I was doing you a favor."

The raw anger soared in Myles. "I handled him before."

"Once." Tyson strolled to the pool table, where the Indian youth was chalking up. "Kutch never loses the second round.... Something to remember," he remarked, leaned over the green cloth, and lined up his shot.

Jostling through the crowd, Myles heard Tyson's gaming voice once more, "Let's make it ten bucks."

It rubbed him beyond reason, a nameless rankling that magnified as he paced to the car. He was thinking of Frank as he drove out of town, thinking that the last thin bond between them had been broken.

CHAPTER SEVEN

WEARINESS DRAGGED at Myles' arms and shoulders. He drove mechanically, his mind fastened behind him, oblivious of the pale night. He was sore of body, still confused and angry. Well, things were messed up good. He turned his head to gaze across the huddled hills. There was a hint of coming autumn in the cool night. Out there, away from the noisy boom towns and the violence, a great, uplifting peace waited for a man. If, he thought, frowning, you can find it.

Sooner than he expected the yellow fingers of his headlights groped for the spread-out bulk of Jeannette Garreau's house. He drove inside the garage, snapped off ignition and lights, felt his way through the darkness to the door.

An instilled wariness made him pause, watching, before he stepped out. The house loomed dark and silent, a citadel of defiant masonry, incongruous here. Wind, wild and lonely, rattled the blackjacks. He felt a tiny shiver.

A footstep fell. He drew back within the shadow of the garage. "Myles?"

It was Jeannette's voice, of course, yet it startled him. He met her a trifle sheepishly. She had been standing well back under the trees. He saw a rifle in her hands.

"Couldn't sleep," she explained, her eyes seeking his face.

He told her about hiring Caldwell, nothing more.

"Good. We can use him."

He eyed the rifle again, the competent way she handled it. "Guard duty, eh?"

"This gun's company, believe me. I keep tellin' myself it didn't happen, but it did. They tried to shoot him—murder him—" She was dismayed, shaken, lost for words. In the soft, tawny light, as she held on to the rifle, she looked terribly young and vengeful—and pleasing to his eyes. "Different when we lost Dad. Drowned. That just happened, I guess…. This, well—I can't figure it, Myles. Guess I'm scared, really scared, for the first time in my life."

Her apprehension touched him and he took the rifle. He wished to put a comforting arm around her shoulders, but he did not.

He saw her as a dark, slender shaft of stone. And she was close, much too close, for him, though she seemed to stand there without conscious design. He was sure of that. And yet she disturbed him in a way no woman ever had, leaving him unsure. In silence, he started them toward the house.

It was she who stopped, her face turned to the night. "Anyone ever tell you Eendians are superstitious?"

"They're just closer to the old days," he answered, not giving it much thought.

"Mighty close… Take these hills." Her voice changed, low-pitched and musing, almost musical. She was gazing off into the dim night distances, and a feeling came to Myles of time rolling back, of standing on a rocky, wind-swept hill beside an Indian girl and not another soul within a thousand miles. "I used to get homesick so much when I was in school, up in Missouri. The other girls called me The Homesick Osage…. This is the prettiest country in the world to me. But sometimes I think it's the saddest, too." Her voice brushed bitterness. "It makes you feel things."

He nodded, understanding. He had sensed it also, coming as a stranger into Two Sands that first late day, and riding over the rounded hills with Happy Adcock. An impression of latent brute force and stillness and space. A suggestion of sadness. He'd glimpsed its shadow in Nellie Tyson's broad, unhappy, full-blood face.

He said, half joking, "You don't have to be an Eendian to feel these hills." He had purposely pronounced "Indian" as Jeannette spoke it, and it changed her mood and stirred her laughter.

"You're making fun of me."

"No, I wouldn't do that. You've been alone too much, that's all. No need to fret about Charlie, long as we ride herd on him here. You call the sheriff's office?"

"Uh-huh. A deputy will be here tomorrow to look around. Maybe an agency man."

"Been thinking," said Myles, "I'd ride over Charlie's way tomorrow. Find me a high spot, look and wait. See if the honey still draws the bees."

He was tired to the bone and apparently she sensed it, because she said, "Let me make you some coffee."

Myles hesitated, stared at the ground. "No, thanks. Big day coming up. Better turn in." He thought Jeannette studied him curiously as they continued to the rear door of the lightless house. He murmured, "Good night," and was going on when she said, "Oh, Myles."

Even as he faced around, her tone indicated she suspected something.

"See anybody in town besides Hill and this Caldwell?"

"The usual bunch."

"Meaning?"

He tried to shrug it off. "Now, who'd I see in Two Sands? Oil field guys, cowhands, some Osages—" He left it there, unfinished.

"You were gone a long time."

"I'm a slow driver."

Her laugh pelted back at him, light and sure. "You're a poor liar, Myles."

"How's that?"

She was scanning his face. "A minute ago," she said, "when you walked into the light, you looked plumb fierce. You don't know it, but there's a welt under your right eye and your shirt's torn—"

His hand lifted to his cheekbone. It felt puffy. He put his hand down hurriedly. "Little scuffle's all."

"With Frank?"

"Didn't say."

"You wouldn't. But I've got eyes. You two don't get along."

"You don't think so, huh?"

"Why, no, and I'm sorry. It's a little odd. Frank's why you asked for a job, isn't he?

"You've got me there." He shook his head. "I wonder, myself."

"You're mighty vague, Myles." She moved a step closer, intently considering him. "Could it be because you don't like that rough bunch Frank runs with? You're afraid Frank's in trouble?" She sounded bewildered. "He could quit—just ride off. But he won't."

"Any other man," he said, low with meaning, "would get married. Settle down to some ranching."

"You might suggest that to Frank some day," she answered archly.

"Better if you'd work on him."

Her chin lifted till he was gazing fully into the enormous eyes. He saw that he trod sensitive, dangerous ground.

"Want me to beg him?" she mocked.

It ended on that unsatisfactory note.

She swung firmly toward the house. As she turned, he got a whiff of her and sensation whipped through him. His eyes followed the straight line of the supple back, the movement of the slim, boyish hips under the riding trousers.

His mouth pinched down. He'd stayed too long. He knew that for certain.

The slamming screen door was like a shot in the stillness.

Nerves, he thought, smiling a little. Nerves and a strong helping of pride. He still had the rifle; it was a reminder. Going slowly to the bunkhouse, he dragged out a blanket and settled down upon the porch, rifle across his lap.

He slept in that position of watchfulness, mostly dozing, till gray daylight came.

It was evident to Myles that, after two days of inaction, of not venturing beyond the yard or barn and certainly never far from Jeannette's protecting eyes, Charlie Blackhorse was restless as a caged bear. Furthermore, because nothing had happened, the Osage seemed unconcerned again.

This morning he ate his breakfast in solemn silence, frequently glancing out the window in gloomy yearning. Watching, Myles wondered if there wasn't some fear in him of being shut up in a house.

When Caldwell, the new rider, finished and jangled outside, Jeannette and Myles exchanged glances. She turned to her uncle. "Tom Bowdre said he'd be back today. Wants to talk to you some more."

Blackhorse looked bored. "Tol' him once."

A sheriff's deputy and Bowdre, the agency man, had arrived the morning following the shooting. After routine questions and a visit to the scene of the attempted ambush, the deputy had left the case with Bowdre, who didn't seem to mind. In fact, Myles decided, he welcomed it.

Bowdre was a wizened, sparse-spoken man with prematurely gray hair and a sun-weathered face. There was about him a mixture of dogged thoroughness and suspicion of everything. He'd come with loaded horse trailer. Coming and going, Myles seldom saw Bowdre's bay gelding in the corral. The first night Bowdre slept in the bunkhouse, at the farthest end from Myles. Last night he'd driven to Two Sands, promising to return today.

"Got chores over m'place," Blackhorse said, shifting his moccasins under the table.

"Now, there's nothing to worry about," said Jeannette, humoring him as she always did. "No chickens or hogs to feed. No horses up. Myles has been over every day. Everything's all right."

Blackhorse stared moodily at his coffee cup. He got up, scowling and unhappy, and scuffed out the kitchen and into the living room. Myles heard him plop into an overstuffed chair.

"We'll have to watch him," Myles said, talking low.

"I know...he's restless." She made a tiny gesture of weariness, of resignation. It passed through his mind that she was tiring of the strain. Her hair was swept back and neatly knotted, as usual, and her face was smooth. But there was a gravity in the full mouth, in the great eyes. She sat with her hands locked. "I wonder how long can we keep him here?"

"Hard to tell," he said vaguely, realizing it was a question both had put off facing. "What's Bowdre say?"

"If he knows anything, he hasn't let me in on it. He's sure full of questions about the neighbors." Her lips formed a faint grin. "Even you."

"Smart man. He's not taking anybody for granted."

"I told him about the lease," she went on, her face darkening. "He was plenty interested."

"He talk to Slater?"

"Don't know."

"Bowdre's close-mouthed."

She thought a second. "Wish you'd ride over to Charlie's again today."

He hesitated. Since the other night, when he'd learned that he had to get out of here, he'd rounded up several excuses for staying. Now, with Caldwell turning out to be an old hand and Bowdre taking over, he had no real reason for lingering on the Garreau ranch. Better if he broke camp. He could operate from town, if he decided to chase the Frank Rikker matter any farther. He was no longer needed here.

"What's wrong, Myles?" She had caught something of his reluctance. "Don't you think we should keep an eye on his place?"

"Jeannette—" His unwillingness piled up, but he rode over it. "It's about time—"

The interrupting jangle of the wall telephone sounded in the living room. He jerked, then relaxed.

She cocked her head to count the rings. "Three shorts … that's us." She rose and started to the door.

But before she reached it, Myles heard Blackhorse's thick Indian guttural, "Hull-lo … hull-lo … "

Jeannette was yelling as she plunged through the doorway, "No, Charlie! Don't answer that!"

In long, quick strides, Myles made after her. He saw her snatch the receiver from her uncle's hand. She spoke into the mouthpiece. "Hello! Hello! Who's this? … Hello! Hello! … Hello … " Her voice trailed off.

She turned with a perplexed and troubled air. "Nobody's on the line," she said slowly. "Uncle Charlie—what did they say?"

Blackhorse peered from Myles to her. "Jus' hull-lo."

"But you shouldn't have answered it!" The gleam in her eyes was raw fear. "Don't you see? They know you're here now!"

Blackhorse scowled, not much concerned.

"Call the Two Sands rural operator," Myles said. "She'll know if it was a town call."

She whirled into action. Her knuckles were white as she cranked the handle. Myles heard the tinny murmur of the operator's voice come on the line. Jeannette listened gravely for some moments after asking for a check on the call.

Very deliberately, she hung up. "The call," she said, drawing a breath, "was put in from the hotel. Some man—that's all she knows."

Myles stared down, mulling it over. When he raised his glance, Jeannette's lips were bloodless. The little-girl expression etched her face. She seemed all eyes, all pupil. Her breathing was ragged.

An angry tide engulfed him that this should happen to these people. He scrubbed a hand across his chin. "Don't let 'em buffalo you, Jeannette. Just a matter of time till they found out, anyway. Not hard to figure, I guess. What counts is you got Charlie, here, with you." He slapped Blackhorse on the back. "Main thing, Charlie, is stick close. Do what Jeannette says and you'll be back on Yellow Dog before you know it."

Gloomy again, Blackhorse stared dolefully out the window. He shuffled his feet, restless, fidgeting.

Myles frowned at the signs. Returning to the kitchen, he took up his hat and wheeled to go. The sound of Jeannette's boots held him there. He turned and met a searching question.

"You're going? Over to Charlie's?"

"Figured so. A quick swing. He'll feel easier if I do." There it was, out of him, his decision of minutes back once more excused.

"I—well—I didn't know. While ago you—I thought—" She moved her head in an uncertain way, blurted abruptly, "You're not obligated to stay."

He said nothing, but his face grew hot.

"I can take care of myself, and him," she said, a backward cant of her head showing the smooth line of her throat. She stood straight and poised, her chin raised.

He eyed her hard, seeing she meant it. Some of his admiration shaded into his voice, "Believe you can. And you got Caldwell and Bowdre."

"I don't know about Caldwell, but I can depend on Bowdre."

Without knowing when it happened, he realized that they stood nearer. It was a dangerous thing. Again, his position became glassy clear in that instant. This thing had to be right between them. "Maybe you got enough help. All you need do is say the word. I'll ride out of here any time. You're not obligated because I'm Frank's brother."

She held his look. He wasn't sure how he knew, because it was gone like a grain of flying sand. But, briefly, he'd caught a vagrant feeling he could not puzzle out.

"You want me to ask you to stay? That it?"

He almost let it pass. "Hard thing to explain."

"Stay," she said, with emphasis, "and you'll risk your neck."

"I don't like to run out on folks."

She added nothing.

The waiting in him got heavy. There was, he thought, neither acceptance nor rejection in her silence. It struck him that she had no intention of telling him, one way or the other.

So it was left, unspoken, unresolved—and at the same time determined.

His jaw settled. Going from the house, he knew that he was staying as long as she needed him. He was all at once relieved and troubled.

The feeling carried him to the corral, stayed with him minutes after when he struck off northeast, riding faster than usual. He found the old wagon road and took it into the layered hills, the first black timber.

He was well inside these hills when he noticed the changing rhythm of his horse, a certain awkwardness, and heard the faint clacking. Dismounting, he discovered a loose left front shoe. With wire pliers from the saddle, he pulled shoe and nails and continued along the road, bound for the Blackhorse range. Time considered, he reasoned it better judgment to go on than return for another mount.

Halfway through the morning he watered the gelding in Yellow Dog below the limestone bluff. Instead of keeping on the road to the Blackhorse house, however, he cut east and circled in toward the landmark ridge. Yesterday, climbing the back side, he'd found a devious trail which took him to the top.

Approaching the trail now, he encountered ranked black-jacks. He ducked low in the saddle, one arm before his face. The sound of his gelding's hoofs came sharp and clear in the stillness as he climbed. When he leveled off near the crest, he reined up a moment to search the black timber shade.

A blur of movement warned him. Even as he tried to swing off the trail and turn, he heard the brittle chop of a horse travel-ing rock.

Before he could take cover, a rider bore out of the timber. He swung straight, alarm leaping in him, and recognized Savannah Tyson. A carbine hung on her saddle.

She saw him at the same instant and stiffened. Her eyes enlarged, then blinked in recognition. "Hello," came her cheerful greeting. "Told you I'd know you. Remember me?"

"Sure do. Just wasn't expecting company."

"Oh, I ride a lot."

"Alone?"

"Most times."

She sized him up openly and he understood. She was specu-lating over him as much as he was about her, except in a different way. "Last time we met," she said, "you were leaving the Osage. Now—"

"On a Chain Seven horse."

Her eyebrows lifted in charming fashion. "You're fast."

"Jeannette Garreau happened to need a man, if you remember."

"What brings you this far, to Blackhorse country?"

"Loose stock."

She turned her head, and there was something unforgettable how the changing light brought the ivory tinting to her face under the hat brim. Into her eyes slid a mocking evaluation of the rocky, timbered crest. "Just the place. Naturally, stock'd drift up here."

"Naturally," he said, going along with her. "And I suppose you're—"

"Just riding," she finished.

"Wonderful place for a ride. No rocks, brush ... "

Her reacting grin became a disarming ripple of laughter.

"But the view's good," he tacked on dryly.

"Yes. You can see Charlie's house."

"Uh-huh. You could see him leave the house, say. On his way to hunt quail along that slope."

She returned an agreeing nod and he felt himself relenting till he noted the carbine again. "Guess they raise mighty big coyotes around here. A man has to ride ready."

"Oh—that!" She smiled so naturally, with charm, that he regretted his suspicion. "Well, I do take it along for just that reason." Her eyes wandered to the leather scabbard alongside his saddle. "Same as you."

Fully at ease, Savannah Tyson crooked a shapely, blue-Levi leg around the saddle horn and jerked off her hat. She presented an arresting picture, he was aware, with the mottled light picking up the reddish gold luster of her hair. Her breasts rose rounded against her shirt. She seemed too lively for dejection, but he could not escape the impression of covered-up loneliness. Somehow he thought of Jeannette.

Her eyes, gauging and interested, rested upon him. "You might let me have a cigarette."

He handed her sack and papers and watched her clumsy efforts. She smoked with an obvious lack of practice. Catching his grin, she said, "I don't do it very well, do 1?"

"Takes practice."

After several unsuccessful drags, she threw down in disgust, straightened, and jammed her boot into the stirrup. "Time to go home. Going down?"

He moved to rein aside, then held up, his mind exploring how to say it. "Other day ... you said something at the house—said you wished I wouldn't leave. How should I take that? Mean anything special?"

"I said that?" And, before he could speak, "I don't seem to remember ... "

"You got a mighty poor memory for an intelligent girl."

Color stung her cheeks. "You seem to know a lot about me."

"Just figured we might finish our talk."

She spurred forward, but Myles reined his horse across. "You're blocking the trail," she said sharply and swung to cut around him.

He leaned and grabbed her bridle, firm and placid as he faced her. "Let's palaver a minute." The skin around her mouth was white with fear and he said, "I won't hurt you."

"I'm not afraid of you."

"I know you're not. So you can talk to me." He let go his grip on the bridle; she eased down in the saddle.

They eyed each other, judging, till Myles spoke up. "I take it you had Frank in mind when you dropped the hint? Wasn't just Tyson hospitality?"

"In a way, yes. But—"

"Keep talkin'. I'm all ears."

Her face clouded, but there was no fear in it now. "Honestly, I don't know why I bothered you."

"Must've had a good reason." He followed up in a weary tone, "So Frank's up to his neck in something?"

"No ... nothing I know about."

He felt an increasing exasperation. "There is, maybe, but it's harder to tell as Sid Tyson's daughter?"

"Stepdaughter," she corrected, heat marking her face. "No, that wouldn't make a bit of difference to me."

"Well, then—"

"I really can't say what it is, because I don't know." There was a tautness about her as she leaned forward. "Except Frank's changed. He's not the same man he was when he came to work for us."

"What can I do? He's old enough to pick his own company. I step out there."

She agreed, nodding in a bewildered manner.

His eyes ranged over her. She was an undeniably pretty girl, fair and blonde, full-bodied. "You don't want him to pull out, do you? Maybe you're why he stays on, instead of going back home where he's got part interest in a good ranch. Ever think of that?"

Her color surged back. "You forget he's engaged to Jeannette."

He shrugged his shoulders. "I'd say we're where we started on this—no place. Now, what else?"

"Nothing."

"Trail's open." He reined off, waiting for her to pass, hoping she might yet talk.

She took up the reins, "Thanks for listening to me," and rode by.

Her expression, as she moved past, rang a distant bell. It was Jeannette Garreau's face in the half-light of the yard—uneasy, disturbed and not understanding fully why. A reflection, he thought, of the ominous dread beginning to grip people in this part of the Osage range.

She rode fast, taking the narrow trail turns recklessly, hanging low to escape the branches. At the bottom she put her horse to a lope without a look for him.

He tailed her for some distance, at loss to figure her. Despite her reluctance, he thought he'd discovered an honest bewilderment.

Swerving west over a hill toward the Blackhorse ranch house, he saw the single spire of a derrick to the north and remembered that Clark Slater's line camp was there. A curious interest drew him. The camp was one place he hadn't prowled in his riding.

Half an hour onward he dropped down a ridge and found the brown wooden derrick, its rusting steam boiler. A crude shack stood resolute at the timber's edge. He rode across to the shanty and stepped down. Wire held the door closed. He unwound it and shoved in.

A circling glance satisfied him. There were blocks of rock salt, a bunk and, upon the shelf over the stove, several boxes of .30-30 Winchester shells and a small supply of canned goods.

Riding west again, he entered the shaded reaches of the virgin creek timber. Untouched ranks of walnuts, pecans, cottonwoods, oaks and the sycamores, whose blotched trunks always reminded him of a scar-faced full-blood woman, seen years ago, whom he'd never forgotten.

Crossing the creek, and south, he rode up to the house. It looked more forlorn than ever, an abandoned relic; no life around. His impression grew of weathered wood and timeless indifference.

Horse tracks cluttered the yard. For no knowing reason the heavy sign bothered him. He reined across to the water pump and halted, frozen to immobility.

The piping that linked well and water trough lay along the ground, torn from its wiring. His glance took in the water trough, kicked in, smashed.

A dull anger needled him, swung him to the barn. The door hung crookedly, ripped from its bottom hinge, the tearings fresh in the old wood. He hesitated, wary and unblinking.

Hurried by the hot sense of outrage, he quick-reined to the kitchen side of the house. The open door told him what to expect. But prior to entering, he spun a look around. For a naked feeling—old by now—filled him.

He stepped inside. Broken dishes and glasses, tinware and iron pots, littered the flour-strewn floor. The stovepipe was a disjointed thing, its black sections kicked into a waste of soot and gray ashes by the overturned body of the stove.

Angrily, he crossed to the next room, into the mess of shredded blankets, the iron bed askew, twisted; the old rocker caved in, the stove and piping wrecked as in the kitchen.

His fury climbed as he glared. Violent hands had swept through here, tearing and hurling, utterly without sense. He returned to the kitchen, and was closing the door, thinking how absurd an action it was now, when he noticed the absence of any lock.

Another sign, he thought, of Charlie Blackhorse's childish, primitive trust in everybody, in everything.

Now, for the first time today, he became sensitive to pressing time. He took long strides to his horse, shaken by the destructive intent here. But in consideration for the gelding he rejected the shorter, rockier route of the bluff road and angled across the easier footing of the grassy basin, toward the high slope that lay as a long wall marking the prairie's limits.

He was traveling the ridge line some minutes later when he saw an angry pall of black smoke far off southwest. The sight held him like an approaching storm, full of foreboding and danger. The blackness was a roiling blanket overlying the country beyond Jeannette Garreau's ranch headquarters. He wondered how long the range fire had been burning.

It seemed a long time before the house rose ponderously among the trees. The distant smoke, he noticed, was no longer growing. He hated to think of the scorched land. That lay heavily upon him as he ran the punished gelding around to the rear of the house.

He was surprised to find Jeannette's roadster parked at the back step, the driver's door flung wide. The car gave off a burning stink.

He shouted Jeannette's name. Almost at once he heard boots running inside the house. Jeannette hurried to the door.

He dismounted, his whole body stiffening. The way she ran toward him killed any hope he'd had. His mind flicked to something terrible: Blackhorse or Caldwell burned.

She was out of breath. She blurted it, the words running together, "Charlie's gone!"

"Gone?" he echoed blankly.

"Caldwell and Charlie—we all took sacks, jumped in the car —drove out there." She had to stop for breath. Her face was pale under the smudges, her eyes big. "We spread out—but couldn't stop it. I told Charlie to stay with the car. Caldwell and I went on. Must've been an hour, anyway. He was gone when I got back. So I came home. But he's not here!"

"Maybe he's still in the pasture."

"No," Jeannette said oddly, knowing. "We looked … Caldwell's still out there. Gone—Miles—he's gone!"

Her eyes lifted dismally to the corral, and Myles wrenched to look.

He saw only one horse, Skeeter. He whirled and found his own damning realization in her stricken stare. As if needing to convince herself, she said between dry, numbed lips, "He walked back … took the paint." Then her inertia broke. She gripped Myles' arm; her fingers dug. "You know where he went! We've got to find him!"

He moved fast to the corral, growling as he slammed the gate bar, "Missed him—I came in from the north. He had to take the old wagon road … Still time."

It was a confidence he didn't really feel while he saddled Skeeter. Within minutes they passed into the knuckled hills of hiding timber and paused to look.

"He could be home by now," came Jeannette's discouraged murmur.

Beyond, the old road wound and disappeared into a stand of blackjacks.

"Come on." Myles went ahead.

"Hold up … somebody's coming."

He saw the riders at the same instant, in the bend of the road. They were milling slowly, intent upon the ground. He recognized Bowdre's bay. The other rider …

Frank Rikker sided Bowdre.

Taken back, Myles hesitated.

Jeannette's shout turned them. Even then they appeared to dally. Her sudden spurring moved them toward her. They rode stiffly, their horses in a slack trot.

Something in their grim approach warned Myles, who came to a watchful attention when they halted.

Nobody wanted to speak, it seemed. For once, Bowdre showed an indecisive manner. Frank's mouth was a set line.

The short silence endured till it became an unbearable pressure and Myles said curtly, "Well—?"

Plain unwillingness entered Bowdre's face. "Miz Garreau ..." He removed his broad hat, forced regretful eyes upon her. "I hate to tell you—but we just found your uncle back there. Dead ... shot."

For a heartbeat she seemed unable to understand, even as she caught her breath. She shook her head stubbornly, fiercely, as a small girl incapable of believing bad news. Her mouth trembled. "No! No!" She dragged her gaze across them, and again to Bowdre. "Let me see him!" she begged and started forward.

All three moved to intercept her, but Myles got there first "No, Jeannette. Not now."

He grabbed reins and swept an arm around her shoulders. He was holding her fast, feeling the tremors jarring her body, when she dropped her head, sobbing convulsively with hands to her face.

Frank patted her awkwardly. She swayed. His arm sought and braced her. As Myles dropped his hand, the brothers' eyes locked.

For a time there was only the sound of the wind, the restless stamp of a horse, and Jeannette's sobs that tore a man's insides. Myles sat by helplessly, touched for her, not knowing what to say.

He stepped his horse away and stayed there, head bent, conscious also that he was left out. He swung to Jeannette once more, only to jam against Frank's searching scrutiny. A vague emotion flickered in the blue gaze, somewhere between interest and guardedness, before Frank turned back to Jeannette. Somehow or other Myles thought he'd interrupted more than a casual study of himself and his horse.

"Helluva note," Bowdre muttered just then. "Me, I was supposed to see this didn't happen."

Shaking his head, Myles looked along the road to the concealing blackjacks. Just now he began to piece things together as they probably occurred. Blackhorse jogging, thinking ahead to home and living his own way, the killer waiting in the timber. No tricky ridge shooting this time.... But why—the question knotted inside him suddenly—why'd a man be posted here unless...

"You—you see anybody?" Jeannette faltered.

Turning, Myles saw her fight for control. She sat rigidly in the saddle, steeling herself. He thought she looked smaller in grief, her well-formed features more accented and sensitive. And seeing her struggle, he admired her for trying. In addition, mixing with her shock, he saw a gathering fury. An Indian's rage. An eye for an eye.

"Just some sign," explained Bowdre, relieved to deal with the tools of his trade again. "Some horse tracks.... Seems to me—" He eyed her, not unkindly. "You better go back to the house. Frank, you take her."

She ignored Bowdre, pulled herself tight. "Mister Bowdre," she began, unwavering. "I'm no little girl. I'm staying here. Now, tell me what you found."

"Horse tracks don't mean much without the rider," Bowdre frowned back.

"Some of those tracks looked fresh to me," Frank put in.

Bowdre blinked. "Did, huh? Maybe I missed somethin'."

"Dunno—" Frank stirred in his saddle. "Been after some of Sid Tyson's remuda since early today. Some fool hunter left a gate down, our south pasture. Happened I gave those tracks a good onceover along the road. Was, in fact, when I ran into you. Just before we found Charlie."

"So ..." drawled Bowdre, in no hurry.

Frank worked his lips, compressed them. "You can take it for what it's worth. On the road I noticed one set of tracks. They stuck in my mind." He hesitated.

Bowdre's cool tone furnished the renewing impetus. "You mean they showed up where Charlie fell?"

"That's what puzzles me, more I think of it. They did." Frank shrugged his shoulders. "Maybe it don't mean a thing."

"I'll decide that," Bowdre reminded and silently sifted things a moment. His jaw jutted. "How you know they were the same?"

"Wasn't hard. One shoe was off the left front foot."

The incredible meaning burst in Myles. He found himself wanting to speak out, too stunned to utter a word.

"Still leaves us in the buckbrush," Bowdre returned gruffly. "Find a man on a three-shoed hoss." His grin was sour. "Could mean somethin'. Maybe not."

"Could," Frank agreed, and said no more.

Relief eased Myles. From all indications Frank had dropped the subject. Further speculation lay with Bowdre.

The agency man's explosive grunt hauled at Myles, who saw Bowdre slide rapidly from the saddle. The old lawman's downward eyes were bright and roving. A new interest burned. His head snapped up.

"Hell, there's such tracks right here!"

Bowdre's stare leaped to Frank's horse, skipped to Jeannette's, then to Myles'. Bowdre's features hardened. "Mister," he droned, "you're ridin' the wrong horse today."

"Not a-tall." Myles felt every muscle in his body grow tense. He tried to give the words a casual sound, and realized he could not. "My horse had a loose shoe this morning. I pulled it on my way to Charlie's."

Bowdre's eyes, pale points in the sun-burned planes of his wizened face, shone suspiciously. "You'll have to talk better'n that. How'd you get here?"

"Rode in from the north. Went straight to the house."

"Out of the way, ain't it? Why'n't you take the bluff road back. It's shorter."

"And rockier. Didn't want a sore-footed horse."

Bowdre snorted. "Anybody with you?"

"By myself." It pounded in Myles that he was damning himself each time he spoke, each word. His temper broke through. "Damn you Bowdre! You've prowled these hills for days and come up with blanks! Now you need something fast—so you jump on the first fool thing you see!"

Anger whetted Bowdre's stare. "It'll do till a better one comes along." His hand moved, blurred. His pistol winked. "I'm takin' you in, mister. If for nothin' else, on general principles."

It was beyond any bounds of conceivable reason. Yet the gun pointed straight at Myles, steady as time.

He couldn't believe his eyes. A long-standing weariness clamped down and he wheeled sharply upon Frank.

"Myles—I—" Frank's hand rose and fell. It was a futile gesture.

"Get away from me!" snarled Myles, suddenly nauseated. Fury shook him.

But what cut deepest was Jeannette's face, blurred in his vision. He saw disbelief struggling with loathing. Then she turned away.

CHAPTER EIGHT

MYLES LAY with his eyes shuttered, trying to blot out the unbelievable images in his mind. Finally, he sat up, the sense of unreality enduring, and looked around him.

Everything was here, however, just as he'd seen it last night in the sickly yellow light of Coon Pollard's smelly kerosene lantern. The narrow cot and the dirty blanket upon the straw mattress. The stool in one corner, the high square of window, and the network of steel bars facing him; beyond, down the short corridor, were the other cells and the door that led to Pollard's office.

Strong morning light slanted through the window. He welcomed it hungrily. Standing, he needed only two steps to reach the window. He remained rooted there, peering out upon the brown buttes of the sandstone buildings, listening to an awakening Two Sands and the throbbing pulsebeat of the distant oil derricks; and actually savoring, he found, the sulphur smell for the simple reason that it rode free on a warm wind.

At length, shaking his head, he turned back to the cot. His movement shattered the momentary illusion of the world outside, opened wide the gates of his dull thinking for the dejection to flood in. His harried brain swung backward to yesterday.

He could understand Tom Bowdre. The man was doing his job, arrest being the only action left for him in view of what had happened. As for Frank—Myles' hands clenched till the knuckles whitened. No, he couldn't savvy Frank; he knew now that he never had.

He winced inwardly as another thought jarred. It was the worst of all. He could still see Jeannette Garreau. Her highboned face, drained of color, the etched revulsion. A look he would remember for the rest of his life with lasting regret.

The other details were merely ill-fitting pieces of a nightmare. Bowdre, competent and cool as his pistol; cautious, too, calling town on Jeannette's phone for Pollard to send out a guard to help take him in. The silent ride through the darkness, handcuffed between Bowdre and another man.

Myles got up and paced the floor, his cornered feeling deepening. His mind was taking strange twists, acting up in a fashion never before experienced, throwing him entirely off balance, so he couldn't think. He called on an iron calm, in a way of desperation. It was as if he dug frantically toward the deep, hidden roots of something he must find.

To his astonishment he discovered that he stood very still, his hands knotted, his heart pounding against the drum of his chest. But he had no fear. Then he felt his fists relax. A glimmer came through the shimmering haze of his thinking. His throat constricted, his mouth went dry. And he was glimpsing a smooth, proud face ... hearing the murmur of a teasing, throaty voice as she moved in the warm shadows of the kitchen ... feeling the electric shock of her inside his arms.

Suddenly, he understood, even as he tried to deny it—understood about himself in one wonderful, terrible moment ... And Frank's girl to boot. How cross-grained could a man be?

He came down to the cot, physically shaken, profoundly shocked.

"Breakfast?"

He recognized at last that someone had spoken. He pulled his eyes to the cell door. The jailer, a wispy, dull-faced man, held tin plate and coffee cup.

"Just coffee," said Myles, not liking the thought of food.

"If you ain't hungry, leave it," growled the jailer, annoyed. He slid the tinware under the cell door and retreated down the corridor in a jangle of keys.

For a minute Myles just picked at the tasteless fare. By degrees a surprising appetite took hold, a reminder that he hadn't touched food since yesterday morning at the ranch. The coffee, black as night, bolstered him like strong drink. A dubious contentment spread. He was thinking clearly again.

He examined the cell, his speculation a sharp, prying inquiry that probed the brown walls, plentifully carved with initials of former inmates and crude, humorless pencil drawings.

His impulsive notion vanished almost as soon as it occurred. For the stone, when he eye-measured it at the window, presented a thickness of two feet. In addition, Pollard had relieved him of all necessities, down to cigarette makings.

He returned to the cot and waited.

During the early part of the morning, Myles heard the corridor door open and clang. Bowdre came forward in the crimped gait of a riding man.

"You kept me up late," spoke Bowdre, minus any expression.

"Didn't sleep so good myself. Missed my feather bed and toddy."

"Too bad." Dislike barged into the agency officer's eyes. He drove his appraisal over Myles and about the cell. "Don't go gettin' any Billy the Kid ideas about bustin' out. Won't work."

"What," Myles inquired innocently, "makes you think a man'd try that?"

"Hell, I know the signs. I can see the tracks in your face. You're like a bull in a chute. Plain as daylight."

"In case you don't know it, that wall is two feet through. It'd take dynamite and friends—and I can't claim any in Two Sands."

Bowdre, whom Myles had never seen grin, permitted a dim amusement to wreathe his face. "No brother, either."

"Not hard to see. Even you figured it out."

"Seen a heap of water go down the crick in my time—sure have." Bowdre's usually toneless voice sounded a note of pleased bewilderment. "But never a brother oblige the way Frank Rikker did. Guess the boy's just extra honest. Can't help himself."

Myles made a harsh noise in his throat. "I'll tell you why. Frank hates my tracks."

"Don't get along, huh?" Bowdre lolled against the cell door, his lean face thoughtful. "Maybe that explains it. Part of it, I'd say."

"You're getting the idea."

Bowdre smiled thinly, with a new alertness. "But that's not all. There's Miz Garreau. I think you crowded Frank's time. Otherwise, he'd kept shut about those tracks."

"Wrong again, Bowdre." Color heated Myles' face.

"You jumped quick enough around the ranch, I noticed that. An' when she got the news about Charlie, you sure slipped your arm around her. Beat Frank to it. Mighty touching, it was."

"Natural thing to do. She had a bad time."

"Mighty natural," droned Bowdre. "Particular, when a girl's worth what Miz Garreau is. Nice big ranch...headright or two...her easy to look at." He peered a long moment. "But you're in up to your neck. You realize that?"

Myles' tone took on a mocking irony. "I didn't know. Thought this was the hotel."

"Don't reckon I told you that Charlie Blackhorse was an old friend of mine?"

"My friend, too," Myles replied firmly.

"Yeah!" Bowdre snapped down his hand. "So you murdered him!"

A powerful anger shook Myles. And before he knew it he faced Bowdre, gripping the bars, and he was mouthing the words at Bowdre, "You're damn hard up for a suspect. Tell me—why'd I want to kill Charlie—tell me!"

"Money—there's always money. Plenty of it around here."

Myles grunted in disgust. "Not for me."

"Somebody hired you," Bowdre decided gravely. "A stranger … you drift into the Osage … act like you're in search of work. Nobody knows you but your brother, who won't claim you, and the gent that hired you. So … you inquire around, get a ranch job near your victim. Meanwhile, there's Miz Garreau—enough to interest any man. You play her, too. After that—"

"Now you're fishing and I don't know a thing."

"Checked up on you," continued the little man, unperturbed. "You had two fights first night in Two Sands. Whipped Tharp Kutch, for one. Other night, in the Palace, you took on Kutch and Rikker. You're a troublemaker, mister."

"They started it."

"Rikker had reason, didn't he? Way you trailed Miz Garreau. The girl he's gonna marry."

Myles lips flattened. There was no arguing with the man. Everything came out wrong. He attempted to route reason through his temper, snapped, "In all this business, you've over-looked what happened first time they tried to ambush Charlie. I mean along the ridge, south of his place. I got Charlie out of there alive—least I did that much. Jeannette knows. Ask her."

"Yeah," Bowdre nodded in cynical agreement. "Looked good. Fooled Charlie. Except he got hit—not you. Him, they wanted. He wasn't hurt bad, so what do you do? Why, you take him up the ridge—you go ahead—like you're riskin' your neck … Trouble was your friend on the ridge spooked after he got the dog. Charlie, a great shot, was just too close for comfort."

Myles threw up his hands in angry resignation, stepped back.

"However," drawled Bowdre, "you might make it easier on yourself … just might."

"How's that?" Myles asked carefully.

A shrewd sizing-up worked into Bowdre's scrutiny. He said in a voice almost friendly, "Sam Ingle, the county attorney, is down at the hotel. Drove over this morning. Sorta figured you might talk with him. Tell him your side. Square-shooter, Sam is. You talk right and, well—" His drawling voice pinched off, dangling a hinted promise.

"Told you—I don't know a thing." Contempt rose thick and sour in Myles' throat.

Impatience cracked Bowdre's mask of friendliness. "Reckon you will after Ingle files murder charges. Then you'll say who hired you, beg to."

"Go to hell," grunted Myles.

"Think it over, mister. ... "

Dragging out the words, Bowdre heeled slowly and, in no apparent hurry, clumped down the corridor.

Myles stared after him, feeling his hot, angry helplessness. He saw through it all. First, the reminders of how tangled his position looked on the surface, leading up to the sly show of friendship, and next the threats. The last rang true, anyway.

The closing door made him think. He hadn't thought of it till now, but he was going to need a lawyer. A smart one. The realization disturbed him. He pondered his reluctance and decided he still desired to postpone the move.

Stretched out upon the cot, hands cupped behind his head, he stared up at the fly-specked ceiling and moodily considered his situation. Heat crawled inside the tiny cell. Smells rose, the unscoured smells of sweaty, sour men whose taints had penetrated even the stone floor and walls and persisted long after their departure.

Lost and baffled, he did not turn his head upon hearing the heavy door grind open. It took the sound of boots approaching his cell before he raised up.

He saw Happy Adcock, flanked by the jailer. Myles swung to the floor, suddenly warmed by the sight of this long, sadlooking face. He stepped to the cell door.

There followed a clumsy pause. Myles looked at Adcock. Did he intend to shake hands? Still, Myles hesitated. Or was he just extra sensitive, seeing things that didn't exist?

He regretted the thought as Adcock thrust out a hand. They shook.

"Figured you might need some tobacco," said Adcock, passing a sack of makings through the bars.

"Why, much obliged, Happy."

The jailer stood close by Adcock, who complained mildly, "You sure do dog a man, Ben. What's the matter? Afraid I'll slip this boy a saw?"

"Orders. I stand right here while you talk. It ain't that Coon don't trust you."

"Course not," replied Adcock, winking. He turned to Myles. One hand tugged at his shirt. He looked troubled, longfaced.

"Well—say it," Myles said.

Adcock ran a finger inside his shirt collar. "Lookee, Myles. Blamed if I know what to say. Except they got the wrong man. Things sure are mixed up." He glanced to the floor, chin on his chest. "Poor Charlie ... they bury him tomorrow."

A soberness threaded through Myles, a profound regret He said nothing.

"I'm a pallbearer. Me an' Sid Tyson, some more old friends."

There came a long silence. It pulled at Myles' nerves.

"Funeral's set over to Nellie's place. She's gonna bury him out there, too."

"What time?"

"Two o'clock. Catholic. Priest's comin' over from Pawhuska." Adcock's head tilted up in surprise. "Danged if you don't talk like a man that's goin'."

"I'd like to," Myles answered earnestly. "Really would. Do me a favor, will you, Happy? Take some of my money—it's in Pollard's office—and buy Charlie some flowers."

Adcock nodded, moved. "You bet. An bld lady lives out the edge of town, raises flowers. Sure does a business. Any special kind?"

"Guess not.... On second thought, make it red. An Indian likes red."

"Roses, maybe?"

"Fine, Happy. Roses."

"Okay. But what if she's out?"

"Anything you like."

"Kinda out of my line." The angular face lengthened. "I'll use my own judgment. What there is left of it these days. Blamed if I don't think Charlie'd soon have a big bunch of fresh prairie grass as flowers around his casket. Uh'd rather, in fact. If you ever been up north, in the Sioux country, y'know sage is big medicine. Same as flowers. Don't see much difference myself 'tween grass and flowers." A grimace of disapproval caught him. "Not many people'd understand, though. Now, would they? Ain't civilized. So it'll have to be flowers, won't it?"

"Guess so."

"Be a big feast. Always is. Neighbors bring in eats when a white man dies—an Injun throws a big feast. All the same, I reckon. Be long tables set up under the trees. Black kettles full. Bunch of wimmen workin'. Plenty of beef. Reckon I'll go, sure will. Bring back what I can't eat in a red bandana, like an Osage," he concluded glumly. "Reminds me when Louis Garreau drownded. That was a real big feast. Bet Nellie spent a thousand dollars. Come to think of it, I was pallbearer that time, too. So was Sid."

Abruptly, his garrulous talk ceased. He scratched his bony chin, rubbed his thin nose and back-handed a yawn. His sleepless eyes left Myles, wandered to the tips of his own boots.

"Ain't you done?" grumbled the jailer.

"Well ... " Adcock turned.

"Happy—" Adcock pivoted at the sound of his name and Myles spoke from the confusion of his mind, "Jeanette ... guess I don't have to ask you what she thinks."

Reluctance kept Adcock's eyes lowered. "You mean about you?"

"Who else?" Myles asked bitterly.

"Nothin's changed, if that's what you mean?"

"She with her mother?"

Adcock looked pained. "Understand she went over to Nellie's last night, but didn't stay. You know"—he spread his hands—"how it is. Jeannette's not very high on Sid. Jesus Christ himself couldn't take Louis' place, an' I can understand why. Sure can. ... Trouble is, that don't leave an ordinary man much to brag about."

"I wouldn't call Sid Tyson an ordinary man."

"You're right there. But he ain't exactly Preacher Jones on Sunday, now, is he? But who the hell is?"

Myles almost smiled. It came to him that he longed to talk about her, even if it hurt. "So she's at the ranch?"

"Where'd you expect her to be at?" Adcock replied, throwing Myles a bewildered look. "She ain't afraid to stay by herself."

"Herself?" Myles felt himself turn tense. "But Caldwell's there!"

"Was, you mean. He quit this mornin', real sudden."

The words struck Myles with the impact of a shattering explosion. He went cold all over. He was all at once afraid, ridden under by a pressure bordering on panic. It was several moments before he could speak, hollow and apprehensive, "But why— why'd Caldwell pull out?"

"Dunno. She didn't say. What with Charlie on her mind, I reckon. Just asked me to look around town for another hand. It's my notion Caldwell decided it was gettin' a little too hot out there."

"She shouldn't be alone, Happy." Myles wiped clammy palms on the thighs of his trousers.

"Aw, she's all right," Adcock insisted, but his voice failed of conviction. "She can handle things till I find somebody."

"I don't mean ranch work."

Adcock's face fell. "What're you drivin' at?"

"Hard for me to say it." Myles had the illogical feeling that if he voiced his fear, brought it into the open, he'd only lend it tangible force.

"Don't know as I get you, Myles. Not exactly." Adcock's frown furrowed to a deep scowl. "If you're thinkin' about what happened to Charlie … that maybe that'd happen to her? Somethin' like that."

"I am," Myles said flatly.

"Nobody'd hurt a woman."

"Th' hell they wouldn't! Listen, Happy. Think you could get her in town for a few days?"

Adcock frowned hard. "She wouldn't leave the ranch. You know that."

Myles dropped his hands. Happy was right. He felt miserable, unable to think straight.

"Time's up," the jailer cut in.

Adcock took a hesitating step and the words, leaped from Myles, "That's not all, Happy. What did she say? Go on, tell me. Guess I can take it. Does she really believe I did it?"

"Well—she … " Adcock's Adam's apple bobbed like a sliding button. "That's just it, Myles. Wasn't what she said. It was—the way she looked. Believe she'd put a bullet in you."

Eyes averted, Happy Adcock turned down the corridor. There was a sag to his shoulders as he went to the door, followed by the jailer.

Myles retreated to the cot, sank his chin in his big hands. For a minute he felt nothing, heard nothing around him. Then, little by little, his mind spun tighter. He shook his head, but the fear upon him kept enlarging.

He snapped to his feet and not till he stood by the barred door did understanding of his intention crystallize. He called loudly for the jailer, his voice sounding like someone else's, called till the sliding bar grated.

An annoyed face became visible at the cracked door. "What's the trouble?"

Myles answered without thought, "Get Bowdre! Tell him I'll talk to the county attorney!"

CHAPTER NINE

Bowdre took his time. An hour crawled past, Myles judged, before the agency officer appeared at the door and strolled inside. After him loomed the moon face and barrel shape of Coon Pollard. Bowdre's pace was deliberate, without hurry.

Bowdre halted. "Changed your tune?"

"In a way," said Myles, casting about in his mind as to how he should begin.

"Gonna tell who hired you?"

"Afraid I'll disappoint you there—since I didn't do it. But I have some information I know the county attorney can use. You, too."

"You can tell me now." Bowdre spoke softly, a tiny flame of interest leaping to his eyes.

"Better," parried Myles, "If you both heard it at the same time." He paused. "Hate to repeat myself."

A bleak suspicion chilled Bowdre's stare. "You make a man wonder. I don't trust you, mister."

"No reason not to." Myles made his voice careful. "I'm simply offering valuable information. Some things I noticed at the Garreau ranch. You want me to tell the county attorney or don't you?"

"Hell, yes, if there's anything to it."

"There is—plenty."

"We'll see." Bowdre turned to Pollard. "Turn him out, Coon. We'll take him over to the hotel. Put the cuffs on him."

FRED GROVE

Pollard, briskly pompous, unlocked the door and entered. "Hold out your hands," he ordered in a commanding tone.

Myles complied. As the cuffs closed around his wrists, he felt a sharp sensation of dismay.

"Wait a minute, Coon," decided Bowdre. "Lock him to your left wrist. Don't want him high tailin' off. Not that he'd go far."

An injured dignity spliced Pollard's round body. "He ain't goin' nowhere," he said. Grumbling, he unlocked the shackles, using a key from the ring attached to his belt, and fettered Myles' right wrist to his plump left. "Let's go."

As they walked outside, Myles felt the warmth of the sun on his face, like tonic. He held up a moment to suck in the fresh air, an involuntary movement which dragged against the cuffs.

Grunting, Pollard hauled Myles forward. They moved on. Pollard's stumpy form seemed to puff and swell as a teamster, harnessing up in a vacant lot across from the jail, stopped to watch. Pollard took the lead and Bowdre fell in behind, intent as a lean gray wolf trailing spring calf meat. They followed the dusty side street a block in the direction of Main Street. Here, Myles figured Pollard would turn, so as to stay on the lesser traveled streets, but he kept going.

Myles was sweating by the time they reached the alley behind Main Street, dreading the crowd.

"Far enough, Coon," said Bowdre, disapproving. "Let's not have a Main Street parade. Just draw a crowd. Take the alley. That way we come in close to the hotel. Ingle's waitin' for us."

It was a command, not a suggestion.

Some of the strut went out of Pollard. However, he gave in grudgingly, his disappointment as keen as a boy called from a game of sheriff and outlaw. "If you say so."

They turned in and paced three blocks down the alley, avoiding heaps of cans and boxes. By now Pollard had recovered his official air.

The change became more apparent to Myles when they came around the corner and saw the loungers in front of the hotel. Pollard shifted his heavy holster. His right hand strayed suggestively to his silver-studded gunbelt, his thumb hooked there. He swaggered. Not too much—just enough to give the impression of assurance. He went slower as they approached the hotel entrance and moved into the absorbed focus of the watchers.

A surge of anger stung Myles when he saw Pollard's design. He thanked Bowdre with his eyes when the little man, frowning at Pollard's play, quickly opened the screen door and flung the words, "Cut out the show, Coon."

The lobby was crowded and Myles sensed Pollard's intentions at once, despite Bowdre's warning. Because Pollard, as if he hadn't heard, was an actor entering on cue. His voice, brisk with importance, filled the lobby. "Stand back, boys." He made a sweeping gesture.

Everybody gave ground, exposing a narrow lane into which Pollard marched his prisoner.

"The stairs, Coon," spoke Bowdre.

Heat burned Myles' face. Pollard, still strutting, was now a parade marshal on the Fourth of July, showing off at the head of a cavalcade of bright-shirted riders and feathered Indians.

Deliberately, Myles stepped faster.

Pollard, caught unawares, snarled, "B'God, you take it easy!" He slowed the pace.

As they neared the stairs, Myles glimpsed two faces—Sid Tyson's, expressionless, and Happy Adcock's, troubled.

They climbed the stairs. At the top Bowdre led off down the hall and rapped on a door. Myles heard an authoritative "Come in!" He had to go in sidewise to make room for Pollard, who announced just as Bowdre started to speak, "Here's your man, Ingle."

A shadow of irritation clouded the notice of the man facing them across a small pine table, improvised for writing purposes.

Myles met dominant eyes, ringed with low-hanging bags of fatigue, which surveyed him through thick-lensed glasses. Ingle looked older than he was, in his late fifties, inclined to stooped spareness and wiser in appearance than most men.

Ingle now ignored Pollard for Bowdre, who grunted his satisfaction, "Pearce says he's ready to talk, Sam."

"Sounds like a very sensible young man," said Ingle, rocking shoulders and head. "Might save us some time. By the way, Tom, may have to call on you for further assistance today. My sheriff is tied up on a little cow-stealing matter in the northern part of the county. Hope you don't mind?"

"Glad to."

"Your prisoner, anyway." Ingle smiled politically.

Bowdre did not speak, but Myles saw his tiny reaction of pleasure.

"Might as well be comfortable, gentlemen." Ingle gestured genially to chairs. "Since I have no secretary with me, it will be necessary for me to take down Mister Pearce's statement in detail." He reached for paper and pen, arranged a bottle of ink before him. With everyone seated, Ingle shed his affability like a too-warm coat. He ground his attention into Myles. "I presume that what you have in mind is in the nature, uh, of a confession?"

Anger, hot and sudden, boiled up. "Who gave you that idea?" Myles asked. "Bowdre?"

"Oh, no—" Ingle, taken back, let his breath filter out. "Of course, Mr. Bowdre did not intend to speak for you. He merely said you wished to talk to me. I took it to mean that you had something vital to say. Now, shall we get on?"

"I want this made straight before we do," said Myles. "I didn't shoot Charlie Blackhorse."

Ingle's smile was knowing. "I'd expect you to deny it, naturally. Notwithstanding an implication to the contrary by your brother." He turned his eyes upon Bowdre as he finished.

Unease touched Myles. He lifted his hand, only to have Pollard jerk it down.

"Suppose you know," said Ingle, "that you can help yourself if you co-operate with authorities?"

"You mean a deal?"

"Not in those words." Ingle coughed judicially. "If you give us the name or names of other people involved, you can ease your situation considerably. If not, we have no alternative but to charge you with murder and hold you without bond for preliminary hearing."

First, thought Myles, the sight of the ax.

A muteness dropped over the room.

Of a sudden he felt he'd need to draw this out to the fullest. He said, carefully, "All I can tell you is what I saw—some of my suspicions."

"No names?"

Myles split his gaze between the two officials. He stayed silent so long that Bowdre, impatient, grunted, "Get started, mister."

"I hate to bring this out," said Myles with reluctance.

"Just give us his name." Ingle tapped the pen, leaned forward. "The man who hired you."

"Now you're back on the old track."

Ingle smiled briefly. "Let's concede the point for the moment. We'll just say you know who did the killing."

"Wrong again. Can't say for certain, because I don't know."

"Hell, he's just out for the air!" Bowdre jumped up, fists squared on hips. "He's goin' back to the cooler, Sam."

"Easy, Tom." Ingle waved Bowdre down. "Want to proceed, Mr. Pearce?"

"Came here to talk, didn't I?"

"All right."

Aversion swamped Myles. Time locked. He was conscious of Bowdre's scowling dislike, of Ingle's chair creaking as he rocked back and forth, of Pollard's lumpy arm like a weight. Through the open window drifted Two Sands' growling murmur, every clashing discord distinct. Somewhere a horse started up and the racket quickened to drumfire upon the sounding board of the flinty street.

Slowly, he realized that he was drawing tighter. His mind seemed grooved, incapable of but this one thing he must do.

"We're waiting," Ingle said.

Clearing his throat, Myles felt an inner shrinking and repugnance. His hands were cold, moist. "It's—like this," he said. "Right after I went to work for Miss Garreau, I noticed she—"

Ingle's pen, scratching steadily, ceased all at once.

"Her!" Bowdre stood up, an angry astonishment flooding his face. "You tryin' to bring her in this?"

"Wait a minute, Tom," said Ingle, recovering from his own surprise. "Let him talk."

Glaring, Bowdre sat down.

"Like I said," Myles continued, "I noticed things. One was how she played up to Charlie. Went out of her way, I thought, even if she was his niece."

"Nothing wrong with that," reasoned Ingle. "A good idea. The way matters turned out, someone should have been with him all the time."

"There was—till he was killed. Why'd she send me off on a long ride the day of the murder? That's another thing. She knew it'd be a long time before I got back to the ranch." Ingle and Bowdre exchanged glances and Myles plunged on, "Appears to me you should bring her in for questioning. Keep her in town."

"Not on that testimony," rapped Ingle. "You may have suspicions, but they are far too vague in my opinion. Particularly"—his voice grated—"in view of the fact that you rode every day over to the Blackhorse ranch. We know that."

Bowdre pinned a triumphant glance upon Myles. So Bowdre had trailed him! It accounted for the little man's unchanging suspicion.

"At least," argued Myles, "you could make her stay in town." He turned to Ingle, then Bowdre. "She's not safe out there. Ever occur to you—maybe she's next?"

Ingle pounced upon the irrelevancies. "One second you hint she's involved. Next you say she isn't. What the devil do you mean?"

"Anything to weasel out of it," sided Bowdre, his leathery mouth fixed in contempt.

"Miss Garreau promised to be available whenever needed," Ingle stated. "As for someone being after her—well, I doubt that. And Tom suggested last night that she take a room at the hotel. She refused. We can't force her, you know." He threw down his pen. "Take him back, Tom. I have no faith in anything this man says."

As Bowdre rose, Myles realized that straight talk would never do. He snapped, "I'm not finished."

"Oh?" Ingle's lagging interest revived, but suspicion made his eyes bright. He picked up the pen. "Proceed, Mr. Pearce."

"Before I start, there's one question, a big one. Why hasn't Bowdre arrested Clark Slater? Slater threatened Charlie over a lease. I heard him in front of the hotel. So did a dozen other men."

"That…" Ingle dismissed it, disappointed again. "Slater couldn't possibly have shot Blackhorse. He was at the Palace most of yesterday. Five men vouch for him. You satisfied?"

Myles remained silent. He could put it off no longer. He said in a lifeless tone, "Maybe I'm wrong." He had the bleak knowledge then that if he went too far he might damn Jeannette forever; that if he failed to make it strong enough. … His mind settled in a distant niche, and cold, firm determination flowed from it.

"I've been slow about bringing her into this," he said. "One thing, she's a damn pretty woman. … It was something I heard at the ranch. After Charlie came to Jeannette's—I mean Miss Garreau's."

Ingle's pen was scratching swiftly. Bowdre sneered.

Myles thrust his chin forward, the import of what he was about to utter racing in his mind. "I heard Charlie say he'd willed his ranch to her, all that fine grassland. He kind of laughed when he mentioned it, said he expected to reach a hundred."

"Talks slick, don't he?" Bowdre sneered.

Ingle chewed on his pen. "Happened I looked over Blackhorse's will this morning. He'd left it on file with the agency, as some full-bloods do. Pearce is right, Tom. Blackhorse did will his land to Miss Garreau."

Myles sat like rock. He'd shot in the dark—and hit.

"What's that prove?" demanded Bowdre. "Charlie was single. Why shouldn't he leave it to his niece?"

"And his headright," continued Ingle, "goes to his sister, Mrs. Tyson." He raised dubious eyes. "In other words, you're accusing Miss Garreau of murdering her uncle for his land? To sorta hurry it up?"

Already, Myles felt himself hedging, fighting a rebellious revulsion. He said, "I'm just passing on what I heard out there," and knew that he was covering up, on the verge of spoiling once more the object which an insistent, hammering voice said he must impress upon Ingle. "Then—the day of the killing—when I was coming up to the house. Well—I saw her ride in from the road where Charlie was murdered. She acted nervous—"

"Have a rifle?" Ingle queried.

"No, but she could've ditched it in the brush."

."He's a liar!" shouted Bowdre, leaping up, his fists balled.

"Hold on!" roared Ingle. "This man's giving us a statement."

"Statement hell!" Bowdre's voice was a wild squall. "He's lyin'! She was fightin' that prairie fire! Her an' Caldwell!"

"Who's to prove she was?" asked Myles. "Understand Caldwell's gone. Left the country. Happy Adcock was just out .there."

Bowdre looked dumbfounded, stunned.

Ingle came alert, and Myles saw that he'd scored. Yet, dismally, a fearful comprehension followed. He'd also smeared Jeannette with a guilt that might be difficult to discount afterward.

"I tell you he's lyin', Sam."

"Let him finish."

"I have," said Myles. Now was the time to shut up, with Ingle hooked. He hadn't expected Bowdre to believe him.

"Realize what you've just said?" The county attorney's tone sounded very official and final. "What it means? You're implicating Miss Garreau. It's down on paper."

Myles nodded slowly, against a rising revulsion.

Lips moving, Ingle read what he'd taken down. As if satisfied, he looked over his glasses at Bowdre. "Tom, we have to consider this from all angles. I want you to scoot out to the Garreau ranch and check on Caldwell. If he flew the coop, Miss Garreau's left high and dry for an alibi. Bring her in, regardless. Caldwell, too, if you can find him. We'll not call it an arrest in her case, just temporary custody." Apology shaded into Ingle's eyes. "My man isn't here, so I guess it's up to you."

Not a muscle moved in Bowdre's face. But if Myles had ever read scorn, he saw it now—withering, hating. Bowdre shook himself like an old wolf hound and confronted Ingle, almost pleading, "I don't like this, Sam."

"I don't either. But I need your help."

"It's all wrong."

"Perhaps. Except we can't take a chance. Furthermore, I'd rather you went instead of the sheriff. You know Indians, Tom. This calls for special handling—uh, understanding."

"A dirty job," said Bowdre. "Touchy, arrestin' a woman."

"I know. Well, what do you say?"

"Damnit," growled Bowdre in grudging defeat. "I'll go. What else can a man do?"

"I feel," said Ingle, relieved, "that we should move fast on this matter."

Still grumbling, Bowdre clumped to the door. He threw Myles a remembering scowl, then went out slowly.

"Now," said Ingle, glancing at the sheet of paper, "you can sign this, Mister Pearce. I suggest that you read it through. Please add your name as a witness, Mister Pollard."

Guilt nauseated Myles as he read rapidly. It was all there — every damning word. He found himself wavering, with the pen in his hand.

"Well—" demanded Ingle.

Sick at heart, Myles penned his clumsy signature. Pollard signed his.

"Now that I've told you all I know," said Myles, "tell Pollard to take off these cuffs. I'll stick around as a witness."

"That, you will," Ingle replied icily. "I'm still holding you without bond. I can, you know, for a little while. Meanwhile —" He nodded to Pollard.

"But you and Bowdre said—"

"We'd let you go?" Ingle beat him to the words. "Hardly wise at this time, would you say? We have yet to complete our investigation. No, we happen to know murder when we see it. This isn't the first time a rich Osage has been murdered. As a matter of fact, it's been open season on headright owners ever since the Burbank boom." Ingle appeared weary. "Take him back to your establishment, Mister Pollard. Later in the day Miss Garreau can confront him. Perhaps, then we'll know about the charges."

"Just holler when you're ready," Pollard assured, and pulled toward the door.

"Say," said Ingle, faintly concerned, "I forgot you're by yourself. Why not call in some local men to give you a hand?"

An offended pride braced Pollard. "Ain't necessary. I can handle him."

Ingle had no time to argue. Pollard marched confidently to the door and shoved Myles ahead of him.

As they tramped along the gloomy hallway, boots echoing on the loose flooring, an odd awareness overtook Myles. From the instant that Pollard had made a show of roughing him through the doorway, he had been calculating the strength in the round man's arm. He let his eyes stray downward to the keys that dangled from Pollard's broad belt.

Pollard stiffened immediately. "Get funny an' I'll bend a pistol barrel across that hammerhead skull of yours."

"You'd like to, wouldn't you?" breathed Myles. Pollard, he decided, might be an officious fool, but he'd not take any chances. If forced, he'd strike brutally.

When they arrived at the head of the stairs, Pollard dallied to eye the lobby. His interest roved, considering and pleased, in the manner of a circus manager counting a full tent before the performance started.

It wasn't long till a man noticed them. All heads craned and Myles heard the buzzing excitement once more. A rankling filled him.

Coon Pollard was ready now.

Head high, he checked Myles with his keenest gunfighter's scrutiny, and started down. Each step was a study in casual competence, as if to impress that escorting badmen were a risky yet work-a-day chore.

Stepping to the lobby floor, Myles had the feeling of a spectator watching an act.

"Make room, boys," Pollard warned and waved them aside. A man grinned, though Pollard gave no notice. Somebody held the lobby screen open.

On impulse Myles swung toward the alley.

Pollard rammed his left fist into Myles' stomach, stopping him.

"Haven't you played enough for today?" Myles asked. "Let's take the alley."

"So you can make a break?" Pollard jerked. "Come on."

His baleful expression left Myles dry-mouthed and angry. Pollard intended to walk Main Street, to show him off in one grand exhibition before locking him up.

That wasn't all. Myles knew the man thoroughly now. For all his outward appearance of softness, of hamming in front of a crowd, he possessed an inner urge toward violence, so long as he took no personal risk.

"Think I'm fool enough to try it handcuffed?" Myles said as Pollard moved to the outside.

"Just wish you would, b'God!"

In silence Myles went along, noting that many of the lobby men followed. Any hopes he'd had for breaking away, already wrecked when Pollard avoided the alley, were made impossible by the size of the tagging, curious crowd.

About midway through the first block, Myles experienced a stab of interest. Happy Adcock stood on the running board of his flivver, peering over the jostling crowd. Briefly, Myles saw Adcock's eyes come across him. There was no friendliness, no recognition, even though their glances met squarely.

It gave Myles a singular acuteness of loneliness. He fought a thought. Did the little taximan wish to avoid any public show of friendship? Going on, Myles was ashamed. After all, Happy owed him nothing. Yet he'd come to the jail to see him.

Soon, to his relief, he saw the crowd beginning to thin. Pollard, drawing the procession out, led into the second block. By the time they'd traveled its length, the pack became even smaller.

At this point Pollard stopped short and appraised the march, reduced to a scattering of Joafers and chattering, long-haired kids. Disappointment emerged in the moon face. He headed up the street, his gait somewhat faster.

At the end of this block, Myles knew, they'd turn off Main. Beyond, along the dusty side street, lay the jail.

It wasn't clear to him just when, or how, he began to notice the change in Pollard—his nervousness. Possibly, back there in the second block, when the crowd started quitting. He didn't know exactly. But he saw, presently, that Pollard walked faster, his body stiffer. Only a trace of his former strut remained. And there was a moistness on Pollard's face. He was sweating; he looked a little uncertain.

A half minute or so passed. They stepped from the board-walk that marked the limits of the third block and made the turn, boots scuffing dust.

All at once Pollard's pace quickened.

The side street was empty, silent save for the chatter of the kids, who maintained an awesome distance from this badman Coon Pollard had in tow. The remaining curious among the grownups, Myles guessed, had quit at prospect of the dusty road.

Sight of the dull-looking sandstone jail so short ahead made him realize that time, if there was any left him, had all but run out. He eyed Pollard from the tail of his eye. He could almost feel the man's caution now, his hurry. Pollard's right hand hovered closer than usual to his holster. His eyes were narrowed. He kept moving fast.

And then Myles slowed, not quite reasoning why he did, unless it rose from pride against being hurried along, or some delaying instinct—

Behind them, on Main, the motor of a car sounded. It grew louder. The driver had turned off Main and was chugging up the side street.

Somehow the noise aroused Myles to wakefulness, but he resisted the impulse to look back. Pollard paced on, unmindful, intent on the jail.

It seemed to Myles, as he heard the approaching rattle and motor racket, that he'd been waiting all along for something.

Another moment and a flivver nosed into view on the right of Pollard, who slowed but did not stop.

Turning at the same time, Myles saw Happy Adcock brake to a crawl. Adcock, ignoring Myles, presented an obliging grin to Pollard. "You got a block to go, Coon. Hop in."

"We'll walk," answered Pollard, annoyed, still moving. A trace of his dignity returned. With an audience at hand, he seemed to swell to the outer dimensions of his padded frame. Adcock lingered.

Then Pollard, with a swagger, lifted his right hand high in his customary sweeping motion and Myles saw his chance.

He slugged Pollard in the belly with his left fist, and as Pollard grunted and doubled forward, Myles grabbed for his holster, got the pistol and shoved it into the thick layers of tallow around Pollard's midsection.

"Get in!" gritted Myles and pushed Pollard for the back seat of the flivver. "Open that door!" he told Adcock.

The taximan froze; he made no move to obey.

"Tell 'im, Pollard!" Myles drove the gun barrel deeper. "Quick!"

He felt Pollard go weak, heard his strangled gulp of terror, "Open it ... he'll—he'll kill me."

Adcock scrambled, slipping the rear door catch, and Myles rammed Pollard up and into the seat.

"Get goin'! Head east outa town—but stay off Main!"

Quickly, the flivver jerked into motion.

Pollard's face paled. His eyeballs were bulging and very round.

Wrenching to look, Myles saw the kids in the road. They stood silent as scarecrows, paralyzed in bug-eyed fascination.

Even as Myles looked, one of them wheeled and ran toward Main Street.

CHAPTER TEN

The flivver was rolling fast, but it seemed to Myles that Adcock would never turn. They ran south on a back street paralleling Main, past unpainted frame houses, shabby and weathered in the glassy sun.

Nobody appeared to notice anything irregular at sight of Happy Adcock driving fast, as usual, with two passengers aboard. A man waved lazily from his porch rocker. Adcock lifted a lazy hand in return.

The houses gave way to beaten shacks and soon the prairie stretched beyond to the oil field, whereupon Adcock pointed east. Within two blocks, he came out on the lower end of Main, swung south again, then east, and they straddled a hill-going road. Myles recognized it as the one that took you to Jeannette Garreau's ranch.

He looked back at Two Sands. As his eyes picked out a knot of men far up the street, he realized that, at best, he had only a few minutes' lead. Jamming the gun barrel into Pollard's soft paunch, he said, "Unlock these damn' cuffs."

The fat mouth trembled. Pollard couldn't speak. His shaking fingers fumbled for the key, snapped the cuffs clear, and then he lay back, fear large in his eyes.

A loathing keeled over in Myles. With one hand, he unbuckled Pollard's fancy gunbelt and yelled for Adcock to stop. The car lost speed, halted.

"Get out!" Myles jabbed and pushed Pollard to the door, flung it open. Pollard had trouble squeezing through, so Myles, in a burst of exasperation, prodded him out with the flat of his boot. Pollard was a tumbling feed sack as he landed on one foot, stumbled and fell.

Adcock gunned the motor and Myles climbed to the front seat and began rubbing his wrists, suddenly loose with relief. "Much obliged, Happy."

"Just happened along."

"That must've been it," said Myles, grinning.

"Now what?"

"Keep driving."

The older man kept his eyes to the bumpy, weaving road. They climbed a rocky hill, boiled down it wide open and leveled off before he spoke again. "Sorry to hesitate on you back there, but it had to look right."

"Convinced me."

"You took a chance."

"Can't do any good in jail." In the same breath, a fresh alarm registered upon Myles. "They'll blame you, Happy."

Adcock seemed not to hear.

Leaning out for another look, Myles saw the road as an empty column of dust stringing behind them. He pulled in, feeling an elation. "Nothin' yet."

"This hayrack can't outrun them big cars."

"They'll stop for Pollard."

"Won't slow 'em long."

They racked on for four or five minutes. The flivver struck a rock, bounced high. Adcock righted it expertly. Another long hill, thick with stubby timber, huddled ahead. Adcock tore up it at full throttle.

Myles, watching behind every few seconds, checked again. The road was clear. His hopes rose.

Just then he caught movement—the body of a black car. It scurried down the slope, swaying, spinning up dust. Another car followed. Gun barrels protruded from the sides.

He shouldered front, every muscle taut. "Step on it, Happy!"

"She's wide open!"

But Myles knew that it wasn't going to be fast enough. He tightened Pollard's gunbelt, trying to frame in his mind the country ahead. Knobby hills and timber patches 'most all the way. A man afoot wouldn't stand much chance.

The awkward bucking of the flivver trapped his attention. They were already losing speed. Steam fumed up from the gurgling radiator. He heard Adcock's stricken curse as he fought the hand throttle. The car was trembling violently.

"She's finished," groaned Adcock.

It wasn't until the car ceased rolling that Myles sized up his surroundings. Timber flanked both sides of the road. He found himself out of the seat and beside the running board, eyes pinned to the rear. So far a hill hid the cars. He took an indecisive step and turned his head, unsure, thinking of Happy Adcock.

"Gonna just stand there?" Adcock yelled. "Git!"

Myles didn't recall heaving around. But he was running, running across the road and ducking into the blackjacks. He felt branches clawing his face. His boots struck rocks. He scrambled over them, still running hard, deeper among the trees and underbrush. He ran till his breath sogged in his lungs, up a high, rough slope.

Sound filled his ears, a roar below along the road. It warned him down to hands and knees.

There in the road stood Adcock, waving his arms. The first posse car stopped. A chatter of excited voices broke out, the words indistinct.

Myles held his breath, his lips compressed. A feeling for Happy Adcock, sharp and fear laden, chained him here when open country beckoned behind him.

He saw them come piling out of the first car, brandishing rifles and shotguns. Close in, raising dust, stopped the second car, which spewed out its men. Everybody crowded around

Adcock. After the first moments of confusion, they stood back. They talked and gestured, formed into a tight cluster.

All but two men, Myles noticed. There was no mistaking the round, outraged form of Coon Pollard. He pointed accusingly at Adcock. Although Myles couldn't piece out the words, the tone carried and the angry arm-waving told the rest.

The second man, who wore a broad, silver-gray hat, took charge. At first Myles didn't place him. A second later, when the man moved, he felt a shock of recognition. Only one man stood like that, in command, and the man was Sid Tyson. To now, Myles had thought of the posse as an impersonal threat.

Tyson roamed his gaze. He pointed east, now north. Stubbornly shaking his head, Adcock jabbed his hand south and waved big.

A gratefulness humbled Myles. And suddenly his concern redoubled as Tyson planted hands on hips. His head bobbed while he talked, his face thrust near Adcock's. Stubbornly, with an obstinate insistence, Adcock pointed south again. He looked thin and old in contrast to Tyson's compact body.

It happened then, a quick, ruthless outburst.

Helpless, Myles saw Tyson lunge and grab Adcock's shirt and shake him. Adcock tried to claw aside the grip, but Tyson's right hand shot out. He slapped Adcock alternately on each side of his face, each clout Whipping his head. Adcock's hat skittered down. Pollard kept edging in, dancing, shouting.

Myles half rose, held by a sinking futility. If he fired a shot to draw them, they'd know Happy lied.

He saw it erupt higher, into a cruel and senseless violence. Adcock managed to raise his arms. In powerful, swinging slaps, Tyson knocked them down and slammed him against the flivver's fender. Adcock strained and struck weakly. The blow couldn't have packed much punch, yet it kindled an unreasonable fury in Tyson. His fist crashed Adcock's face and thumped him, spread-eagled, almost upon the flivver's hood.

For awful, powerless moments, Myles fought a silent battle to rush down there. Through his own blazing, protesting anger he saw Adcock sway up and try gamely to fight back. He saw Tyson punish him.

One blow did it. This time Adcock sprawled loosely along the fender, no spring left in his wizened body. He rolled off and pitched to the ground. He lay there, jerking. Tyson stood over him, fists knotted.

Sickened, Myles thought it finished.

Except Tyson wasn't. His right boot flashed back and forward. Adcock's flattened body jumped. Pollard shouted. Several of the men shuffled, averted their eyes. But something told Myles nobody was going to stop it. Tyson kicked again, and Myles heard Adcock's lifted cry. Myles found his fists clenched, his insides balled. He made himself see it through, wincing each time Tyson kicked, watched till Adcock's cries quit and Tyson seemed weary of the game. Afterward, so casual it might never have occurred,. Tyson faced the posse and singled out men. A bunch slanted south across the road. At the timber's edge they deployed and stalked in. The others still waited for Tyson, who delayed only briefly. He considered the road east, now the north side.

A cornered pressure pinched Myles, for it was coming. Another moment and Tyson hand-signaled the others wide, spreading them out, and they advanced north.

That stirred him. He'd already waited too long. Hence, low in the thickets, he began legging up the slope. When he panted to the top and gave the road a final inspection, he could make out only the cars and Happy Adcock, hoisted up on an elbow.

A trembling anger seized him, undercut by a bottomless regret and self-reproach.

He tore his eyes away and broke into a long-legged run, thinking coldly of the distance ahead. An instinct aimed him for Jeannette Garreau's house. For out of the wild ride and the ruthless beating he'd witnessed, an idea had emerged. He knew only one thing: he had to find Frank at once. And he could quit worrying about Jeannette. The efficient Bowdre would have her in custody; in fact, considering the time elapsed, Bowdre should be on the return trip to Two Sands. His lying had accomplished that much for the present. But he hated to think of Jeannette's furious reaction and he tried to bury it inside as he ran down the brush-studded hill.

Hot sunlight bored through the black-boled timber, exposed a hay meadow close beyond. The open space sent him veering north, so as to place hill and woods between him and the road. Several hundred yards on he turned east again. He was soon sweating, his senses sharpened to the impression of stillness and vastness through which he moved. Now and then he'd stop to rest and listen. Once he heard men calling, their voices alarmingly close.

After that, he struck a steady dogtrot, pacing himself, and felt his own smallness in this rough and tumbling range country... The thickly wooded places made him think of the Argonne forest, dark and deadly; except there was a silence here... As he worked onward the needle of his mind kept swinging from Jeannette to Frank to Happy; always it returned to Happy. And when it did, he experienced a surge of frustrating anger.

He'd been going hard for half hour, anyway, despite the heavy, high-heeled boots, when the growl of a motor shattered the deep hush of the hills. He faced in direction of the unseen road, stiff and listening, feeling the fire in his chest. The noise, building in the afternoon quiet, peaked to a pulsating roar approaching from the ranch.

Some of his tenseness eased as he placed it. The timing could mean only Bowdre and Jeannette. No car had passed going to the ranch. He was relieved, deeply so, and he wondered if Jeannette would ever learn how glad he really was.

Muttering, the motor's voice hung over the hills for a time after the car had passed. Myles went on. Bowdre, he figured, wouldn't join the manhunt till he'd delivered Jeannette in Two Sands. Even so, it made an uncomfortable thought.

Much later he sighted the high, alien wedge of Jeannette's ranch house, massive and proud as a monument among the blackjacks on the long ridge. Its red stone seemed on fire, in dull flame under the lowering sun. Despite his roundabout traveling and the frequent pausing, he'd covered considerable distance in fair time. Only once more had he caught the calls of pursuit, and then distantly.

A thin elation pulsed in him, tempered by caution. He hid in a thicket near the road and noted that his view was limited to the upper part of the house and barn. After some moments of this, he faced up to his situation. He had to cross the road and that left still about a hundred yards of open prairie to the nearest scattered timber. From there he had cover to the barn.

His heart pounded faster as he quit the thicket on trembling legs and stood an instant by the road, squinting into the low sun. The urgency of lateness hurried him over and into the trees. Out of breath, he dropped down against the base of a blackjack, suddenly dog-tired and hungry. He thought of food, of Jeannette's well-stocked kitchen. His desire rose so keen that saliva quickened in his mouth. He stood and started up the hill, scowling over another possibility. What if no horse was up?

The lip of the ridge, bedded with limestone outcrop, slowed him. When he made the crest, his eyes tracked eagerly to the corral. He blinked. His heart became cold, his mouth dry. There wasn't a hair in the corral.

He accepted it doggedly, mouth drawn; all his expectancy drained down. Still—

It was then, searching the yard and around the house, that his gaze located the brick garage and settled there, upon the back end of Jeannette's roadster. He moved without thought. He'd clean forgotten her car, left behind when Bowdre took her in town.

Before he'd stepped far, he realized his mistake. Hardly more than a wagon trail wound from Jeannette's to the Tyson ranch, the bad place entering the valley worst of all. A car would merely hinder a man. His only course was to follow the Two Sands road and chance slipping past the posse.

A cold logic came. It wouldn't work. He'd take open country anytime, even afoot.

His doggedness returned. He cut for the corral, slipped the gate bar, and trotted toward the barn, the knowledge strong that he was wasting time. He saw the first stalls, all empty. The open rear door streamed light and he could see the stalls on one side now, everything vacant. Going farther along the stable runway, he shifted his glance to the other side and halted instantly.

Greasy light shone on the blood-red rump of a horse. Coming to the stall opening, he recognized Skeeter, Jeannette's mount.

A sweeping exultation stirred him, sent him in a search of gear. He found bridle, blanket and saddle hanging on a partition.

He was leading Skeeter to the corral gate when a latecoming realization tripped his mind. Why had Jeannette left a horse tied in the barn, though knowing she'd be gone an indefinite time? He mulled it over as he opened the gate, faintly puzzled, but not concerned.

No call for him to question it, except it ran counter to the way you were used to handling saddle stock. Better, if she'd left the gelding to run in the corral for water and loose hay. More likely, expecting to be gone a day or more, to have turned Skeeter out in the horse trap below the house. However, it was a small thing, and he dismissed it. She had just forgotten Skeeter during her angry excitement.

He turned to mount. But just as he lifted boot to stirrup, the back porch held his eyes and he dropped his foot.

That porch door, open as usual, raked up all his clamoring hunger. It forced him to balance it against impatience. The road showed empty yonder. He had time if he hurried.

In sudden decision, he tied reins to a corral post and ran to the house. Letting himself in on the porch, he swept his eyes about. Against the kitchen side of the wall hung a canvas-wrapped canteen, yellow slicker, a sweat-darkened hat and work clothes. On the floor lay a pile of gunny sacks, neatly folded.

A notion occurred and he picked up a sack. As he straightened for the door, a shred of familiar fragrance arrested him. It anchored him still, as if Jeannette herself stood near and unseen. It affected him powerfully and he scouted his glance.

Now he saw it. In his hurry, he'd missed seeing her blue riding shirt hanging to one side.

He set his mouth and entered the kitchen, his mind filled with her. Jeannette could have just stepped from the room. Everything looked in the usual neat order. Skillets and pans hung beside the black stove. A coffee pot was shoved back on the stove. An empty cup rode the red-checkered tablecloth.

Remembering the long narrow pantry, he dumped canned goods into the sack from the stacked shelves. He saw an extra coffee pot and so added it. Returning to the kitchen, he gulped a cup of the black, cold coffee and helped himself to leftover biscuits from the breadbox. The remaining biscuits he wrapped in a newspaper and stuck in his grub poke. Still chewing, he went quickly to the porch and came back with the canteen, which he began filling at the water bucket.

The stillness inside the house pulled at his nerves as he set about the awkward job. He became engrossed, hurrying, head bent over the bucket, the drip-drip of the spilling water from the dipper magnified in the high-ceilinged room.

Almost imperceptibly the atmosphere in the room changed. One instant Myles was pouring water into the canteen, his eyes on the narrow neck. In the next he realized that his eyes were wandering. And across his back lay a sense of prickling coldness, the feeling of a door being opened behind you. Only he knew it wasn't that, for he hadn't closed the door.

He dropped the dipper and wheeled, somehow knowing then that he was too late.

Inside the porch slouched a man, a dim bafflement upon his sharp, dark features. But the rifle he held straight before him remained steady. He kept peering. His expression tightened. He was stringy and somewhat stooped, a high frame of bone without much flesh. Yet his extreme leanness told of a cat-like quickness. The hands on the rifle were wide, big knuckled. His coal-black eyes were shrewd, bright beads in the stubbled sheeting of his slack cheeks.

Recognition grabbed hold. This was Wiley, one of Sid Tyson's men.

A caution warned Myles. "You don't need that rifle," he said. His voice sounded strained and at once he was measuring the scant time left him.

The flattened line of Wiley's mouth cracked a trifle, show-ing uneven, yellow teeth. "Kinda figure I do." He peered again and limped warily inside the kitchen. "Got you placed, all right. Hell, you're Frank's brother! They took you in yesterday for kil-lin' Charlie Blackhorse."

"Yes, but they let me go. Found out they had the wrong man. Released me. So I came back. I work here. Maybe you didn't know that?"

Moments slipped by while Wiley's stare pecked at the sack. "What's in that?"

"Why, grub. Going over to the Blackhorse place. Miss Garreau gave me orders to keep an eye on things a few days."

The button eyes lifted. There seemed no reaction in the man. In a voice so matter-of-fact that he might have been speaking over a store counter, he said, "Canteen? ... This ain't desert country."

Myles shrugged his shoulders. "Happens I don't like water out of cow tracks." And then it flashed that Wiley, in the country, hadn't had time to hear about his escape.

"Miss Garreau around?"

Myles shook his head. "In town."

" ... notice her car's here."

"She rode in with Tom Bowdre."

" ... comin' back, is she?"

"Didn't say. Just told me to hustle over to Charlie's." Myles made a slow motion. "Late as it is, I'd better make tracks." He decided that maybe he'd won, and he leaned suggestively toward the sack as if to go.

"Wupp, now." Wiley's flat voice straightened him up, Wiley's rifle barrel following him. "Gunbelt on, too ... Part of your reg'lar gear?" Wiley's mouth split in a grin, except it wasn't a grin.

"Since Charlie was killed, yes." Myles' palms were slick with cold sweat. Silently, he damned the hunger that had drawn him to the house, when he could have ridden on free. He felt an acute reminder of slipping time. The pressure piled up. "Same reason, s'ppose, why you lug that thirtythirty Winchester? But not why you bull in here, cocked for trouble."

The black eyes were points pinning Myles in his tracks. "You're a fine bird to ask questions. Charlie Blackhorse was a great friend of mine."

"Seems," Myles answered dryly, " 'most everybody was a great friend of his. Never knew a dead man to have so many friends that couldn't help him."

"Wouldn't say that." Wiley, drawling, dropped each word into the room's pool of waiting silence and slouched in time-killing indolence. He showed no hurry whatever, as if he had a secret and superior knowledge. Myles strained for sounds along the Two Sands road as Wiley mumbled, "No ... wouldn't say that a-tall. See, I watched you come up the hill. For a minute I figured you wanted Miss Garreau's big Cadillac. Took me a spell to scout across the road, so I could look good. Make you out ... But when you snaked out that horse, I knew. Made me think, Here's that bird what killed pore Charlie Blackhorse—my friend. Now he'll sneak in the house an' murder that purty Garreau girl ... what's her name?" Wiley showed a mirthless grin, not expecting an answer, and nodded to himself. "Jean—Jeannette. That's her handle. Names slip my mind sometimes, but I never forget a face. No, sir … "

Anger belted Myles. A dangerous anger, he acknowledged, watching the man. Why, Wiley knew all along he was running!

He heard himself saying, overruling a better judgment, "You were snooping around the house." And he was viewing Wiley in the light of a stabbing comprehension, yet afraid to utter it.

"Call me a liar!—you!" Alive as an animal's, Wiley's shrewd eyes darted to the sack and up to the gunbelt and canteen. His voice leaped from its rooted calm and knifed at Myles, "That's travelin' stuff! You broke out! Reckon I'll just take you back!" Wiley's voice changed and dropped to the flat drawl. "Unbuckle your gunbelt." He elevated the rifle barrel up a notch, till Myles faced into the muzzle.

Myles had no breath; it was all squeezed inside his chest. He let the canteen go first. It made a clumping disturbance, overly loud. He drew his hands to his belt and hesitated, "Miss Garreau won't like this."

"Don't give me that," said Wiley, impatience capping his voice. "Drop it!"

Very slowly, Myles tugged at the buckle. The belt slid and he heard it thud. He became erect, catching for wind that had become too thin. His heart hammered and there came a brassy taste at the back of his tongue. He watched Wiley miserably, a gathering desperation kicking the pit of his stomach.

Wiley took a sidewise step, which drew him nearer Myles, and then he pointed with the rifle, indicating the door.

Without any warning, a deep and throbbing note had gradually invaded the room. A faint but growing noise. It threw all Myles' senses pounding. But he did not stir; he kept his attention frozen.

Wiley seemed to catch it a moment later, belatedly, through his concentration upon Myles. His eyes peeled off Myles for a fraction.

Almost mechanically, Myles flung himself forward in a low dive. And just before he hit, he saw the muzzle tilting and heard the ear-splitting roar. He drove his doubled right fist, punching with all his weight.

The blow shook Wiley's shoulder. But too low—too low. Then Myles grabbed with his left hand for Wiley's rifle and slugged with his right and encountered the stringy swiftness of this squirming, cat-muscled man. Myles felt his fist strike bone, higher this time. As yet, though, he couldn't jar Wiley loose from his weapon. Locked, they rolled over again and again.

Upon his knees, Myles clamped his right hand to the barrel and wrenched savagely. The rifle tore lose—and caught. Wiley still had one hand fast. Half rising, Myles bunched his shoulder behind his left fist. Wiley's neck took the brunt. He sank down suddenly, near limp, his gasping a sick and sodden sound. One hand clutched emptiness.

In a wild burst of elation, Myles spun up with the rifle. He worked the lever and ejected.

But Wiley rolled like a greasy cat. His right hand streaked, clawing frantically inside his belt, and Myles knew that he hadn't hit him hard enough. Myles said, "Don't!" but Wiley didn't heed. His hand cleared and Myles saw the upsweeping glint of metal.

So Myles fired, feeling the recoil buck against his hands, smelling the gunpowder stink and his ears ringing with the deafening roar in this confined space.

On the floor Wiley was just a long slack shape, the pistol loose in his fingers, unfired. His head rolled and he gagged the last of his life away and then he didn't move any more.

Upon which Myles, gripping the rifle, ran from the kitchen and outside. He had the gelding going in a slamming run across the yard when he heard a roar, and he jerked and saw the car.

CHAPTER ELEVEN

FADING INTO THE TIMBER below Jeannette's house, Myles ran through it to the first break of prairie and rode without letup till the blackjacks massed a second time. Here he hauled up. Although he couldn't see the house, he looked in that direction.

It seemed mighty quiet back there. No sounds followed.

Thus, in pausing, reaction caught up with him. Nausea rolled in his stomach. He kept seeing Wiley's stubbled face and the shock etched there when the bullet hit. It didn't seem to matter so much that Wiley would have killed him if he hadn't fired first.

It was a minute before he turned Skeeter. He just drifted, the gelding in an aimless trot, himself irresolute and shaken. If he'd had any sense he'd have scooped up the grub sack and gunbelt. Way it was, he had nothing but Wiley's .30-30.

He held the rifle across the saddle while he struggled for a grasp on himself. He guessed he had breathing space for a short time, possibly an hour or more. Without horses, the posse couldn't follow. However, he could count on them to telephone neighboring ranches for mounts.

Going ahead, he began to take notice of his surroundings. Wind, pulsing from the southwest, rustled the branches above him and the tall grass when he rode the open stretches. Somewhere a crow scolded, its solitary clacking reminding him that he was alone. Off to the northwest the upthrust spikes of oil derricks reached for the late afternoon sky, and he saw that he was going in the general direction of the Blackhorse ranch.

Some of his doggedness revived. He remembered what he had to do first. It hadn't changed since he'd left Happy on the road—circle around to the Tyson ranch and find Frank for a showdown. Beyond that he could not figure.

He stepped up Skeeter's gait and soon came to the old wagon road, followed along it to the gate that opened into Blackhorse range. Not long afterward, quitting the high tableland, he dropped down to Charlie's sleeping valley and noticed Yellow Dog creek as a ribbon of shining silver short to his right. Swinging under the trees, he stayed within their cover till Charlie's forlorn house hunkered left.

He didn't linger and in a few minutes passed into the upper part of the Blackhorse country. On his right tumbled sprawling hills, studded with blackjacks. Yellow Dog, sweeping the base of these hills, split them from high-grassed prairie. Without hesitation he forded the creek and put it between him and the plain's nakedness. He was traveling north now, below the first low ridge, the gelding clicking over sandstone.

Daylight was fading from the changing sky when he reached the fence line that fixed the boundary side of this pasture. He swam Skeeter over the creek and debated a time before leaving the woods. The barbed wire also represented for him a certain line of safety, for here onward the land lengthened to folds of undulating prairie. Clark Slater's lease ranch, now a place to be shunned, lay straight north as he recalled; and Tyson's holdings touched the northwest corner of Blackhorse land.

Once in the open and the grasses talking around him, he felt a premonition of being unsafe. It spread strong and pressing, a growing perception, as he halted by the fence. He regarded the strands of thorny wire gloomily. In his haste he'd taken Jeannette's saddle, which carried no wire pliers. The discovery brough a groan, and he began working along the fence and looking for a stock gate.

He found it some distance on, farther than he liked, where a grassed-over trail curled in from the pasture and struck dimly in a wavering line for the Tyson ranch. Dismounted, he upped the wire loop from the gate post and led the gelding through. As he straddled the saddle he had the feeling of letting himself in for more trouble; at his present rate he'd reach Tyson's about dark.

From that moment he rode uneasily, glad for a shallow draw now and then, or an infrequent stand of blackjacks from which to scout before he continued. Twice he halted in low places and smoked off the edge of his hunger. A deep-settled weariness gripped him.

About sundown a silver twinkling glinted northwest—dying sun on the steel fans of a high windmill. Grouped about it, he saw tall trees that joined prairie and sky.

He was disturbed to find himself this near on a treeless level, no cover between him and the ranch. He reined north, toward rounded nipples of hills, holding up there. Early darkness came on and day's heat left the prairie; grass smell rose. Finally, it was time to go.

He heeled Skeeter in motion alongside the hills. Minutes later he saw sheds and corrals, blurred in purple shadows. This was close enough before a man closed in. He reined up on the off side of the main corral, tense and watching, realizing how blind he traveled.

One square of light shone in the tree-guarded house, and he thought of Nellie Tyson, alone, brooding over her dead.

His eyes shifted, snared upon the long bunkhouse. Light, dim and yellow, sprayed a puny glow out the rear door. Frank's bunk, he remembered, was at the rear. He drew on and left, his intention to circle the corral.

Upon Skeeter's just-audible tread a horse snuffled suddenly inside.

Myles checked hard, his stomach churning up in a sick kind of flutter. He could glimpse the animal, a tall-shadowed shape, suspicious head pointed this way.

A lengthy and hard-breathing waiting followed. But the snuffling did not repeat and Myles relaxed. Gradually, he slow-walked Skeeter away and rounded the corner of the corral. Beyond its long length stood the low-framed bunkhouse with its cone of drawing light.

He was approaching, of half a mind to tie up and go in afoot, when a shrillness tore apart the night—the calling nicker of the loose horse.

The sound, like a signal, dropped him down flat over the pommel, his upturned eyes searching the doorway.

His breath quit as a chair scraped plank flooring. Boots sounded. He saw a man come to the door, silhouetted, all but blacking out the light. In a moment, behind him, a taller figure filled in. They muttered low. Afterward, one man stepped to the yard. The other leaned in unconcern against the door siding. "Aw, come on back," he said. "Let's finish the game. Loose stock, I reckon."

"I ain't so damned sure."

"You would quit just when I'm winnin'."

The man in the yard kept silent.

Myles, hunched low in the saddle, realized quickly that Frank wasn't one of these two.

Somewhere in the gloom, boots tapped toward the corral. There fell an interval of silence, when Myles missed even the bootsteps. He tried to pierce the dimness, and discovered he'd lost the man.

An instinct made him draw in. Nerves tingling, he plied his gaze along the rim of the corral. He caught a low call. Instantly, he saw the man in the doorway stiffen and pace to the yard.

The meaning raveled through Myles as he picked out a sliding figure on the corral's far side. The man over there had changed course, coming this way, as if he intended to scout around the corral.

Step by step, Myles started reining off. But before he'd gone a rod, he heard a shout, and boots thudded. At once a shot blasted.

He kicked his horse, beating away. A second bullet whined from behind, and he heard the crash of the gun as he flattened down in the saddle. He reined right, evading, and left. He straightened Skeeter out in a low run. The gun banged again, but the bullet wasn't very close.

Sweeping a look over his shoulder, Myles saw figures milling in the yard. He thought, the whole damned nest of 'em.

Rushing on, he bore back the way he'd come in. The hills where he'd waited short minutes ago came up skylighted and he ran to them and along their base before he stopped. He heard Skeeter's heavy heaving and nothing more. He'd lost all sound of the men, no horses putting out as yet; he'd lost as well any sense of a working plan, somewhere to go. But when he moved out and swapped directions, he pointed without thinking for the trail he'd followed near all the way. There was no solid reason for retreating to Blackhorse country, unless it could be his wanting familiar footing.

The thought urged him upon the dim trace as revealed by the mellow fight of a rising round moon. Very soon the night would be almost like day, like soft twilight. He welcomed the clearness at first and then silently damned it. He rode in haste, craftily, saving, a steady lope, a steady running walk. Later, through the gate, he hesitated to consider his next move and remembered the Blackhorse house several miles below.

He had no more than started off when a sound filtered across the night. He wasn't long finding its source in the filmy light, a wedge of motion down the fence line, approaching the gate. Knotted shadows—that could mean some of Charlie's ponies.

He pulled his horse up, his alarm leaping as he saw the knot materialize into horsemen—much closer than he'd supposed. Without running, he dropped down a long slope and cut for the black cloak of timber. Whipping to look, he saw the file of riders still jogging parallel to the fence. They showed no indication of changing drift, and he could breathe again. Another half minute and he'd have been caught. Second-guessing himself, he recognized that he should've run north from the Tyson ranch, not easing up till he'd placed the Osage behind him and arrived on the Kansas side. There a man could hole up. Trouble was, you had to come out of a hole sometime.

Thereafter he maneuvered just within cover, in order to fix an eye on the prairie flowing westward. He moved in a kind of unreal mist, his mind tight and tired, the silver paleness out there playing strange tricks with his vision. The leftbehind grub kept taunting him. Hunger dominated. He found himself thinking steadily of the Blackhorse house, not far now, no more'n a mile maybe. He left the timber, eyes straining. Everything looked open; he felt better.

Some distance on he shook his head, not trusting his eyesight. He was seeing things. Phantoms.

Quite suddenly they came nearer, out of the prairie's brown and yellow dimness. He heard a drumming. Somebody whooped and horses ran in violent rhythm. A bullet whirred and a gun cracked.

Over them he drove two shots, high and quick, and swerved. The horsemen came on. He'd merely spurred them on by shooting. Jabbing Skeeter, he covered the open stretch and piled under the dark arms of the creek timber. A short race into this blindness—and he felt Skeeter hump up, balking.

In the same instant, he saw streaky light, glassy upon water. He kicked hard, flat-handed the bay along the rump. The gelding hesitated, trampling, trembling, then took off.

They traveled through a black void. A breath after they struck with a jolting splash, sinking, and Myles felt the water rising cold around his belt. Skeeter lunged, swimming, kicking out for the invisible bank. It bulked close ahead, a shadowy wall in the darkness.

All in a moment Skeeter slammed against the solid earth. Humping, he churned the slippery slant with forelegs, unable to climb, and Myles felt the stay of motion and the sickening give. He sighted the ledge above too high, too steep. Shifting his weight forward, he strong-armed the gelding's head downstream. They floundered under, thrashing, before they could get underway again.

There seemed no end to the sooty depths down-creek. As Myles held the rifle high, trying to urge Skeeter still faster, he saw what had happened; they'd jumped into a deep-bottomed pool. True, they swam steadily, and yet they might have been crawling, so damnably slow did it wear on a man in this murk. And that was when he heard the hoofs pound and roll off the prairie.

It happened suddenly, just when he thought the pool had no limit, no bottom. Skeeter's front quarters shot up so unexpectedly that Myles' head crashed the high-tilting head. Pain flashed clear to his shoulders. Rock clacked under Skeeter's hoofs. They climbed out, dripping and sliding for footing, and Myles headed left over the flat, slick rocks and up the sloping bank.

Skeeter's shoulders banged a tree trunk, making him grunt, and the impact threw Myles loose and adrift in the saddle. He clawed for the horn and righted himself, already aware of a heady triumph, because they had the other side of the creek under them now, solid and sure. He reined up and felt the punished Skeeter quivering and jumpy as a cat. His own head still rang.

Across the creek rasped the scuffing of bunched horses in leaf litter and underbrush; their location seemed above him. So Skeeter had made better time than he'd figured. The restless sounds faded but did not move off and he heard a weighted voice, "Spread out. He's in this timber."

"Maybe he crossed over, Sid."

"Hell, guess I know this country. You can't cross here. We'll fan out. Work up and down."

Rigid, Myles heard the scuffling strike up again. This time it reached him as a softer, slower cadence behind the screen of trees. The padding of riders in careful motion. He traced the sounds directly across from him as another fainter shuffling bore upstream. He heard men calling cautiously in the timber, heard them go on; presently the woods were still.

The night was warm, but he felt cold in his soaked clothing. Here, with the wind shut out, a man sensed a complete loneness and indecision. The punishment he'd absorbed this day swarmed up through his body; it tugged at his nerves and dulled his drive, leaving him dry-mouthed and without ballast. His empty stomach growled.

An opening yawned beyond the timber and he entered it, coming out under a climbing yellow moon, and followed onward to a low hill. As he rode, he squeezed his mind down to what was left him, if anything. He couldn't get to the Blackhorse house for grub; he'd almost slipped in even trying. Worse yet, he had only the shells left in the magazine. His thinking mulled darkly upon that, beating him down, then leaped into the brightness of sudden clarity.

Why, he'd overlooked the line shack by the old wildcat well. It wasn't very far. He could find it, light as the night was. In the shack, he remembered, he'd seen shells and canned stuff. Not much, but enough. Certainly enough to keep a man going. His hunger quickened.

Clapping heels to Skeeter, he forced down his circling thoughts and drew the surrounding country onto the map of his mind and tried to orient himself. Everything looked different in this pale, fooling starlight. Objects that seemed near took on the mystery and elusiveness of space. He rode more by sense, by feel, than by knowing, till something grew in the edge of his vision.

Not far below him the tower of a wooden derrick floated up from the floor of a brushy ravine, imprisoned between two low-knuckled ridges. They kicked up a clatter going down the rocky slope as Myles hurried the gelding. At the bottom he overcame an impulse to rush on and, instead, walked the bay in.

The place seemed changed somehow, more lonely and oddly unreal in moonlight. The rig forming a jagged crag against the sky, the motionless walking-beam like a forgotten arm left behind by the disgruntled drilling crew, and the squat ruins of the steam boiler nearby. A short distance on he noticed the dull face of the shack edging out from the crowding blackjacks. He went eagerly forward, then.

As he stepped to the ground and tied Skeeter to a brush clump, the emptiness of all this returned and bored into him. Almost furtively, he strung his gaze around the grown-up clearing. Afterward, he stepped to the door. It was shut, as it had been the day he stopped. And that day seemed long ago, never happening.

He shouldered the door inward, scraping it over the uneven flooring, then stopped dead. Wire, he recalled, had been twisted through the lock hasp that first time. The realization delayed him just a fraction; he shoved the door wide. The musty staleness struck him and he paused, blinking into the darkness, pierced dimly by the shanty's one small window.

A coolness crept along his neck. He moved his stare, deeply disturbed by something he couldn't yet determine. Now, standing there in the moonlit doorway, he had the eerie sensation that he wasn't alone in the room.

Before he could swing the saddle gun a voice bit at him from the blackness. "Put the rifle down."

A woman's voice.

CHAPTER TWELVE

MYLES FELT a flash of recognition. That voice! He'd know it anywhere—except it was changed, loaded with an unmistakable fury. And suddenly he understood what had bothered him: the faint violet smell, the kindling scent of her. Carefully, he placed the Winchester down, leaned the barrel against the door.

"Turn around."

He did so, still slow.

"Outside."

He paced out a few steps and halted, feeling the edge of her wrath like a knife at his back.

"You can face around now."

During all this time she had not raised her voice, and Myles let himself hope a little.

But in the next moment, facing Jeannette Garreau, he saw how wrong he was.

Light glinted dully on a pistol which she held unwaveringly upon him. She stood straight and tense in the doorway, bathed in the moontide, her coppery face engraved with anger. She looked slim as a reed, and she wore no boots. In spite of her disarray the rumpled shirt still outlined her unconfined breasts and the riding breeches accented her supple legs. He'd never seen her with her long hair down before, and it gave her that little-girl look which he thought could so deceive a man. For she was burning mad—Injun mad.

Suddenly, her voice drove against him. "Damn you, Myles! I ought to shoot you!"

"I can explain everything." He took a forward step.

Her hand tightened around the pistol grip. "Don't you move another inch—and you can't explain anything I don't know about."

"If you'll just listen—"

"Listen—to you!" Her full mouth curled. "After you told Bowdre I shot my uncle. After he came out to arrest me..." She choked on the thought and her anger soared. "Like a common criminal!"

"Well, I see he didn't."

"No—despite your lies," she said bitterly. "He didn't want to, but he had no choice. He's a man, if you know what that means— and you don't. I left him with a cup of coffee in the kitchen. Told him I had to get my things... He trusted me. I slipped out of the house. Ran—walked." Her angry eyes flicked away, darted back to him, and Myles sensed her deepening indignation. "My horse, too!"

He squirmed and spread his hands. "Let me talk."

"I won't listen to you—you and your smooth talking." She sounded hurt and resentful, and he saw the gun tremble slightly. She flounced her slim shoulders in a mimicking gesture. "So noble about Frank's girl... so concerned. Yet you made love to me!" She raked him up and down, her large eyes narrowed to points of scorn. "You're lower than a potlicker—that's the lowest thing I can think of!"

He felt himself flushing. "Kinda high on yourself, aren't you, claiming I made love to you?"

"You did! Don't deny it!"

"Just because a man kisses a girl... once."

"Don't try to back out of it! You weren't just kissing me. I knew... don't think I didn't."

Of a sudden he became deeply angered. He said, "You will listen to me!" and automatically reached for her.

She retreated a slow step. "Come any closer, I'll shoot!"

He stopped, his breath catching. "Put it down, Jeannette. Let's talk."

"I told you I won't listen." New suspicion seeped into her tone. "You know what I think, Myles? It's like Bowdre said. Somebody hired you to kill Uncle Charlie. You did it for a fat price. Then you tried to blame me. Tell you what I'm going to do—" She broke off and he was close enough to her that he got the heady perfume of her again. "I'm gonna take you into town. I will—yes, I will!—even if it means I go to jail, too. You hear me, Myles?"

"I hear you," he said softly, watching the gun. It wasn't trembling any more. She looked mighty attractive there, young and hurt and confused, and he felt a regret over what he had to do. "I said put it down, Jeannette. I won't hurt you." He ventured a careful pace.

"I told you—not another step!" Fear gleamed in the wide pools of her eyes, uncertainty shrilled her voice. She backed up and came against the low sill of the door, stumbling. The impact threw her off balance, startled her.

Her pistol wavered and Myles moved swiftly.

He lunged for the tilting revolver. His left hand caught her gun wrist. She cried out as his big hand clamped down. He knew his grip was cruel, but there was no other way because of the determined hold she had on the pistol.

He twisted, at the same time catching her flailing left with his right. Slowly, he felt her right hand loosen. He heard the weapon plop in the grass. And yet he had no elation and eased up before he thought.

Too late he realized his mistake.

For she made a crying, hating sound and tore loose. She came in savagely, swinging and clawing. Her fingernails raked his face before he could imprison the hands again. Then she kicked him, kicked him so violently that she cried out in pain when her stockinged toes struck his booted shins.

He thought he had her now as he gripped her arms roughly. But she wouldn't quit, even then. Unexpectedly, her strength surprising, she thrust one foot behind him and shoved desperately. The quickness of it caught him off guard, for he was still trying not to hurt her.

They fell sidewise in the tall grass, rolling over and over.

Without any warning, she was clawing him again, kicking and twisting. His face burned from the rakings; he tasted warm salty blood. When she almost scrambled up, as if to run, Myles lost patience. He caught one thrashing leg arid tripped her, brought her down heavily and heard the wind sog out of her. At once, he switched around, upon his knees beside her. He trapped the elusive wrists once more and he pinned them flat while he glared down at her weaving, furious face.

She fought him several moments more. Then her strength seemed gone all at once and her breathing became a series of ragged gulps. But the hate still simmered in her eyes. He recognized that and, despite it, was ashamed of the way he'd been forced to handle her. Like a saddle bronco in a corral. All but earing her down.

So he just held her, her arms fastened, till his own breathing slowed and he could think. She was a hell of a mussedup sight, he thought, in one way. In another, she had a loveliness he'd never noticed before in a woman, made still greater because it lay forever beyond him. The mass of her sweet-smelling blue-black hair strayed loosely around her high-boned face, sort of framing it. During the tussle he had ripped her shirt front down several buttons, almost to her narrow waist. Under the filmy light her skin shone softly bronzed. The open shirt revealed the bare point of one shoulder, the smooth shaft of her throat and the rising roundness of her breasts.

For the first time she seemed aware of his gaze. She said in a husked-out tone. "You tore my shirt. Let me up."

"So you can claw me?" He shook his head. "No—I'll fix it." He slid a hand and tucked her shirt front together, keyed for her free hand to strike. However, she made no move and he released her other wrist. Instead of rising, he merely straightened a trifle.

He discovered that he watched her intently. Her upturned face stood out. The soft mouth, the wide eyes. She seemed without expression, too weary to get up. And as he considered her, he noticed a change in the night, a sudden stab of excitement. Where there had been struggle barely moments before, there was now something added. A different quality.

Not till he bent his head did he realize that he meant to kiss her. He did—and briefly he thought her lips lifted to meet his. An instant later, sensing her rippling quickness, he jerked upright and caught her swinging fist aimed for his face. Seizing it, he said harshly, "You really do think I'm a killer, don't you?"

Her eyes didn't meet his. "How'd you guess it?" Momentarily, he thought her voice lacked conviction, an impression erased by the contempt he saw in her eyes.

"I'm a little slow," he said, touching fingers to his cheek scratches, "but maybe I'm catching on."

He did it then, half angrily, not conscious of motion. He bruised his mouth over hers and knew he'd ached to kiss her again, all the while tensed for her to whap and claw. She tried to squirm away, her body rigid and resisting, her hands beating and pushing against his face.

Disgust for himself, sudden and sharp, overtook him. But just as he started to raise his head, he felt an astonishing change in her.

She ceased struggling. To his surprise, her lips became slowly and warmly responsive. Her hands, pounding him a briefness ago, slid to his shoulders. There they seemed to hesitate, then brushed to his neck. He could feel the growing pressure of her fingers—and suddenly she pulled him even closer, the blur of her face swimming like ivory in his vision.

For a long-running moment, as she held his kiss, he knew the harsh truth about himself. Finally, when he lifted his head, her throaty murmur pulsed in his ears, "Guess I can't whip you, Myles ... so I'll just join."

He looked down at her, still taken back, still filled with the wild sweetness of her hair. Her eyes had an expression he could not define, and for the life of him he couldn't decide whether it reflected genuine emotion or a sort of speculation.

"You tried hard enough," he said, unsteady and somehow yet wary of her. "Sorry I had to throw you. Now, you're going to listen to me."

He forced aside his reluctance to rise and stood. When she showed no inclination to stand, his unwillingness returned, strong as ever.

"I'm tired," she said in a lazy voice.

Except her eyes failed to match her tone. He reached swiftly, grabbed her hand and pulled her up.

Her lightness surprised him. Just the touch of her rocked him again. Before he knew it she was in his arms, no resistance left. She came close against him, willingly, her dark head scarcely up to his shoulders, her pliant mouth just parted.

He kissed her, and the tremors rolled through him. If he had any doubts, they vanished in his overwhelming awareness of her.

It was he who broke away. "Posses all through these hills, he said, with a gruffness. "We can talk at the shack. I want shells and grub."

He wondered about his hurry, knowing it wasn't all linked to the posses. He was, he recognized now, running from himself— something over which he had no control. Jeannette was Frank's girl. He kept telling himself that. Yet, when he'd held her in his arms, she had been his completely.

He took her arm. She traveled several tentative steps and checked up. She began hopping on her left foot, holding and gingerly rubbing the other. "My toes! I think they're broken."

"Never kick a man with your boots off," he said.

"Had to walk all the way, and now I'll have a devil of a time getting my boots on. You see, Bowdre could watch the barn from the kitchen. I couldn't sneak Skeeter out."

Lending a supporting arm, he assisted her, limping, to the shack. Beside the door he remembered Jeannette's pistol, stooped, searched the grass and came up with a .38 special. She threw him an inquiring glance as he checked the safety and slipped it in his hip pocket. "I'll just take it in tow for a while," he told her, and realized that he didn't fully trust her.

She appeared not to mind and went inside, where she crossed to the single low bunk and resumed massaging her toes. "Canned beans on that shelf over the stove," she said. "Help yourself. I've eaten."

After bracing the door wide, he could see fairly well. Rummaging along the shelf, he found the scant supply of boxed Winchester .30-.30 shells, two cans of beans and a thickbladed butcher knife. First, he loaded the saddlegun and stuffed his pockets with the remaining cartridges; then, seated on a block of salt which he dragged against the door, he knifed open the beans. He had wolfed down the first can, scooping out the beans on the broad blade, and was starting on the second before he felt like talking.

His contentment grew. The posse seemed distant in his mind, miles off. He finished the last can, rolled and lightetd a cigarette from a cupped match, and leaned back, letting the ease strip away the stiffness of fatigue in his arms and back.

Across from him he saw Jeannette sitting on the bunk. She was putting up her long hair, piling the raven's mass on the back of her neck, her movements rubbing softly out to him as intimate rustlings, almost lost to sound.

Feeling stormed through him. He had to fight down the desire to go over there and wrap his arms around her again. I could, he thought, I could. And what did he owe Frank? Nothing—nothing to a man who had lied up murder about him, thrown a cloud of suspicion upon his name.

His unrest rose. He couldn't take his eyes off the bunk. In this gloom he couldn't see her face clearly, only the outline of her small figure, but he could imagine the rest. The sensation of her, the unbelievable sweetness of a woman he'd never have.

The rustling ceased. He saw her straighten, and he knew that she watched him.

He said, "Well—here goes. I'm going to tell you this and I want you to listen carefully. Every word. You can decide about the truth after I finish."

"I'll listen," she said, talking around a hairpin. "Maybe I'll even believe you."

At this moment, he found, her trust was the most important thing in the world to him, something he had to have. And so he told her tersely why he'd made up the story that sent Bowdre after her, and how he'd escaped; how he had been forced to shoot Wiley, what happened afterward when he approached the Tyson ranch, and his brush with the riders.

There fell a period of silence. He realized that he had related an awkward, loose-ended story and without enough conviction. "That's it," he concluded, "except I say again I didn't shoot Charlie."

"Frank same as said you did. Same as accused you in a roundabout way. Those tracks—"

"Sure, I rode that way—earlier." He struggled to keep his voice steady. "But why should Frank hint—" His anger burst through. "I'll run him down yet and get the truth!"

She stirred on the bunk. As she drew her long legs up and sat with her feet crossed, he glimpsed the indistinct frame of her face. She seemed to ponder before she spoke, "You still haven't sold me on why you had to cook up that arrest story." A note of reserve cooled her tone.

"I told you Happy said Caldwell quit. Sounded too sudden to me. I didn't like the idea—you at the ranch, by yourself. I was—well, I was afraid something might happen to you. How else could I help? Me in jail, you at the ranch—too stubborn to come in town if I sent Happy out there. You wouldn't have believed him."

Her rejecting laugh stung. "Coming from you—no. Anyhow, I can take care of myself."

His hand strayed to his cheek. "You do pretty well. But Charlie figured he was safe, too. Not an enemy. And look what happened—he's dead and we don't know who killed him."

"Unless Frank had the right man."

"To hell with Frank."

"I'd like to believe you, Myles . . " . Her voice trailed off and she gazed away.

It occurred to him that, in his mental lurchings, he was merely sinking deeper and strode to the bunk. Looking down, he said, "You've got to believe me."

Her dark head tilted slightly. "Maybe … "

Her voice was a guide wire, leading and drawing him down beside her. He found her hand—it was unsteady, almost withdrawing. In it he sensed a struggle going on inside her. So, then, he wasn't certain at all that he had convinced her, even halfway, despite what she'd said.

Always tonight, after thinking he'd won back her confidence, some tiny gesture or expression of hers left him wary and cast doubt upon her talk or willingness to come to him.

Now, all he could find to say was, "If you'll just go on believing in me, till I get to Frank." She had become a stiff and silent shape and he added, "Listen, you understand why I shot Wiley? How it happened." An inner voice belied it and suddenly he was bombing his words at her. "He went for his pistol. I had to shoot him—it was his life or mine. You understand that, Jeannette? Tell me!"

He waited and he hoped. He was rising when her voice roped him back, "I—I'd like to, Myles. I would … "

But she still hadn't really said and that could mean only one answer: she did not believe him. He eyed her, straining to pierce the shadows around her face, wishing that he might see her eyes and read in them her true thoughts.

"You mean," Jeannette said after a moment, "you think you killed Wiley."

"Not much doubt." The smoky kitchen and the impact of dull surprise on Wiley's dirty, stubbled face swam afresh in his mind. "He took the bullet in his chest. He—he looked dead. I've seen dead men before—in France."

Swiftly, her hand took his. "I hope not—for your sake."

The words rang right and he felt relieved of a tremendous load. "That's almost as important to me—for you to know it straight—as it is about Charlie. Who killed him."

"Wiley was always a mystery to me," she said in a thoughtful, recalling way. "Nobody around Two Sands ever heard of him till he started working for Sid."

"When was that?"

"About three years ago. When my father was alive. About the time Sid closed his law office in town and started ranching on north Yellow Dog." She paused and seemed to gaze back briefly in time. "I remember the first time Wiley rode up to our house. He stopped for dinner. Didn't talk much; of course, nobody asked him where he was from. You don't do that in the Osage. But he looked on the rough side to me, and he wasn't friendly around the boys. No, don't believe he was ever there after that. In fact, I forgot about him till here lately, when he started coming to my place with Frank."

"Funny. Frank needing a chaperon."

"Oh, it wasn't anything like that."

Her denial followed so quickly that he gave a low laugh. "Don't believe that fits—for Frank. He's a lone wolf ladies' man. Always was."

"Frank didn't seem to mind. Least he never said anything to me."

"He wouldn't."

Her voice took on a somewhat bewildered tone. "Wiley showed up twice, alone. Right after my two hands quit. Then he was there this morning."

"This morning?" Myles felt a prickling interest. He leaned forward. "Were you by yourself?"

"No—Happy was there."

He straightened, the distant flare of a forming thought pinching out in his mind. "What did Wiley have to say? Give his reason for showing up? Don't tell me he was looking for strays?"

"He said Sid told him to ride over and see about me. See if I needed anything … I remember he was pretty talkative, for him. Almost friendly. Said he was sorry about Uncle Charlie, and I invited him in. But when he saw Happy there in the kitchen having coffee, he cooled off, I thought. Oh, I don't mean he and Happy didn't talk; they did, about Uncle Charlie. Pretty soon Wiley rode off."

"He brag what a good friend of Charlie's he was?"

"Not that I remember. If he had—"

"Well," Myles interrupted, "he did to me. Made a point of it."

"But that's not true!" Her voice broke on anger. "He wasn't, I know! Charlie hardly knew the man."

Her rapid breathing beat across to him, and he realized that his mind had quit circling, that it was settling upon a cold knowledge. "So Caldwell wasn't there?"

"No. He left early this morning. Came in and said he was drifting. His excuse was he didn't like this part of the country. It made me mad, with everything else happening. I wrote him out a quick check and told him to travel."

Myles scrubbed a hand across his chin. "I'm not putting this together right. I mean, did you tell Wiley that Caldwell quit you?"

"When he first asked me about needing anything, I told him I was shorthanded again, but guessed I could get along."

"I see," Myles said slowly. There the thing shaped now, not just faintly glowing, but bright and clear-cut. "So when Wiley came back later, he knew you'd be alone? Instead, he ran into me. And this morning he'd already buffaloed Caldwell—maybe bought him off—and was just checking up to see if Caldwell had pulled his freight. There's a pattern here, Jeannette, there is. Maybe it fits those other two men of yours."

"What're you trying to tell me?" She sounded bewildered and frightened.

"Just this—Wiley came back to murder you." He heard her sudden gasp as he plunged on, intentionally making the words brutal. "He was there in the barn that day, waiting for you—not me. I just blundered in. He had to knock me out or be discovered."

"But why—why would he want to?"

"That's something else, though we're getting warm, I think. Could be Wiley shot Charlie, too." He saw the dead end as soon as he spoke. "Except—if Wiley's dead—it'll be hard to prove." He fell silent, brooding.

"If he is…that sort of ruins your own alibi about Uncle Charlie, doesn't it?"

He gritted his teeth and seized her arm. "What have I got to do to make you see this?" His fingers gripped so hard that she winced. He released her and drew back, aware of a certain order to his cluttered thinking. He spoke rapidly, his voice rough with feeling. "I just remembered something. The county attorney said he checked Charlie's will at the agency. Charlie left his land to you—his headright to your mother. All right. Say somebody wants Charlie's grass land. How would they get it? Charlie won't sell it, so they murder him. Then what? They still can't get their hands on it legally. Maybe they know he willed it to you. They decide to get rid of you next. You don't have a husband.

That makes it simpler—everything you own would go to your mother."

"But—"

He spoke bluntly over her angry protest. "I'm not accusing your mother. Hell, no! She's out. That leaves just one person who would stand to profit in a big way." He paused, his mind racing. And swiftly, without his really thinking about it, the name rolled off his tongue, "Tyson—Sid Tyson. Wiley's his man. Tyson would have control of all this—Charlie's land and headright, yours—through your mother, wouldn't he?"

She sat stunned, not moving. Her voice, when finally she spoke, came squeezed out and unrecognizable. "You—you really believe that?"

"I can't be sure. But it seems to add up. Part of it, anyway."

A sob shook her. He saw the dark head drop suddenly to her hands. It knocked some of the harshness out of him, and he slipped an arm around her, sorry for the blunt way he'd had to talk. And, again, the exciting scent of her flowed around him. "Believe me a little?" he asked, between tight lips.

She buried her face against his shoulder. He heard her sniffle and felt her nod. Despite everything, even while holding her, he wasn't quite sure and could find no reason why. "Listen," he said impatiently. "We're getting out of here. North—clear to the Kansas line if we have to." She pulled away, glancing up, and he pushed his voice at her again. "You can't stay here. We're both running now. No safer for you than it is for me."

Remembering Skeeter tied away from the shack, he left her and led the gelding to the door. Entering, Myles found her struggling with her boots.

"You'll have to help," she pouted.

Between them they tugged on the tight boots. She stood and stamped her feet deeper into them. She seemed eager as they went outside. Myles motioned her to the saddle and straddled on behind.

Leaving the blackjacks, they jogged past the derrick and headed up the ravine. As he scanned the light night, alive with bird sounds, it struck him how great their disadvantage was.

An old cow trail snaked out before them. This they followed for a space, halting when it twisted off for the creek and left them at the base of a rock-layered ride. It sat in Myles' mind that humped-up country massed north and northeast, that east of the creek, where they rode now, was mostly a succession of crumbling hills and strung-out ridges which pinched in stretches of small, irregular grassy valleys.

At his word, Jeannette reined northeast. They moved through brush and scraggly timber. In another hour, crossing a ridge, he noticed that Jeannette rode wearily in the saddle.

"You're tired," he said. "We'll rest in this timber. Skeeter can stand it, too."

He dismounted and held up his hand to her. She slid into his arms without hesitation. He held her briefly, then turned and tied Skeeter. When he looked around, Jeannette was curled up under a blackjack. He took position against a rock, the rifle across his lap. It wasn't long before he became drowsy.

Myles had no idea how long he dozed. He awoke startled and glanced skyward, jarred by a pressing lateness and guilt. He hadn't just dozed. He had slept like a bone-tired man, and now the sky looked pale.

Bolting up, he swung across to her. Then he halted, arrested by the picture of a small girl sleeping there, one hand thrown back, the added light casting a tawny haze about her face. She slept with an utter exhaustion, her torn shirt alternately rising and falling. Regretfully he touched her shoulder.

A long, sighing groan escaped her.

"Time to travel," he said.

She raised herself and sat up, rubbing her eyes.

"It's late," he said. "I overslept."

"Oh..."

He reached for her and she pulled up, light under his hand. He dropped his hand, but she kept coming, swinging into him. And, suddenly, she flattened against him and seemed to wait, her face upturned.

The unexpectedness of it made him hesitate. His hands swept to her shoulders—and stopped there, not going around her. He realized his restraint with something near to wonder. It was the second time tonight. Now the moment was gone. He said, "We've got to make time," and walked over to the gelding.

"You're right," she said. "We better hurry." It was curious, though, that her voice lacked hurry.

Without another word, he brought Skeeter over and she mounted easily, no trace of weariness in her movement. As they rode from the timber, Jeannette looked up at the sky, "It's getting lighter."

His mouth hardened. "Plenty time to cross the fence, if we speed it up." He'd been dreading that fence ever since they left the shack. Lacking wire clippers, he would have to kick the strands loose from the posts.

Farther on, not liking the openness, he said, "Let's ride higher up. Closer in to that timber." He figured they traveled about straight north now.

After she climbed the gelding and they straightened out, Myles turned his gaze front and back. The land lay sleeping in a bed of thinning gray light. The opposite line of hills, furred with black-jacks, loomed quiet, deceptively quiet, he thought. Despite a wavering course, they had covered some distance. The creek, he figured roughly, lay a mile or two left. The fence wasn't very far. And with the bay horse moving steadily under his double load, Myles began to feel they would cross the fence before full daylight broke.

Some minutes onward he realized the land was tilting. The rough ridges were dropping away, smoothing out, swelling up to the high brow of the prairie across the fence line.

Thus, as his eyes kept searching the dissolving murk, he turned rigid and cold. A shudder of alarm kicked him violently. Yonder, between a split in the hills, leaped the bold cone of a campfire. Around it dim figures stood or reclined. A darker mass indicated horses.

At first warning he grabbed for the reins, but Jeannette was already jabbing the horse into the nearby timber. Sliding down, Myles looked again and spoke to her without turning, "They haven't spotted us. No commotion down there. We're blocked off, though. Better work on east, go around." He was still speaking as he started off, "Let's go. I'll walk a while."

"Myles—"

He stopped and turned, just now realizing that she knew this country far better than he. "What's the matter?" he said. "Am I headed wrong?"

She seemed to hesitate longer than necessary before she answered, "I'm—not sure. Keep going. I'll have to look some more."

He half turned. Then some quality in her voice brought him about with the swift conviction that she disagreed. He said roughly, hurrying her, "If you know a better way?"

She flung him an inconclusive shake of her head, and he delayed no longer. Leading off, he stalked farther under the trees. Almost at once the low limbs and brush slowed him. Around him the gray gloom deepened. He pulled up, searching for an easier way.

The absence of sound behind rang an alarm. Jeannette wasn't trailing along, in close, though the rough footing could account for that.

Whipping around, he saw her dimly on the horse, farther back than he figured she should be. But Skeeter's head bobbed. She was following, all right. Satisfied, Myles returned his attention to the thickening underbrush.

He was struggling forward when a warning voice spoke inside him, low and cold. He whirled and glanced backward. First, he thought he saw her. Or was it the fooling shape of things in the dim light? More looking and he couldn't be positive in this murk; then he knew that he did not.

His feeling of trouble came clamoring. And he was running, unmindful of the stinging, tearing brush. He heard nothing beyond him now, saw no sign of her, the noise of his own passage deadening all sound save his pounding boots.

He ran to the timber's edge and stopped, panting, and he caught sound now—the ringing racket of shod hoofs racing across rocks ... going away.

He knew even before he saw Jeannette. She had the bay horse running recklessly down the rough slope, toward the posse's camp. And she was shouting and gesturing as she rode.

Understanding crashed through Myles. He continued to watch her, frozen into shocked immobility. Here, in this fast-shifting light, he stood as a sleepwalker emerging into cruel consciousness. He understood everything now. Why she had come willingly into his arms. Why she had pretended to believe him. And the faked weariness soon after they started.

Still not moving, he watched nightmarish figures come alive around the fire. He heard a drawn-out yell. Finally, a tardy warning pierced his sick disgust.

Bitter-mouthed, deeply shaken, he slipped back under the trees.

CHAPTER THIRTEEN

EYOND HER WINDOW the rounded hills should have been framed in strokes of brilliant sunlight, their wooded sides shaggy as the buffalo robe upon the floor; the clean, high grass of the prairie a green sea lapping the foot of those hills.

Sick at heart, Nellie Tyson moved her head back and forth. It was like trying to see through a black cloud over the land, only the cloud wasn't out there but in her.

She groaned and the stirring of her heavy body set off a series of tiny squeaks in the old cane-bottom rocker. She had no notion how long she'd been sitting here, just rocking and staring into space; maybe hours. Well, tomorrow was the funeral and she'd have to pull herself together. She tried to lay back, to rest her pounding head, but the turmoil inside denied her even that small comfort. Her mind was a dull and useless thing, without order or benefit.

The first crushing impact of her grief had passed. She no longer stayed in her bed, inert, drowned in sorrow, in blackness. But she felt lost, lost completely in a haze of unreality. She attempted once again to convince herself that good people like Charlie were never murdered—that it couldn't be true—an irrational line of reasoning that brought her flush against the brooding memory of Louis.

Thinking of him, gone so long, she started crying again and dabbing her face with a lace handkerchief.

Sobbing, she got up and half lurched, half walked to the closed bedroom door and put her back to it and leaned there for support, frightened, every part of her body and mind a separate ache. In confusion, she took an uncertain step back to the rocker.

The dresser mirror flashed her puffed image. She drew up, swaying, and inspected herself. She recoiled at the red, swollen eyes, the bloated mouth and cheeks, her once-braided hair wild as a crazy woman's who'd run through brush.

The sight forced a tiny trace of command to her thinking. Her fingers worked absently at her hair. But when she thought of powdering her face, she shrank back in shocked protest. On leaden feet she reached the rocker and slumped down.

Sounds in the house came to her remotely.

The old Oto woman was in the kitchen, she knew, busy cooking for the cousins and others who'd been driving in since late last night and were still arriving in their long cars. At the beginning, Nellie had seen them all, but each handshake or arm around her or sharp wail only blew up another storm of grief which she could not endure. So she had taken refuge in her room.

The feast ... it occurred to her again.

She had forgotten till Sid brought it up, as if he should. Familiar with Indian ways, he said he'd make all arrangements in town at the trading store for the meat and groceries they'd need at the house.

Sid it was who broke the unbelievable news about Charlie. Sid, his arm gently around her as he spoke, the one who held her when the full and terrible sense of loss struck.

It was like the other time, when Louis drowned. Sid had come to the house to comfort her, to do small things you appreciated and to run business errands. Jeannette, home then, had taken care of other matters.

An uncontrollable moan burst from Nellie. It hurt to think that Jeannette, her own blood daughter, hers and Louis', hadn't stayed overnight, now of all times. Nellie could understand why Jeannette resented Sid. Was natural. He could never take the place of her real father, which was true.

But did that explain it all? Why Jeannette hadn't spent a single night in this house since Nellie had married Sid? Why, if Jeannette didn't like Sid, was she so friendly with Savannah, Sid's step-daughter?

But Jeannette had promised to come back today, and Nellie was grateful.

Now she stared out the window. The morning was gone. Mus' be afternoon, she thought uncertainly.

The realization worried her. It grew out of proportion and spread to fear. Her mind groped and settled. She found that she was on her feet. Glancing down, she saw the knuckles pale on her clenching brown hands. Somehow, despite her confusion, she recognized one distinct longing: the burning, all-powerful desire to leave this house as soon as she could. To drive and drive and drive, to lose herself.

Jeannette wasn't here. She'd drive to Jeannette's.

Time seemed to drain through her hands. Nellie moved quickly. She opened the closet door, searched swiftly along the row of crowded dresses hanging there till she found a black one. Changed from her robe, and clutching her pocketbook, she left the bedroom and slipped down the quiet hallway.

Murmuring voices rose from the front part of the house. She froze at the sounds, wishing to avoid anyone. Then she took a long breath, relieved. Sounded like everybody was out on the front porch, having a visit, talking old times. But there would be someone in the living room, sitting up with the body.

Just the thought of Charlie nearly gave her away by triggering the convulsive crying again. Sid had made arrangements with the Two Sands undertaker, the same man who ran the trading store. Funny, but she couldn't even remember his name today, and she'd known him ever since she was little .... Everybody said Charlie "sure looks nice an' natural-like." After one brief look, Nellie had started wailing and broken to her knees. Dead people never "looked nice" to her. She knew people just said that to cover up how bad a person did look, so stiff and the color of wax. Nobody looked nice dead....

She managed to get a grip on herself. Braced against the welling-up sobs, she went quietly downstairs.

At the foot of the stairs she darted a sorrowful, reluctant glance to the living room, in the direction of the casket she could not see because of the wall, while the sickening scent of carnations filled her nostrils and turned her stomach.

The smell became unbearable. She felt faint.

She must have made a noise in the whispered stillness, for suddenly Savannah was near, her blonde hair like gold against her dark, plain dress.

"Nellie," she asked, low, "where are you going?"

"Jeannette's," said Nellie, surprised at her control.

"Let me drive you."

"No—" Nellie's voice all but broke. "No—you're needed here." She motioned toward the porch. "All these folks . .."

Savannah Tyson put her arm around Nellie's shoulders, though not restraining her. "You shouldn't go alone."

"I'm all right."

"Yes, but I'm afraid—"

"Don't worry. You know I'm a good driver. Be back pretty soon."

Nellie squeezed Savannah's arm and, in near panic, swept to the kitchen. The old Oto woman looked up with solemn, understanding eyes. Her shapeless lips parted, baring the toothless gums.

Nellie spoke first, quietly, "I'm going for a ride, Grandmother. Over to Jeannette's. Feed everybody good."

Already stepping to the back porch, Nellie was thankful that she'd met no one else. As she walked fast over the yard, she had to think hard in order to remember where she'd left her car. For once, her carelessness helped. She saw the roadster parked to one side of the house, out of sight from the friendly but curious faces on the front porch.

Glancing behind her, she saw Savannah watching worriedly from the back porch. Nellie waved.

Some moments later, driving through the black pools of shade under the cottonwoods, she noticed many cars parked in front of the house and many people on the porch. The number surprised and pleased her, and she hoped they wouldn't think her ungrateful in leaving. It was a comfort to know that she could count on the old Oto woman and Savannah, who would explain.

Driving off, she realized how much she owed Savannah for her understanding. The knowledge humbled her and her eyes blurred. Why, she was just like another daughter!

Yes, it helped getting away from the house. Somehow the wind and the sun approached reality out here, because she could feel them.

She drove automatically, she drove fast, in a stupor of fixed concentration that was also aimless. When she came out on the county road, she realized she had crossed the cattleguard without knowing it.

That startled her. So she stopped and sat and gathered herself before shifting gears and going on.

Before her the empty road climbed and dipped between lonesome hills, through a sad emptiness of space that pierced her shell and made her feel insignificant and lost again.

She pressed harder against the foot feed, hardly conscious of it. The car swerved on the sharp curves, slewing gravel and dust, but she seemed strangely unafraid. A wonderment stirred her, for always before she'd felt fear when her car skidded dangerously, expert a driver as she knew she was.

Now, she gunned the roadster wide open on a level course of prairie, eased off roaring into the curve close upon her, and cut the wheel in a hugging, screaming turn.

The car hung, tenacious as a wildcat clawing bark. She straightened out.

Running smoothly at floor-board speed again, she had a stab of understanding: she wasn't afraid at all. That explained why she could take the curves so fast and with ease, coaxing the roadster till it quivered on the verge of flipping over.

And there was yet another reason: she no longer cared.

She shuddered, her heart racing in an uneven beat, high in her dry throat. Yes, it was there—far back in her mind—ugly, terrible, cowardly, something she'd tried to hide even from herself since the day Louis died in Yellow Dog....

She moved in the encircling grip of it now. She felt an overpowering indifference, no desire to fight back. And she knew it was wrong.

Her eyes closed upon trees very near, upon the low framework of a narrow bridge leaping a creek. During a flick of time the railing loomed as a challenge over the rushing hood of her car, daring her to crash.

Her eyes seemed fastened in fascination, her body unable to act, helpless in the sensation of sweeping relentlessly toward destruction.

At the last moment, Nellie Tyson screamed. She spun the wheel with an instinctive desperation to live, and heard a crashing and ripping. She was pitched sidewise; her hands caught the wheel—held. She felt the roadster lurch wildly, come right, come free, and she was across.

She never remembered stopping. But she found she had, and she looked behind with incredulous eyes and saw the wilted guard-rail. She had slammed and scraped along it, she realized, the last twist of the wheel saving her from ramming it head on. She shuddered, thinking how close she'd come.

Trembling, she went slowly around the car and discovered the crumpled right front fender and torn running board. As she inspected the damage, a sudden shame slapped her. Shocked at herself, she returned to the driver's side, got in heavily and sat a long time.

Much later, judging by the sun riding far down its westward slope, she drove away.

Entering the outskirts of Two Sands, she thought herself under control. She'd go right on through town without stopping. Nevertheless, approaching the first side street past the red depot, she caught herself turning off as if by habit.

The dirt road took her along a fringe of shacks, a quarter mile beyond to the base of a limestone hill. She turned and the way narrowed roughly; it made a right angle and ran erratically to a small creek, straggled beside it some hundred yards and ended in disappointment facing a woodpile just outside a hog-wire fence. Inside, humped a two-room shack of cottonwood lumber, by now well weather-warped.

Stepping from the car, Nellie saw a face blur at a window, a face quickly hidden. She heard a dog barking.

Something made her glance around before going to the house. Often as she'd come to Stoke's Place in the last two years, she could never escape the feeling of guilt, of being furtive and sneaking; and not just because whisky wasn't legal. Stoke was dirty personally and his house dirtier. Yet he always had whisky, dubious though it was.

Pocketbook under one arm, she walked rapidly to the gate. Her pushing started a cowbell clanging, Stoke's first outpost warning of visitors. A brown dog romped up, still barking, and suddenly he turned silent and wagging.

Nellie patted his head. He always knows me, she thought ruefully.

She knocked at the door. There followed a lengthy pause, as there always did. Just as she was getting impatient, the door cracked and she saw a familiar face, thin, unshaven, unwashed.

"Want a pint, Stoke," Nellie said.

Stoke poked his long turkey neck out a notch, cast the road, and drew in. "Okay," he grunted, and Nellie entered, her nostrils pinching down upon the rancid smell of fried meat and grease.

Shuffling, he drifted through a gunny-sack curtain. After a series of rustlings, he returned with a pint bottle. Its contents, Nellie noted with some misgiving, were white and beady looking on top.

Stoke, however, handled his stock in trade with the manner of a benefactor about to bestow a great treat. "This here's extra good," he muttered.

Unimpressed, Nellie opened her pocketbook. "Three dollars?"

Stoke swallowed nervously. "No … four. Went up, Nellie. Had to. Gettin' tough the way them Federals bird-dog a man, watch him day an' night."

She paid without argument, dropped the pint inside her roomy pocketbook. Looking up, she saw a curious expression overcome his habitual nervousness. "Been up town today?" he queried. "Heard the big news?"

"You mean about Charlie?" she answered resentfully. Did he think she'd been out hooting around and didn't know?

"Nope," Stoke went on importantly. "About the feller breakin' away. The man they had in for shootin' Charlie. Seems he kidnapped Coon into Happy Adcock's taxi an' drove east. They's a big manhunt on out there."

The words trickled through her dullness. Till now, submerged in grief, she'd had slight time to consider Charlie's murderer. All she knew was what little Sid had been able to tell her before she broke down: something about Frank's brother being held as a suspect.

"East … from town?" she echoed, fixing him with her eyes. "That's on the road to Jeannette's!"

"Never thought—but it is—"

Watching the pale, jumpy eyes, Nellie read in them a discovery of her own fear. Uncertain, her throat contracting, she left the house and stood outside a moment.

There her fright broke through and she hurried to the car and started the motor. She gunned the roadster in a tight circle, spinning the wheels and kicking up wood chips. She drove off in a rush, her mind reaching out to Jeannette, the whisky beside her forgotten.

Approaching Jeannette's house, Nellie noticed cars and horse trailers parked beneath the trees. She scrambled out and thought it strange she saw no one. Hurrying, rounding the corner of the house on her way to the kitchen, she almost collided with Happy Adcock. He stopped in surprise and started pressing a red handkerchief to his face.

"Happy! Your face—what's happened?" The sight of him made her draw back. One eye puffed shut, his lips cracked and swollen, one side of his face skinned raw.

"Nothin' much," he answered, evasive all at once. "Heard your car. Was just goin' out to see who it was."

She said impatiently, "They told me in town Frank's brother broke out; was headed this way. I got worried about Jeannette—a killer loose!" She sprang toward the rear door.

"Don't go in there!" Suddenly, Adcock had her arm. "Wiley's in the kitchen—dead as stone!"

Her breath wedged in her throat. She shrank back from the door. "But Jeannette—"

"Ain't here," he snapped, not ungently. "Now, you just hold on a minute an' ol' Happy will straighten you out." He tried to, in his clumsy, well-meaning way, and finished up with, "The boys lost Myles in the brush and gave up. Bowdre joined up, so they came on to the house. Just as they drove up, they seen somebody take off on a horse. Looked like Myles. Then they found Wiley—in there. Undertaker be here any minute. I'm just waitin' around." He added reluctantly, "Nobody's seen Jeannette, except Bowdre. He said she slipped out on him earlier, when he came to take her in—"

"Take her in!"

"Yeah." Adcock stared at his boot tips. "Bowdre claimed the county attorney wanted to ask her about—well—about—" He stumbled in his talk.

"About Charlie?"

He nodded glumly and Nellie felt a leaping astonishment, then swift anger. "She wouldn't do such a thing! Not Jeannette!"

"What I told Bowdre. But they're huntin' her—just the same! An' I don't think Myles shot Charlie—know he didn't." He shook his head dolefully. "Ever'thing's gummed up, if you ask me."

Her drive of moments ago collapsed. His battered face held her attention. "Who beat you up—Frank's brother?" She couldn't seem to call the man's name, though Happy had just said it.

"No—not him. Nothin' for you to worry about, Nellie."

She read him like a book, his obvious evasion. She faced him squarely. "Don't lie to me, Happy."

"Oh, now, I just got caught in a bind. Little boys shouldn't play pool." He was far too casual with his words.

"Happy, you're tryin' to hide something." She grabbed his arm. "You're gonna tell me!"

"I tell you it's nothin'."

"But I know better, Happy."

He ran his tongue across his broken lips. His slight shoulders sagged. He brought up the unwilling words with his good eye gazing down. "All right … You'd find out soon enough. It was Sid, Nellie … Coon put in his two bits' worth first. Blamed me—claimed it was a frameup between me an' Myles. Sid got ravin' mad. He—sure dressed me down prime."

"But you said you drove by and stopped—and this Myles got Coon's gun—"

"Exactly right," he agreed, almost too readily, she thought. "Just drove by." But his eye slid away from hers.

Her impulse to defend him hammered stronger. "Sid was wrong," she said, and realized she was getting angrier by the moment.

"Forget it, Nellie." He was trying to act indifferent.

She ran her eyes over the punished homely features, deeply shocked and outraged. Just because Sid got mad didn't excuse this; it was cruel and uncalled for. There wasn't any reason in the world that gave Sid the right to beat up Happy, who couldn't whip a chicken, who had never spoken one unkind word to her or tried to cheat her, who had gone out of his way many times for her—and for Louis.

She turned suddenly, astonished at her fury toward Sid. In her mind's eye she saw a different man, changed in size. The knowledge hurt.

Adcock broke the silence. "Ever'body left soon as they could phone out for horses. Somebody called your place." There was a question in the last, as if she should have known.

"Don't know … I went for a ride."

Some of her despair edged into her voice, and Adcock considered her gently. "Go home, Nellie. The boys will find Jeannette. Reckon she got scared an' just plain spooked."

He took her arm and started her slowly toward her car, continuing to talk in his rambling, soothing fashion. "She'll be all right, even if she is afoot."

She whirled on him. "Afoot—in these hills?"

He had the pulled-in expression of a man who had let his mouth flap. "Why—uh—Bowdre said so. You see, she left her horse in the barn."

With a swarming fierceness Nellie knew now that she'd never go home till Jeannette was found. "I'm gonna look for her," she announced firmly. "She needs me. Where'd the men go?"

"Off toward Charlie's. They're searchin' all this country."

"Then I'll go to Charlie's."

"No, Nellie! There'll be trouble!"

Jerking away, Nellie marched straight to her car. She had the motor roaring when Adcock, limping, caught up. He placed a detaining hand upon the door. "Road's bad—"

"Stand back or get in," she told him.

Happy Adcock worked his swollen mouth. Their glances met, and he saw his own defeat. "Got yourself a passenger," he said dismally, getting in.

She shifted gears, grinding them, and the roadster snarled across the yard.

CHAPTER FOURTEEN

MYLES DELAYED some moments, with the mocking enormity of Jeannette's betrayal beating hard upon him. Then he took long-reaching strides into the black timber, not pausing till his chest burned and his legs felt like rubber.

In the increasing light he was beginning to see where he stood, straddling the saddle of a broad-backed ridge. Off to the east he got glimpses of prairie, a wide river of grass running between the slopes, and to the north the discouragement of more open country, of the ridge ending naked. So he dodged south, keeping to the only cover left him, back in the general direction from which he and Jeannette had ridden.

Soon he heard sounds of chase: horses running, strident yells. Somebody's gun went off, its echoes slapping and flat-sounding off the ridge sides. As a curious youngster of twelve he had tagged after a Flint Hills posse hot on a murderer's trail. Some of the men acted foolish that day. Some swaggering and careless with their weapons; talking too much. Men at a circus. Myles had thought of the hunted man and wondered how he felt. Now he knew.

He came rock-still, seeking to judge the pattern of the noises, and decided the riders were fanning out to sweep the ridge. He also knew they'd have to dismount, once they rode inside the timber and met the brush.

Now followed a taut time, while he ran and tried to listen. Without any warning the footing roughened. Long slabs of sand-stone and man-size boulders cluttered his way. Past them he tore through a growth of low plum bushes, there in a place where the trees had thinned and the ridge sluffed off sharply. Here, in thick concealment, he checked again for noises, while his heart seemed to swell and pound till it drummed out all else.

Far back a hoof struck rock.

Then the bristly, secret woods were quiet and the wirestrung tension of being hunted built up in him. His heart still tugged, his throat dry and cottony.

It was full daylight. Somewhere horses were running again.

The sound jolted him up, hurried him. He heard nothing more and traveled faster. Several minutes of this and he made out an emptiness through the trees. He refused to admit it, not till he could see for certain, but he recognized a dead end. Even as he stumbled forward, yet some yards from the edge, he saw the ridge shelving off, bare of trees.

He ducked into brush and lay heaving, popping with sweat, gauging his chances. Timber formed in the distance, where the broken land pieced together again. He scrambled up—and immediately jerked down.

Three men were swinging horseback around the base of the ridge. As they watched the crest, he flattened lower. He thought maybe they intended to search the next chunk of highland, where he wished he was this moment, figuring he'd legged it that far.

As the thought rose, they halted. He could see them nodding in talk. His hope pinched out when they deployed at short intervals and started up the slope, walking their ponies.

Myles wiped a hand across his wet face and swore. He was hemmed in; they had him boxed.

The need for haste whipped through him. He eased back on hands and knees from the tangle and crawled to the next knot of brush and came to his feet. He broke out running. Wincing, he slammed into the plum bushes, teeth set against the tough branches ripping his arms and thighs, the slungup carbine guarding his face.

A warning welled up: he was heading straight for the others. Yet a gambling piece of his mind said that only among the big rocks, studded with brush, had he a chance—if he got there first. Hide, slip by them, if they overlooked him, and grab a horse.

His momentum carried him through, and now he felt the pressure redouble. It plucked at his nerves and loaded him with the panicky expectancy of seeing men stalking toward him. But he saw nothing ahead or to the flanks, nothing in motion. However, he missed the rocks, where they should be. Had he swung wrong? He placed himself and plunged on. Brush thickened and pulled, and then he was free of it.

As he burst from the snarl, his boots struck stone and he stumbled. He'd found his rocks, though he still doubted his sense of direction in this twisting and turning. Around him the brown sandstone spilled in a careless, jumbled mass, spreading fan-wise along the ridge. Ducking low, he went as far as he dared and snugged in against a broken layer, fairly well shielded by brush.

He pulled the carbine to him and waited.

A minute drifted past, sluggish and heavy. Silence was a growing weight overhanging the ridge; it piled in about the rock and searched him out and pushed like a battering ram out of the emptiness. Despite the cool, early morning wind, his shirt was sopped through. And even after his heart ceased racing, and he'd lain there a time, the tightness persisted in his body. Every muscle seemed a single string, twisted taut.

Head cocked, he listened toward his blind side from where they would come. After a while he began catching the tiny murmurs and shufflings and stirrings of early morning.

Down on the prairie a meadowlark whistled. There was a rapid rustling, so faint and light he dismissed it. He thought, Funny, no boot sound yet. Cramped in, he tried to imagine the ridge top. The brush should warn him when—if—somebody began scouting this way.

The moments dragged. He drew tighter.

It seemed a lifetime before he heard anything more, a thin, raveled-out scurrying. He froze, his eyes fastened to the limited view beyond the rock's end. Just then a tiny lizard darted past his hideout and disappeared under a sandstone ledge.

His grip on the carbine relaxed. He breathed deeply.

But a few counts later his ears picked up a faint though definite intrusion, the crunching a boot might make upon rock.

He dragged wind into his tight chest, knowing it wouldn't be long. All set, he tensed for the slow-paced fall of other boots. He found himself in the awful waiting once more.

Nothing happened for a while. When movement finally registered, it was closer to a feeling than actual sound, very near. Seconds passed. Next he saw the toe and foot of a black boot planted down noiselessly, just past his rock. Another boot followed, stepping on and pausing.

Myles' eyes widened in recognition upon Tom Bowdre.

Bowdre hesitated, his dogged glance flicking left and right. He gripped his pistol with careless competence, looking sure of himself.

In the same breath, Myles realized he had Bowdre easy. Just tilt the barrel a trifle. The thought climbed and fell swiftly, broken by revulsion. So he sweated it out and wondered why he didn't hear the others. On the other hand, this was Bowdre's style—alone.

He saw Bowdre, silent as smoke, slip on and disappear.

Now was the time. Now... Crawling, Myles nudged along the length of the rock. Indecision, the dread of leaving his hiding place, stopped him when he reached the end. What if Bowdre came back?

He breathed to the bottom of his lungs and edged around the rock corner. Onward reared the dark wall of blackjacks. Not many steps away the rock clutter ended. He started off, crouched low, still worried by the unusual quiet.

His boots scraped as he rounded a hunk of sprawled stone, the faintness jangling his nerves. He waited and no sound came. His confidence returned, strong, hurrying. Faster, he dodged to the last line of jagged rocks. As he stepped to a boulder, his attention sought the greenery....

It looked clear. Nobody there.

But when he left the stone's shoulder and straightened, something went wrong, swiftly wrong. A feeling... He glanced right, saw nothing. Before he could jerk back, a voice cut in behind him.

"Don't move. Drop your gun." It was Frank Rikker's voice, cold as ice.

It pinned Myles to the spot. He stayed stiff, too stunned to move, while his stomach keeled over. For a brief, reckless moment, he held on to the gun.

"Drop it."

Little by little, Myles lowered it. His fingers loosened and he let go.

As he heard the metallic thunk of the carbine, he saw a man spring up. And another. The rocks kept growing them. Men bobbing up and closing in from their hiding places, and he realized with an angry disgust why he hadn't heard them. They'd waited for him. Bowdre the only one catting ahead. Why, Bowdre had him figured all the time!

He was suddenly played out, beaten to his bones. He placed his hands on his hips and breathed through his teeth. A man he didn't know came up. He tapped Myles' shirt and belt line and pockets and thereby found the .38 special. He fished it out and they all stood around Myles, looking him over. Everybody talked at once, relieved, high-pitched and nervous, some swaggering and heedless with their weapons.

"By Gawd, we got 'im!"

"Hey, Bowdre!"

Frank's pistol covered Myles and Frank said, "Stay put—right there against that rock."

Slouched wretchedly, Myles damned him with his eyes. In that instant he knew a withering disgust that surpassed even Jeannette's betrayal. This was different. The crushing disappointment and sick regret you felt when a man failed to pan out right. When he let you and all his own kind down. This man cut from the image of Dow Rikker.

Glaring, Myles couldn't even feel an honest anger. Frank didn't rate it, not any more.

"You're doing all right by yourself," Myles said bitterly.

"Shut up!"

There wasn't much you could read in Frank's handsome face. It was set, the blue eyes almost without expression. He wasn't as noisy as the rest of the posse.

Bowdre ran up, calling, "Nice work, boys. Wanted him alive." He faced them in command, pistol swinging, his eyes alight with a brittle pleasure and triumph. "This winds her up good," he said in a satisfied voice, then turned to Myles. "Figured you'd throw a little lead before you gave up."

"Could, Bowdre. Could have stopped your clock back there in the rocks. You club-footed right by me."

"Then why'n hell didn't you?" replied Bowdre, surprised and stung.

Shrugging, Myles let it pass. He was already thinking of the long ride back to Two Sands.

"Guess you got soft," prodded Bowdre. "Maybe scared—after shootin' Wiley."

In cold anger, Myles said, "He drew on me. No choice."

Bowdre gave a cynical nod. "Oldest song in the hymn book, mister. Frank tell you Wiley's dead?"

Myles stood very still, feeling an instant remorse. Still, he wasn't surprised. An old knowledge had whispered it to him, even as he fled the kitchen. He dug the probe of his glance into Bowdre, hoping yet to read there the denial, knowing Bowdre was full of tricks.

But Bowdre's expression held steady. "No reason for me to lie about it—he's dead. Gives you two men to answer for now." He made a half turn and impatience ripped through his voice, "Let's clear out of here, boys."

The possemen stirred, and Myles saw them all for the first time. Small bunch. Seven-eight men. Not so many as he'd first thought. He recognized only one face—Coon Pollard's resentful moon features, slick with sweat, and made the quick guess that Pollard had posted himself safely on a flank before the capture.

At Bowdre's growled command, Myles moved out. Several steps and a formless unease grazed him. He turned and cast the posse's face again, halting.

"Get along!" Bowdre ordered.

Dragging on, Myles wasn't clear in his own mind what nagged him. It was as if something failed to fit.

As he hesitated again, a shout sounded far to the rear. He heard a man say, "Looks like the Harper boys. Them an' Morgan. Bet they're peeved, missin' the big show."

Turning with the others, Myles saw three riders appear on the south rim. The same trio he'd run from earlier. They reined up before the rough horse footing. Bowdre armsignaled them off toward camp.

"Damnit to hell!" he compained in general. "You'd think this was a picnic hike. I told Morgan to help Tyson an' Kutch bring up the extra horses to our bunch down the ridge. But Tyson offered—his headache. Well, let's get along."

An unexpected perception stopped Myles. Facing Bowdre, he heard himself saying, "Jeannette—she give herself up?" He had the unsound hope, he realized, that she'd struck across country after pointing him out, instead of going to the camp.

"Bet your bottom dollar she's a prisoner. If she ain't mixed up in this, why'd she run? Think I'd bring a woman up here—risk gettin' her shot?" Bowdre pushed his chin at Myles. "Mister, you better move!"

Even then, Myles failed to budge. He understood now about the faces—Tyson and Kutch not among them. "You left her with Tyson and Kutch?" he demanded. "Her—alone—with them?"

"What difference it make?" The lawman's jaw hinges clamped till the muscles bulged. "Hell, yes, if that'll make you move faster!" When Myles stayed motionless, Bowdre quick-stepped forward. He seemed unable to control his angry impatience. "Pearce—damn you! You're stallin'! Wish t'God I had me some cuffs!" he swore.

Sick desperation took hold of Myles. He heard the charged words explode from his throat without thought, "You damned fool, Bowdre! They'll kill her!"

An off-guard astonishment enlarged Bowdre's stare, then bewilderment and, quickly, a hot irritation. "What's the matter, you crazy? Sid Tyson's her step-father, ain't he?" He made a short, chopping gesture that dismissed the whole incredible thing. "Now take your choice. Come along quiet or we tie you up. Right now it'd be a pleasure to drag you through brush, mister."

Their eyes clashed, Bowdre's immovable skepticism maddening. "Off your nut, I'm thinkin'," he said and pointed to his head and twirled an index finger. "Plumb loco … or just an act to make trouble."

"My God," Myles said miserably. "Send somebody down there before Tyson does something!" It struck him that his pleading lacked logic. He groped frantically for some plausible explanation he might use and knew there wasn't one. All he had was his own crystallized fear, clear only to him. "I tell you Wiley—no! I can explain later. Bowdre—you go—anybody—but hurry!"

Bowdre chewed his lip, his wind-burned face changing slightly, and Myles' hopes leaped high. As suddenly, the eyes switched to a cold suspicion. "All right, boys," Bowdre ordered. "Fooled around long enough. Somebody snake off his belt. Rest of you put up your guns and lend a hand. Throw him down. We're gonna hog-tie this here gentleman," he promised grimly.

They put down their pistols and rifles and, empty-handed, gauged Myles menacingly. In slow step they started for him, and he drew back a pace. He saw Bowdre's pistol swing up, and he heard Bowdre's voice, stripped of its final patience, "I'm warnin' you, mister. Take one more step . .

Myles stood fast.

A square-built puncher, younger and stronger-looking than the others, stepped forward. He had resolve smeared all over his sun-blackened face, his work-hardened hands spread wide like a carnival grappler's.

"Stand back—"

It came clipped, cold and firm, and the voice belonged to Frank Rikker.

The puncher stopped short, his head swiveling. Myles followed the man's eyes with swelling astonishment.

Frank Rikker, his fisted hand sliding his pistol back and forth, had a side angle on Bowdre, the only armed man. Frank's eyes were as dull points of flint under his brows, his mouth a pinched line—compressed, thinned flat. He didn't so much as notice Myles.

"What th' hell!" exploded Bowdre.

The needle of tension now teetered between him and Frank. Bowdre still gripped his pistol, too surprised to use it in the first moment of opportunity—his chance gone.

Yet Myles saw speculation whet Bowdre's eyes. He saw Bowdre tense a fraction, his left shoulder dip.

"Don't try it!" Frank warned. "I don't want to shoot—"

The pressure of waiting knotted Bowdre's wizened, dogged features, sketching them in straining concentration.

"—but I will," Frank finished.

Bowdre's gun knuckles whitened and gradually eased. Quite slowly, his hand opened and the pistol bearing upon Myles dropped.

"Not much time left," Frank said, snapping it out. "No time to draw pictures. But it's pretty clear." He jerked his head at Myles. "Grab a gun—get started! They'll be down there end of the ridge, if it ain't too late. All Sid has to claim is she tried to escape. Already got his alibi—damn his heart!"

From the nearest man Myles unbuckled a gunbelt and scooped up a pistol. As he ran for the timber, he heard Frank speaking in a low, steadfast tone.

Something told him there wasn't much time left.

CHAPTER FIFTEEN

NOW, TRAVELING in a stiff-legged run, Myles entered the false twilight of close, black-boled timber. As the breeze fanned across the ridge, it rippled the blackjack leaves, turning them lazily, and this was the ony movement meeting his eyes. Stillness lay behind and ahead of him, as if he trod a forgotten backbone of land, shot through with tricky shadows and uncertainty.

His body wet with the sweat of running and nervousness, he came to a flat-footed stop. He breathed sluggishly, his thigh muscles twitchy. He carried a sharp premonition of lateness. His eyes swept wide and the quietness rolled in, mocking him. Picking up the pace, he told himself that he had to go fast but he also had to use caution, else he'd be worse than useless to Jeannette.

His eyes strained for horses. Had to be horses. Tyson would make it look good. But he saw only the blank, somber woods. His doubts piled up, and he wasn't entirely certain of what he should do. Constantly sweeping his glance, he ran till his tortured lungs seemed on fire, till every stride became an effort in itself.

At last he discovered a break in the solid rampart of trees. The light grew. He saw the clear space that showed the limit of the ridge....

But he found no horses.

His fear knotting, he scrambled to the timber's edge and gazed downslope, staring at distance scrubbed bright and dazzling by sunlight—staring at emptiness. He moved his gaze, thinking darkly of the camp, wondering if it had happened there already.

Moments ... and he located smoke to the northwest, between bold hills. Wisps feathered up, rising till the downdraft from the hills scattered them into streaming ravels of gray flannel.

His eyes lowered—fell upon a vacant camp, empty of horses and people—and he knew then that he had to hurry.

He was in groping motion, not knowing which way to turn, when a shot slammed the stillness.

He thought, Oh, God, and one of the flashes of his mind said, You took her pistol and made up that story, and abruptly he knew a soul-breaking sense of guilt.

He fought out of it, fought for a sort of shaky control.

That gun—it'd crashed to his left ... back a way ... where the ridge crooked out.

The woods were deathly still now.

For the briefest of time he wavered, while the pieces of the ridge fell into place and gave him the answer of direction. He understood what had happened to him: running through the ranked trees, he'd angled off right.

He spun into a ragged run, with the sensation of too late a sick knot balled inside him. Yet his mind seemed cold and clear as he ran, lips drawn against his teeth.

The going climbed roughly to rock and leveled off.

He was looking down when he spotted the horses, brushtied in a shallow ravine. That was all. Just the horses. Plenty horses.

He plunged past them and took the opposite side of the ravine in long, rapid strides, making noises he didn't like, and reached the top.

The quietness drew him on, the land flattening and then rising all at once, cowled with brush and rock....

His eyes caught upon a patch of bright brown. He halted, almost afraid to go closer. Letting go, he stepped carefully on and saw a dead horse. Stopped again, he looked and felt as if someone had kicked him in the stomach.

The dead animal was Skeeter, his bay coat glistening.

Anger struck him. Through it his mind rallied to Jeannette, realizing there'd been just the one shot. He saw everything in one awful picture: Jeannette breaking away, Skeeter taking the bullet as he ran up the ravine... gamely driving on, running till he dropped dead.

She had to be somewhere in this dense brush, afoot.

He was already past Skeeter.

The ridge seemed blanketed in a sinister stillness. Around him tall brush flowed in tangled matting to an outcrop of splintered sandstone. Nothing moved; no sound came except his own uneven breathing.

Rocks high as a man's shoulders confronted him. He swing around them and halted in his tracks. The heavy silence bore down, mocking him, reminding him how tardy he was. He could feel the sticky clamminess of his hands.

He swept his eyes forward, to another heap of rocks. For a terrifying moment he thought he'd missed them. But no—this had to be right. A knowing told him. His mind kept twisting to her as he moved, faster now, as he met merely more maddening rock and brush....

Except over there the high growth stirred as if by a strong wind. Only he felt no wind in this shut-off hush. It bothered him; it fired his nerves.

He saw a blur of white in a thicket. It materialized slowly to the peak of a man's hat, followed by face and shoulders. At the same time, in the edge of Myles' vision, another figure sprang up. Both men were advancing.

His breath locked, Myles lifted his pistol. In a rush he got it: the two of them stalking in toward the rock rubble, which dead-ended under a high brushy ledge. She...

Suddenly, he lost the hats. The pair had dropped down.

He'd waited too long. He planted a shot, guessing where the lead man stood. Even as he fired he knew he'd missed, and saw the two shapes bob up farther on, whirl and fire backward, the gunshots so jammed together they sounded as one.

Ducking low, Myles drove right as another bullet whinged brush behind him. He couldn't see them and he held his fire.

Now an old instinct, deeper than thought, guided and directed him. A clawing perception told him to wedge in between them and the ledge. He maneuvered a rod or more that way. ...

The sharp crackle of brush, of stomping, running boots, chained him down again. Caution seized him, a swift insight. He couldn't reach the ledge, because somebody was cutting across. Somebody was waiting for him.

This was the moment. He let the rustling tell him. He still caught it as he reversed direction, then reared up, his eyes jumping with a cold prickling.

Swinging, he glimpsed a crouching shape, yellow eyes, a wide-jawed face—Kutch. And Kutch, intent on Myles' position of seconds ago, pivoted and snapped off his shot—too hurriedly.

Something bit past Myles' ear as he pulled the trigger.

He heard the deafening roar of his gun. He saw Kutch fold. He heard Kutch cry out, and now Myles squared for Tyson and heard the panicked pounding of boots—but not where Tyson should be.

Myles jerked toward the sound.

Tyson made an indefinite figure, low, crouched, obscured by brush, going away.

Myles started after him, only to haul around on a queer hackling. He flung Kutch a glance to make sure. Kutch was still down, all right. But somehow it seemed too easy. Kutch had squirmed back. He wasn't—

Distrust warned Myles. It kept rooting him there while Tyson ran. His indecision bound him, even as he saw Kutch sprawled, partly hidden by brush, not moving.

It happened as Myles straightened for a better look, as he stepped forward. Kutch rolled violently and brought up his arm.

Their gun blasts roared and blended, Kutch's weapon flash flaming in Myles' eyes. Strange, but he felt nothing. Blinking, he saw Kutch in the thin grass beside the green thicket. Kutch's head moved; he groaned. The pistol still bulked in his hand, flat alongside him. He couldn't seem to lift it.

Myles broke brush getting across to him. He booted the pistol loose from Kutch's hand and swayed over him, ready to kick and hammer if need be.

A second later, stepping back, he saw force was no longer needed.

Kutch's head slacked to one side. He didn't seem aware of Myles and the gun in his hand. His eyes, white and frightened, were filled with shock. Then a new and awful insight crept into them.

It made a lump of Myles' insides, though he'd seen this often not many years back. He saw the thick mouth wobble, the lips strung across teeth strong and yellow.

"Sid—don't leave me!" Kutch had difficulty mouthing the words. For all that, they carried clearly in a straining call.

Fading, yet distinct in the muteness, over by the first stand of rocks, Myles heard boots traveling fast and the crashing of a body through brush.

He lunged to follow, but came to a standstill at sight of Kutch, who had picked up the sound, too. Something was dying in Kutch's face, something like belief and watchdog worship. A frightening look of comprehension forged live coals of the burning eyes.

Kutch strained up on an elbow. The heavy, ugly lips moved. "Sid! Damn you! Come back! Sid—y'hear me?"

The racing boots dimmed out.

Kutch collapsed, breathing hard. There wasn't much spark left in him.

Then it burst up through Myles: Tyson was making for the horses.

A hot and killing violence ached in him. Its single purpose shut out all else and swerved him toward the rocks in a long-reaching run. He rounded the outcrop, thinking, She's all right—just one shot—

A horse rapping over rocks drove him faster. But the drag of these past days had caught up with him, and he stumbled. The ground rocked before his eyes. Angry at his slowness, he forced himself to keep on.

Panting up to the ravine, he found the horses in restless wake. Glancing down slope, he saw Tyson spurring and whipping, not slowing for rocks.

Myles threw up his pistol. As he fired, Tyson suddenly reined west and passed from sight, untouched.

Finding himself along the ravine's edge, Myles jumped down and on trembling legs he reached the first horse and pitched into the saddle. He was well down the ravine, in a slamming run, when a shout pecked at his ears.

It shouldered him around and he saw them. Men running from the blackjacks. Frank in the lead. Myles waved him across and turned front in the saddle again.

As he came to the turn Tyson had taken, another yell sounded. He whipped backward and slowed down.

Frank was storming up the ravine's far flank, the possemen spaced out behind. And something in the way Frank hurried breathed it to Myles. He shifted his gaze, and a high wave of relief, warm and good, rolled over him. ...

She stood a rope's toss away in the brush and she looked all right. Even from here her full-bodied trimness stood out.

Without really knowing why, Myles continued to delay. He saw Frank top the ravine and race across. For a long moment Jeannette appeared to wait, uncertainly, as if not sure. She took a sudden step toward Frank, and another.

Still watching, Myles had one indelible impression of her upturned face and mouth before she went into Frank Rikker's arms.

Dropping his gaze, Myles turned the horse. He rode some distance before he could think. Then it came to him why he'd waited when haste meant everything: he wanted to witness for himself the one thing he had to be certain about. And there wasn't any doubt now. Because in that brief space of time, as they came together, he sensed a complete apartness from them.

Well, he thought, that's it. . . .

Steadily, he saddled down the western slope of the ridge. For once, even though Tyson had a sizable lead, he felt no pressing hurry. He reloaded, mechanically punching shells from the gun-belt, while he paced the gelding to a trot.

He could never recall such a weariness as this, not only physical but also of the mind, when thought lay so buried and his body so dull and sluggish to respond to command, as if he weren't capable of feeling. Little by little, he let the horse out in a warming-up lope, saving him for the punishing grind ahead, for this chore had the earmarks of a drawn-out business. Soon he was pushing the gelding in steady gallop. All the while he wrestled his mind to functioning again, to thinking ahead. Invariably, it returned to her, changeless, ever there.

Time seemed stopped, of no matter, himself and the horse lost in these frowning, rounded hills, ancient for an eternity before the Osages quit the flat Kansas lands and moved south, seeking space away from the crowding white man and never finding it. During this interval Myles seemed in a vacuum—

Till, skirting a hill, he thought he saw a horse blur in the timber half a mile onward. One of those flutters of movement, of shifting shadows, you couldn't tell about from a distance; just a suspicion of motion, quickly vanished.

He made a fast, straight-on approach, refusing caution. Yet, when he got there, all he found was trackless sandstone and bunch grass, no sign whatever upon that dour terrain. Reining in, he let the horse blow and found that his head had untangled and was fixed in a surprising clarity and straightness of intent.

Afterward, still traveling west, he settled down to an increased pace.

Later, when he forded the creek and rode out upon the turfted prairie, he faced a decision. Had Tyson run northwest for his ranch? Had he hurried south to the Blackhorse ranch, then struck for Jeannette's place? Either bet looked sound.

He dragged it across his mind and decided he needed the advantage of higher ground, a point where he could see better.

From the top of the first rise he noted the cheerless Blackhorse house—solitary, bowed down in age under the sun, oppressive with memories of good-natured Charlie. He found no motion down there, but the off sides of the house and barn were concealed from him here.

He felt a sharp disappointment, an end to his patience. Since leaving the ridge, his mind had been building on the Blackhorse ranch; he'd gambled on finding something there. As the likely headquarters for the manhunt, it offered Tyson the nearest opportunity to catch up a fresh horse or help himself to a car.

He held up, realizing that some of the impetus had drained from him, and that the lack wasn't only in his body. Scanning the northwest, in the direction of Tyson's ranch, he rejected that possibility as too far off for a running man. He turned once again to ponder the silent house, galled by fleeting time.

He had made up his mind to ride down there when he saw a car shoot out from the far side. It gained speed rapidly, racing up valley in fuming dust, its roar rising in Myles' ears.

He waited no more, already kicking the gelding's flanks.

CHAPTER SIXTEEN

FINALLY, the old wagon road shook loose from the tousled hills and bent across rolling upland. Nellie Tyson fought the ancient ruts, now and then dodging a rock or depression.

She could not remember the last time she'd come this way, but it was in a wagon. Charlie, a horseback man, had never bothered to fix the road, not even the bad place entering the valley. She wondered if he'd had a purpose. So people wouldn't bother him...to keep hunters out. For a countless time she regretted that her visits with Charlie had been necessarily limited to the infrequent occasions when he rode by the ranch or when she saw him in Two Sands.

In her younger years, in the years that Louis lived, she used to go horseback to Charlie's and often Louis rode beside her. At this moment those happy days seemed lost in years, never existing.

The road, crawling from a draw, emerged smoothly upon high prairie. She drove faster. Now the road pointed straight for the valley's limestone rim, as if to leap off, and in breath taking suddenness dropped without warning to a narrow, twisting descent.

Braking hurriedly, Nellie felt her stomach go queasy.

Happy Adcock said, "Let me walk down there first."

"We can make it," she told him, but her heart was pounding fast.

"Wait a minute. You want to get wrecked?" He got out.

At sight of him, limping stiffly down the steep incline, her banked outrage fanned up. She'd ask Sid about that! As her eyes followed Adcock, she saw him reach a sharp crook in the road, just where the bluff changed and sloped and the hugging trail turned abruptly and plunged to the valley floor. Water pouring off the rim had gouged the wagon ruts still deeper, leaving treacherous furrows. And past the lip of the road, down the side, she could see clinging brush and the teeth of jagged rock. She trembled a little.

Happy Adcock studied the road a full minute before he returned. "I don't know," he puffed, shaking his head. "Might slip off. If we had my flivver, I'd risk it. But—"

"You walk down," she said. "I'll go slow."

"Slip off that high center, you're stuck for good. Get too far out ... " His shrug told the rest.

"I'm going down there, Happy." She scarcely recognized her own voice. "That's all there is to it."

"An' get yourself killed."

Her answer was to shift the gears into low.

Resigned, Adcock got in, his swollen face worried.

As easily as if she traveled this precarious road every day of her life, Nellie eased the car onto the narrow ledge and guided the right front wheel upon the high center between the scoured tracks. The trick, she realized, was to prevent dropping off into a deep rut, else they'd stick, nor to let her left wheels slide off the outer edge. They'd roll fifty feet, anyway. Rocks and brush.

Icy with sweat, she stiffened against looking down.

They edged cautiously downward, squeezed out on the far side, for there was no other possible way. From the corner of her eyes Nellie was conscious of dizzy space on her left, the gray limestone bluff on her right. She hardly breathed, fearful that her perspiring hands might slip from the wheel. Upright beside her, Adcock gripped the door.

They made it to the bend without mishap. Nellie stopped, pulled in her breath and exhaled.

"Doin' fine," he encouraged, not looking at her. He sat like a passenger, pointedly enjoying scenery.

"Maybe you better get out," she suggested again.

"Never walk when I can ride. One of my rules."

She smiled at that and slowly let out the brake. The roadster inched forward. She turned the wheel. Another few feet, she saw, and they'd have the road whipped ... It narrowed sharply, then, more than she'd thought from higher up ... The nose of the car came around, and with it her instant relief. They were creeping ahead, safety but a leap beyond.

A sickening lurch set her heart racing. Her visualizing eye swept to the left rear wheel, breaking the road's crumbling rim, as she halted the car. She froze, braced against the seat, her knuckles white on the steering wheel.

"Happy ... " she breathed. "Go see ... "

He slipped out and quickly she heard his steadying voice, "Turn right—sharp—give it the gas ... slow—"

She turned the wheel and fed the gas.

For a fleeting count the rear wheel seemed to dig the car lower. The next instant she felt the catching surge of traction, and the roadster bucked forward.

"Left! Back left! Watch them ruts!"

As Adcock yelled, the front end started dipping dangerously.

With all her strength she twisted. She heard rubber crunch gravel, became aware of a grabbing progress ... and the roadster shivered up and free. Instantly, she stopped on the spot and leaned back, weak with the lifting of fear.

Adcock climbed in, grinning big. "We're all right now. Nobody can drive like you, Nellie," he said admiringly. "Got to hand it to you."

Voiceless, she returned him a slack smile.

It was moments before she drove carefully down the slope and gained the bottom and pressed faster.

The dark tresses of the virgin trees along Yellow Dog creek blurred by, cool and quiet, shaded in loneliness. Above the roar of the motor, she heard the throbbing of the well across the creek. Soon the timber bent back and there was the house.

To her surprise she saw no one, not even a horse, when she had expected a swirl of activity. She parked near the porch and walked around to the kitchen side, Happy Adcock trailing. The presence of Charlie haunted her as she pushed open the door and entered. A moment later she jerked still, stunned by the litter meeting her eyes—the broken dishes and scattered pots, the overturned stove, the torndown pipe sections.

Her anger hardened and deepened, as striding, she went to the next disordered room. One glance sufficed. Swinging again to the kitchen she surveyed the wreckage, both angered and bewildered.

"Why in the world," Adcock echoed her mind, "would anybody do this?"

She could only stare; there was no answer. She gave him a dull look and wandered out alone, in the grip of a frightening reaction. Her head pounded. She was actually afraid now because of this thing she could not see, which followed poor Charlie even after death.

Shivering, she gazed at the solemn, mysterious distances. The sun was sinking, poised to plunge behind the far western ridge; sunset a slow-dying fire, bathing the prairie in crimson and yellow. She dreaded the thought of aproaching night. Wind, cool and clean, turned to a gathering murmur in her ears. Yet it came laden with an isolation which made her feel small and uncertain, on the verge of self-pity.

Swift shame engulfed her. Why, she wasn't even tryin' to help herself! Givin' in to everything that went wrong!

By the time she returned to the house she could almost smile at Happy Adcock, awkwardly wielding a broom. She took it from him and swept up the mess. That done, they righted the stove and, after a crude fashion, pieced the bent pipe together.

There occurred to her now the vital need to stay busy. She said, "I found some flour. I'll make bread and I think there's some coffee."

He grinned at the prospects and went to the front room. She could hear him rummaging about. He came back with a kerosene lantern. "Thought I saw one," he said, grinning again.

The lantern pleased her. "I want to keep that going all night, Happy. If Jeannette sees it, maybe she'll come in."

His face looked doubtful, but he said humoringly, "Good idea, Nellie."

During the sparse supper, she took only coffee. Later, they left the lighted lantern upon the table and turned from the smoky kitchen to the yard.

Evening had crept in, just the last fading light hazing the purpled western ridge.

"Why don't you get some rest?" he asked. "We're in for a long wait."

"Couldn't sleep if I tried."

He didn't argue the point, seeing it was futile.

As the moon climbed in its circle across the sky and changed the gloom to a pale silver, they sat in the car. In silence. Watching and listening.

Beginning night sounds held Nellie's attention. The weird, vibrant call of an unseen whip-poor-will, and she could imagine it drifting low, shadow-like, in the dimness. An animal scurried through the creek brush. High-wailing and drawn-out, a coyote cried from a distant place. . . .

Her body shook as if with cold. She had learned in school not to place stock in superstitions, but when you heard such sounds far out in these lonely hills, you thought that maybe what the old full-bloods said might be true.

The coyote sounded again. She located him, straight west, right on that ridge. And presently she heard a chorus of yipping answers, wild, far-scattered.

"Happy," she breathed more than spoke, "you believe what folks say about coyotes and people dyin'?"

He considered it a while. "You mean … same as it's a death sign when a bird gets into a house?"

"Yes. Only the coyote don't have to get inside. Somebody dies if he just howls in close to the house."

His disdainful snort was like a dash of cold water in her face. "Sure, I've heard that said. But I don't believe it. Don't tell me you do?"

She stayed hushed, and then she said heavily, "Sometimes you wonder."

"Nothin' more harmless than a coyote. To humans, that is. Anyhow, them coyotes are a long piece off, sounds like."

"They are … now." Her voice trailed away.

Happy Adcock turned all at once. She could feel his steady eyes.

A little later she sat up straight, listening intently. In from the north rolled a drumming over the ground, faint against the wind. The sound sharpened to distinctness, and she heard the shuffling cadence of horses scuffling tall grass and metallic jingles and squeaks of leather.

Walking rapidly from the car, she waited where the kitchen lantern thrust its yellow haze over the yard. Adcock, she felt rather than saw, hung back in the shadows behind her.

Horses padded into the glow, the pale light throwing a greasy sheen across the riders' faces. She recognized Tharp Kutch, Frank Rikker and Sid Tyson. Before she could speak, her husband demanded incredulously, "What in hell are you doing here?"

She told him, cutting it short as she sensed his severe disapproval.

His glance was a quirt laid upon her. "You shouldn't be here, Nellie." His quick eyes searched beyond her, questioning.

"Happy's with me," she explained, unsure of herself, and saw anger slide into her husband's face.

"Him! He let Myles Pearce get away!"

"I asked him."

"Don't give a damn! This is no place for you—him in particular!" She thought Tyson made an effort to control himself before the others; instead, his voice raged at her, "Nellie, you're being very foolish, coming here. Very foolish. There's a manhunt on. Pearce has already killed one man today. He won't give up without a fight. We're looking for Jeannette, too. Nothing you can do."

Till tonight, she'd always heard his arguments without show of anger, quietly accepting or turning them aside. But as he finished, a defiance stiffened her for the first time. "She's out there—alone. Can't you understand that, Sid? She needs me. If you find her, I'll be here."

Tyson lowered his eyes. Yet, when he spoke, it was bluntly. "I hate to say this, Nellie, but Jeannette's mixed up in Charlie's murder … She ran off when Bowdre tried to arrest her. Now she's wanted as bad as Pearce."

"She didn't kill Charlie!" Nellie, unknowing that she had moved, stood at her husband's stirrup.

"If she's not guilty, why'd she run?"

"It's a lie an' you're crazy to believe it!" She charged the posse with her blazing eyes. "Ever' damned one of you!"

They shifted uneasily in their saddles. Nobody spoke till Tyson, on a note of crackling sharpness, said, "Nellie—I'm ordering you to go home!"

"Well"—she knotted tighter—"I'm not going!" She held his stare, unyielding, realizing that she was fighting him openly for the first time in their short married life. Only once before had she bordered on it, over firing Kutch; never this far.

Tyson changed his tone persuasively. "You're upset. I can't make you leave, of course." He shrugged in a fashion that said she was denying his better judgment.

Nellie's mind raced ... caught. He'd talked like this often, it seemed now, in the injured voice when other people were around. Never before, though, had she discovered in it the hint of something false.

"Better swing back," a man raised his voice. "Work the north side."

"Plenty time, Bowdre," Tyson answered, irritation tracing the words. "Had to check the light, didn't we?"

"We have," Bowdre replied gruffly, "so let's go." He reined his horse and the others followed.

Tyson, the last to leave, pinned his unforgiving glance upon Nellie as he joined them.

Watching him go, she groped for the feeling she had once held for Sid Tyson. Somehow or other it wasn't there, and she fell into a deeper despair.

Minutes afterward, while she walked the yard, shots crashed in the direction of the posse. Pulled taut, she heard the distant running of horses. Pretty soon all sounds faded.

"Happy!"

"They've flushed somethin'," he said.

"If I had a horse!"

"Thank God you don't!" He was very firm. "We wait here."

She accepted that in her helplessness, though struggling, and continued to walk and scan the night. A thick and troubled lull seemed everywhere.

It was late when, at her insistence, Happy Adcock took an Indian blanket from her car and made himself a pallet upon the porch. Nellie checked the lantern for kerosene and paced the yard in an unending beat, till weariness ached in her. When she got in the car, thinking to sleep, her unrest built up stronger than ever, heightened by the fear of not knowing.

By the dragging hour she watched the sky change with a tortured slowness, and she heard the sad coyotes crying on the ridge. A whole chorus of them. She felt cold. ...

Along toward daybreak she must have dozed, because she came awake in struggle, her breath short, her tense muscles resisting. She'd been bad-dreaming, and she heard a sound quite close in the dream. A sound she couldn't locate—obscure, half-heard, and yet terrifying.

Bolt upright, she realized daylight approached. She could see Happy Adcock's form, rolled in the blanket. The reality of tangible objects brought her some relief, helped shatter the frightening aftermath of the bad dream. Almost, she convinced herself that she'd heard nothing unusual, just dreamed it.

Encouraged, she slid from the car seat. Some instinct stayed her from closing the door and making a noise.

Drowsy and dull, she found herself stalking in silence toward the kitchen. She passed the corner without stopping.

Then she heard it. A wailing bark, close, yet unseen. The wild notes flashed through her body and numbed her brain, freezing her with fear. She tried to call out, but her mouth was dry as dust. Her widening eyes shifted ... sank upon movement there by the kitchen door. A shape, gray and gaunt, low to the ground.

She heard her throat-torn scream at last, as it shrilled and the shape, slinking like a dog, wheeled and padded swiftly away. It dissolved at once, merging so soon with the mealy grayness that it seemed unreal, might never have been there at all.

She heard footsteps running, very real. "What is it?"

She managed to point, feeling foolish because the unreality persisted. "I heard him—I saw him, Happy!"

"Talk sense! You saw what?"

"A coyote—"

"I didn't hear a thing."

"You been asleep. Thought I was dreaming at first. Woke me up, I guess." She fixed her eyes upon him, appealing to him, hoping that somehow he'd prove her wrong. "But I wasn't dreaming," she heard herself insisting. "I saw him—right there—close by the house!"

He looked for himself. And when he turned, calmly, he could have been comforting a frightened child. "What if it was a coyote? They prowl all 'round. Come here 'most any night, I bet. Nobody's here. Hills full o' the blamed things."

"But I tell you he was by the house!" she argued, eyes wide.

"So what?"

"But you know what that means! Bad sign—somebody—"

His scoffing laugh rang out. "Aw, that don't mean a thing, Nellie. Just superstitious talk. Reckon I've seen fifty coyotes 'round houses in my time. Nobody even got the chills. . . . Come on. Let's start a fire. You need some coffee."

At his urging she walked to the kitchen, but the sense of foreboding followed her inside. He built a quick fire and made coffee, which she drank listlessly. Waiting soon became intolerable and she compelled herself to finish cleaning up the wrecked kitchen.

The early sun attracted her outside, into the fresh light showing everything in relieved detail. Seeing again that place by the house where the coyote had skulked, she wondered if she had actually sighted such a dreadful animal. The next moment she knew that she had.

Her unease returned and she threw herself into timekilling motion, either tramping around the house and continually watching, or going to the barn and corral and back.

At length she tired and came to a stand in front of him. "Happy—" she began and suddenly lost her words.

His head was cocked in a listening pose. He turned and gazed northeast.

She picked it out now—distant cracks of sound, like guns, muffled by the hills. A short silence. Another clap. The wind turned soundless.

"What can we do, Happy?"

"Nothin'. But I'd take that horse you spoke about."

She resumed her constant pacing, straining for sound, watching for some tell-tale sign. The sun rose higher. Now she tramped to her car, now back to the porch, where Happy Adcock slouched, smoking, an air of gravity in his hammered face.

At that instant she heard a horse in violent action. Heard it running like wild, a split pause before it flat-struck creek water. Heard its roiling passage and the mad hoofs dulled upon the spongy creek-bank soil, then suddenly sharper in racket upon hard-packed ground.

She stiffened to attention, arrested by a stabbing fear.

The pounding filled the yard, and she saw a rider tear around the house on a beaten-down horse, its mouth foaming.

Sid Tyson leaped down. His animal swayed on wobbly legs. Tyson's eyes cut to the car. He lunged one step, then pulled up, as if changing his intention at the final moment

"Jeannette...?" Nellie spoke, unable to go on.

Tyson seemed to inject control into his rapid breathing, to speak carefully. "She's all right."

Except, she thought, the words had an odd ring. Despite that, she clung to a hope and knew a humbling thankfulness. Tyson's figure blurred in her sight. Her knees felt weak.

"Nellie," Tyson said flatly, and something in the ring of his tone alarmed her. "Get in your car. Take me to town."

She did not answer for a moment, seeing in his face an inflexible decision. "But—I want to stay here," she said, shaking her head. "Wait for Jeannette—"

"You take me now."

A warning sparked in her mind. "Sid! Something's wrong!"

"Nothing is wrong."

His speech, so cool and weighted with persuasion, almost convinced her. She longed to believe him, and yet—

She asked suddenly, "You have to go now? Can't you wait—till I see Jeannette?" The warning winked again. "Sid, don't hold out on me! Don't!"

Beyond them she was vaguely aware of Happy Adcock.

"Don't ask questions." A mingling of haste and cold ferocity bristled in Tyson's eyes as he advanced toward her. "Get in that car!"

Before she could edge back, his hand clamped upon her shoulder. His roughness angered her. When she pushed at his grip, he spun her at the car.

"Leave her be, Sid—"

Nellie flung around, her breath caught. She'd forgotten Happy Adcock, who now stood in close, his long face stubbornly framed. He looked very old and thin.

"You!" For just a thin slice of time Tyson gave him his full contempt.

"You heard me!" Adcock spoke again, much louder, his voice ringing with a deep and vibrant emotion.

As Tyson took a menacing step, Nellie found her voice. "No, Sid—no! Take the car! You can have it!"

"He's on the run, Nellie! It's smeared all over him! Look at that horse—near dead!" Adcock was hurrying the words in the brief time left him. "He wants you—nobody else can drive that bluff road—"

Fast as he spoke, Happy Adcock barely got it all said.

Tyson drove a fist to his face. Adcock semed to totter tenaciously, as an old tree will when uprooted by violent wind, and then he fell.

The next thing Nellie knew was the blink of a pistol in her husband's hand, the cruel bluntness of the barrel being thrust into her. "Get in that car!"

Even then, she couldn't obey at once. She was seeing him in the cone of a new and terrible light, just now breaking through the cloud of her mind. Seeing a stranger—the pleasant mask ripped off and underneath an alien face, starkly ruthless and determined, every pretense gone. ...

Her dark world was spinning. She felt a sudden pain; his gun hurting her. His hand became a club, whapping and knocking her to the car. She found herself slammed behind the steering wheel. Her mouth hurt. She tasted blood, warm and salty.

"Sid ... don't ... " she tried once more, while a cold, tiny voice said nothing could stop him.

"Shut up! Drive—damn you!"

Mechanically, her foot pressed the starter. It made a protesting grind. As she prayed it would fail, just this one time, she heard the motor catch and roar. She shifted and the car lurched forward. She turned the wheel, turned short, and they were moving.

Sid held the pistol against her ribs.

As in another bad dream, she saw the trees flashing past, the empty prairie, felt the wind strong on her face, smelled the pungent grass. Her whole life, it seemed, was filing swiftly before her eyes. ...

Thus, beyond any reason, her mind lurched to Louis Garreau. His image so near that she could all but touch him, feel him, very close, somehow lending her courage, dispelling some of her terror of this total stranger beside her.

Snapped off, as if a part of her being also had ended, the smoothness of the valley floor ceased.

She saw the frowning slope beginning, the treacherous ruts winding and twisting upward. She slowed down, shifted to low gear. Hesitating, she made her final plea. "We can't go up there, Sid!"

"Came down it, didn't you!" he snarled and jabbed the gun barrel harder.

She winced away, crying in protest.

"You dirty squaw! I'll show you!" Raging, he raised the pistol. "I'll knock some sense into you—Goddamn you, I will!"

Out of nowhere, without thought, she blurted, "Why don't you get it over with—kill me!"

He darted a look down the road and swung back savagely. "There's time, b'God! Oughta throw you in the creek—it's close!"

His free hand batted her face.

A sudden daring made her bold as she tried vainly to fight him off. "Go on! I can swim out!"

"Not if I knock you in the head first!"

She continued to wrestle his arm, helpless against his impossible strength.

Then her whirling mind slowed and clung, fastened. She stared as she fought him, feeling herself growing weaker. Maybe it was how he said it, sort of popped out, and the way his thin lips locked down after, too late to hide it. Now, as he swayed over her, and she met the chilled brightness of his eyes, something snapped within her.

It was almost as if the whole thing had been simmering quietly in the farthest recess of her head these past few years—and, now released, had emerged in one lightning perception.

A cunning she did not know she possessed took hold of her. She smothered an accusation; she quit struggling slowly, as if beaten. Then, in a voice so dead and bare of feeling that it seemed not her own, she said, "Don't hit me again ... I'll do it."

"That's better!" Tyson dropped his fist, shoved the pistol against her. His eyes were queer and gleaming.

Nellie's breath sawed. She fed the car gas.

They bounced up grade, gaining speed despite the steep rise.

Soon she saw the ruts in close focus, where the road bent in its sudden, narrow turn.

"Slow down!" she heard him warn. "Wreck us, I'll kill you!"

She obeyed slyly, enough to silence him.

The turn loomed just before her. And at that moment, very close, she thought she heard an oil well pumping—its throbbing strangely like the frenzied beat of Indian camp drums.

Her jaw firmed. Every part of her came knotted.

All in one breath she gunned the car and yanked the wheel fully over and aimed for the edge ... Tyson's startled yell broke ... and even as she tried to twist away from him and failed, she felt the burning iron tearing her body and heard the thundering blast of his pistol.

The last she saw was Sid Tyson scrambling to get out ... the brush heaving up at her, the teeth of the waiting rocks.

But somehow she wasn't afraid, just fiercely resolved, because she knew by now that Sid Tyson had murdered Louis.

CHAPTER SEVENTEEN

RUNNING HIS HORSE across the yard, Myles first thought it empty. His sensation of lateness got heavier. He'd lost the car some minutes back, beyond the curving line of trees.

But as he came around the house, he saw a loose horse dragging reins and a man humped on the ground. He swerved violently that way and recognized Happy Adcock, head between his hands. At the nearing horse sound Adcock lurched to unsteady feet and peered dazedly.

"Happy!"

Adcock worked his distorted mouth without getting out a word. He swallowed and coughed, spat blood, swallowed again, and his speech seemed dragged up from the bottom of his chest, "Sid—he made 'er drive him," as if Myles should have known.

Myles felt his heart beating high as he searched the blood-shot eyes and saw something terrible filling them. "Made who, Happy? Who?"

"Nellie!"

"They can't get up that bluff road."

"Nellie can—"

Myles kicked the gelding with his boot heels, sending it forward in labored jumps. Turning the bend, he hunted his glance to the crooked scar of the old wagon trail slashing the distant lime-stone bluff. In the sun-shot brightness it showed empty. Being late, he'd expected that, and yet he kept thinking of the bad road.

Onward, across the creek, he saw the dark finger of the single derrick above the timber, its pumping a low, unbroken throb.

Now the bluff massed in size, sharpened in detail. Again, he scouted his vigilance up and along the road. It was hard to believe that a car could travel it, this washed out, though Happy and Nellie Tyson must have come down it. He dropped his gaze below the rim and, after a moment, looked away.

But his eyes went back suddenly, persisting, fixed on an unnatural object. Something was out of place, neither rock nor brush, about three-quarters down the bluff. ...

Sun flashed.

He pulled up, eyes hawked to the spot. Cutting sharply away from the valley road, he loped for the base of the rugged slope. He could see the location better now, but whatever it was the brush hid pretty well. He closed the distance and halted.

As he looked up, an awful certainty overwhelmed him. A car—what he could make out of it—lay shattered above, pinned against a boulder. He saw the twisted hood, blood red, like a bird's broken wing.

He came down from the saddle and started scrabbling up the uneven slant. Far above, the ragged edge of the road hung as a torn underlip across the limestone face. The tumbling drop inspired fear; thinking of Nellie Tyson, he felt a dread of what he might find.

It wasn't till the wreckage lay within paces that a delayed caution rang in his mind. His eyes pried at the crumpled metal. He climbed and stood quite close, considering the bloody seat cushion, catching the smell of spilled gasoline. The roadster's top was crumpled; a jagged piece of windshield still hung in place. This or the hood, he realized, had flashed light as he loped up the road.

Nelie Tyson filled his mind. He moved quickly and began searching away from the car, realizing he'd all but forgotten Sid Tyson. After a tramping swing through the brush and no success, he returned to the wreck with a puzzled haste. It was hard to believe that anyone could walk away from this.

The rocky ground, thinly grassed, drew his eyes to the driver's side.

He raised his gaze and there he found them ... spots ... overlooked in his hurry. The spots were bright red and they dripped into the brush, down slope, to the opposite side from which he'd approached.

In dread, in revulsion, he followed them and parted the first low brush clump. He stepped once and recoiled ... almost stumbling over Nellie Tyson.

She lay on her back, her left arm crooked, odd-angled. Stooping down, he discovered the great crimson blot high on her right side, along the ribs. But what knocked the bottom out of him was the fixity of the eyes in the broad full blood face ... strangely unmarked, peaceful, upturned to the warm Osage sun as if she'd wanted to face the light at the last.

He straightened slowly, shaken with the impact of this, seeing an Indian woman's face as she roared by on a dusty road, her impish wave; large and genial among her guests in the vast house under the giant cottonwoods. His mind went regretfully to Jeannette.

Then came a sudden unease. Had Tyson jumped from the car? Crawled off after the crash and left Nellie to die alone? Somehow he couldn't see Sid Tyson getting caught here. The man was too sharp, a back trail always handy.

Myles angered and swung a step, to be checked by a colliding sense of impropriety. If he left her here, concealed, anybody coming up would have the same trouble locating her that he'd had. There was plenty time for Tyson.

Grimly, he went about the painful business of lifting Nellie Tyson's heavy body and carrying it to the car. There he laid out his burden, though not yet satisfied, and decided that the rocky ground was unseemly for her. So he dragged forth the seat cushion and raised her upon it. Next, going again to the wreck, he found what he wanted—a gaudy Indian blanket.

He was drawing it over her when he noted again the crimson smear on her dress. The meaning slammed hard. How had he missed it—a bullet wound—thinking it was caused by the wreck?

He jerked up with a renewed fury. The little he could do now finished, he gave her a long look and scanned the defiant brush, up and down the bluff, back and forth. On impulse, he climbed a high rock.

Standing, feeling a pushing wind from the creek's direction, he circled his gaze to all sides. ... There wasn't a thing. By now, he suspected glumly, Tyson had taken cover or legged it over the bluff for Jeannette's ranch.

He was shifting his .attention to his grazing horse, and beyond, when he froze. Something had moved down there. He to fool a man. He blinked and squinted again, slowly beginning to doubt what his eyes insisted.

Even as he questioned himself, he saw a white-hatted man near the road, running jerkily. At the same moment it raced across Myles that he stood out like a sign post on the rock. He squatted down just as the man, limping but striding fast, spurned all concealment and ran for the horse.

Myles' pistol filled his hand, as if it had been there all the time. He fired at Sid Tyson, for it had to be Tyson, driven into the open by desperation.

Tyson kept going until the solid report banged against the hillsides. Then he stopped with the quickness of a trained horse haunched against rope slack, apparently unhurt. A fraction of a second after he whirled, off in a stiff run toward the road and the sheltering creek timber.

Myles put another bullet, high, knowing it futile at this distance, and jumped from the rock. Fighting brush to the base of the bluff, he reloaded quickly and mounted up.

Tyson, he saw, was just now entering the timber.

About halfway to the road, Myles heard a vibration drumming the prairie, then a shrill yell. He hauled in, taken back, seeing Frank Rikker swerving across on an over-used horse. By the way Frank scanned the bluff, he decided Happy Adcock had told him what to look for.

Running his horse in close, Frank called, "Myles! Kutch spilled the works back there! He—"

"It can wait," Myles cut him off bluntly. "Nellie's dead—Tyson got away—come on!"

"Dead! My God!" Frank slumped as if from a blow.

"Come on!" Myles repeated, swinging his horse. "He's in that timber!"

Frank Rikker followed, his face stricken.

Abreast, they soon rode the bluff behind them. As the twilight shading of the trees showed, Myles felt a clubbing caution.

"Space out," he called. "Watch sharp."

Frank swung wider.

Myles slowed as they came under the timber. In the dingy shadows the creek cast a dull glimmer. He didn't like it, this going in bold as daylight and not knowing. He thought rapidly of Tyson's maneuver, trying to fathom its intent. Nothing past the creek but brush and the old pumper. Tyson, curbed by a game leg, would be thinking of a place to hide—a way to ride out. . . .

It happened all too fast for Myles. The bullet's whip, the sagging give of his gelding, the crack of the shot. This, in a twinkling, before he glimpsed the spurt of flame from Tyson's gun in the thicket across the creek. . . . Then the stumbling fall and the scream of his wounded horse, the smash to the leaping-up ground.

Stunned for an instant, Myles sighted blurred light. Swinging his eyes, he saw blood streaming from the downed gelding's head.

A gun crashed near. Once, twice. Very close together. Frank, he thought.

Then, silence. As Myles swayed up to look, he saw a horse rushing across and Frank getting down swiftly.

Dragging to his feet, Myles felt his head clear. He heard Frank swearing. "Got away—that damned brush!" His eyes pecked over Myles. As if satisfied Myles wasn't hurt, he wheeled toward his horse.

Myles, lunging low, was there an instant before him, before he realized what he was doing, jamming himself between Frank and the stirrup. "Slow down! Rush out there, Tyson'll blow your head off!"

"Get back from that horse!" Frank's mouth flattened in a bitter line.

Myles stood fast. He said slowly, "Listen to me. You hustle back after Bowdre," and heard how superior he sounded without wanting to be. The older brother, talking down to the younger. But cold, matter-of-fact reasoning told him that Frank's recklessness, almost wild, was a dangerous thing.

"Bowdre, hell! Sid's gettin' away!" Frank's glance flecked to the creek and back, suddenly bright with suspicion. It seemed, then, that they had retracked in time. That they stood outside the Flint Hills dance hall, while Buck Hoyt screamed on the floor inside, while Frank spiked his wounded pride at Myles. "You're stallin' me!" Frank challenged. "Won't you ever learn?"

"No—not that." The only real clarity Myles had was of Jeannette coming into Frank's arms as Frank ran through the brush above the ravine. This guided him in a slow but sure-feeling way. "Just better wait on Bowdre—the posse."

"An' let Sid skip!"

Frank, closing in with his words, swept up his hand to shove Myles aside, and Myles knocked it down and grasped Frank's shirt in his fist. During one fugitive moment they struggled, rigid bodies straining, wrestling away from the horse.

Myles said hoarsely, "Don't be a fool—why take the chance—now?"

"You won't stop me!" Frank grunted, breaking free.

Myles eyed him, breathing deeply. His mind was a pincers, closing now upon a single object. "No," he said, dropping his hands. "I can't. I'm wrong. We're both going, Frank."

Frank's mouth fell. "You mean it?"

"Sure..." Myles waited. It was a dirty thing. He saw it coming.

For a pause Frank Rikker's attention stayed upon the horse. He was saying hurriedly, "Better leave..."

Myles' big fist, his shoulder weighted behind it, cracked Frank on the point of his chin. Frank's head snapped back. His eyes turned glassy. He fell like a loose log and did not move.

Without another look, Myles swung from him and started wading the rock-bottomed creek, his loathing for what he had done squeezed inside him. He gained the spongy bank, climbing out beside a lightning-shattered cottonwood, and faced into a steady wind. It grew stronger as he advanced into the open.

No more than a minute or two had elapsed since Tyson's gun flamed from cover, and yet the time seemed measureless. Off to the left he saw framed the point of ridge where he had routed the rifleman after Dog was killed.

The sound of the pumping unit on the wooden rig, laboring between creek and stony ridge, built to an ominous chant. He spied a storage tank far back, the faint trace of a road straggling off south.

He walked in tall grass, dry and crisp under his boots, and entered a waist-high wilderness of brush. He searched his eyes wide and decided Tyson would scorn the ridge. What ruled it out was the man's desperate need for a horse. He had to stick on this side to rate a chance, maneuver around. Myles' boots swished softly. The derrick, some hundred yards ahead, shaped nearer against the backdrop of blue, windy sky and the glowering ridge.

Suddenly, everything got too simple. Tyson in the brush, merely waiting? No, it didn't add up. Myles worked his glance here and there, wondering at the emptiness.

He had no notice of warning. Smoke puffed. His eyes centered there, his nerves snapping. But he could find no man in motion. As he stared, more smoke flurried up near the first, this side the rig.

Hardly had he halted when the smoke billowed and the wind-fanned fires took snarling hold. They ate steadily, hungrily, rushing faster now, leaping, summer-dry brush and matted grass cracking in his ears. It rose to a roaring upon the stout wind.

His reaction was a stubborn, unwilling shrinking toward the creek. And yet he felt himself balking, still playing for position, moreover angered. He'd fought prairie fires before, swinging burlap sacking and bedding, but this one had the added element of complete surprise. He'd been tricked.

He angled off almost before he understood his purpose, trying to skirt the first fire before it widened. He ranged left, running, the rig by now a confused shaft in the lifting smoke. The wind seemed stronger and the two fires, joined up, licked forward in a red wall, throwing up grayish clouds of showering sparks.

At once the heat feel got closer.

For a dozen long strides he matched the fire's march. Then he saw the reddish column dart ahead, like an angry tongue, outdistance him.

With a frustrating smarting of defeat, he broke pace. A warning heat whipped his face. His breath shortened. He had to turn.

Reluctantly, as a leaf before the wind, he reversed and took the only remaining direction. He sprinted for the creek, guided by the line of timber, hacking hard, his bandana matted to mouth and nostrils. Step by step, he felt the hot breath lessen against his back and neck. The brush thinned. He stumbled under the trees and a coolness took him in, though smoke was even beginning to gang in here.

He shook in a sudden fit of coughing, his lungs raw. When he could look around, his position startled him, for he'd come out some distance down valley from Frank and the horse.

Another qualm jarred. He saw it late, clearly defined. Tyson, slipping behind the smoke screen, could make for Frank's horse. The realization clawed at Myles.

In violent haste, he drove into a woolly world of windblown smoke, gray and blackish, swirling and layering the woods. It produced an instant eerie, floating sensation, aroused his distrust. He stifled a cough, had difficulty locating trees just rods ahead. The overhanging smoke, piling up and dammed by the timber, made the water appear greasy, unreal...

In a little while he came to the place where he thought he had crossed, and knew for certain when he saw the broken cottonwood, its shattered fiber like exposed bones.

But, searching the other side of the creek, his eyes ran against the same unvarying gloom. Not trusting it, he stepped to the bank's edge and peered again, right and left. In his fixed watchfulness, he noticed how the wind kept roiling the smoke.

It was as one of these whimsical shifts occurred that he saw the indistinct frame of the horse. He looked lower, hopefully, but Frank wasn't there.

He jerked uncertainly, with a condemning fear. It sent him prowling farther into the timber. He started to call, only to silence it as heedless. Everywhere he looked the gray smother gathered, filing upon his nerves. Beyond a few feet, he realized now, you couldn't tell a man's face. But there was one concrete thing he could fix to, and that was the horse, the stake in this waiting game.

So he bent to the creek again and stayed fast, where he could eye the animal. He stood long moments, bothered hard about Frank....

When he first felt it, he never knew. It came by degrees— an obscure sensitiveness to sound, a whispering crush of dead leaves, maybe, a pressure of movement that he could not see. His senses hinged abruptly upon a noise, behind to his left.

Spinning, he saw a shape—two shapes, unrecognizable—emerge in the pall. The nearest man lunged, his back turned to Myles. A shot blasted apart the stillness and a voice cried out. Another report slammed as though late.

One figure spilled down. The other, beyond, dissolved into the smoke, pounding away. Running over, Myles heard the boots strike briefly and fade.

He knew before he saw the turning face, knew it with a racked inward sinking.

Slackness was dulling Frank Rikker's features. He jerked an arm, trying to point.

Myles bent down, hit by a damning self-reproach.

"Damn it—go on!" Frank tried to twist up, then flopped back.

Myles shook his head. But as one part of him demanded that he stay, another said this was the time, if ever. He stood slowly. He looked at Frank, both fear and a great killing anger shaping.

Then he moved.

He was stomping on, reckless to hurt, to kill, when realization exploded: Why, Tyson had come up behind him—had him!

He dodged from tree to tree and heard the bellows of his jerky breathing. Some yards and he stopped, fearful he'd lost his man. An urgency prodded him forward, fueling a wildness that he knew was bad. He hunted into a thickening screen, now and then pausing to listen, keeping in mind the location of the horse.

Still, he met only grayness. So he waited again, slowly circling his glance.

He picked out sound. He skirted a tree and halted, all weight upon the balls of his feet. The sound magnified to boots, and Myles turned a tree, seeking to locate the source of these sounds. He took a deep gulp of wind and held it. He thought he heard Tyson, but as yet he could not place him. The boots padded up creek, dimming, and suddenly they beat back.

Then he knew Tyson was circling, aiming for the horse he had to have. As Myles stilled, his senses leaped to a muffled cough, barely audible. Straight ahead, now.

But he heard nothing more. He had the tingling that Tyson had finished running ... that he waited.

It had to come. Myles, behind a tree, stepped around it.

Motion pinned his eyes. A head and shoulders formed in the smoke, a body slowly pivoting.

He froze, not understanding why he didn't shoot. Then Sid Tyson faced him head on. For a second he stood there. He had lost his hat. Soot rimmed his face, blackened his white, benign hair. He blinked. He stood tough and dominant. His eyes showed a relentless will.

These impressions flashed and died as Tyson's arm came up with a mighty jerk. Myles heard his own weapon roar just before Tyson's. He felt his pistol jump in his hand.

Tyson broke his stance, driven backward one step. His gun wavered oddly. Straining, he sought to lift it level again ... did, almost, and the bullet spanged dirt at Myles' boot tips.

Without feeling, Myles fired again, and again.

Tyson seemed to droop, his legs crumbling. He fell all at once, upon the gray mantle wrapping in these woods. He rolled over, face up, his eyes already dead. Lumped there, he looked old as sin.

Staring, Myles felt something akin to regret, only that and short-lived. Now thought of Frank Rikker, somewhere in the murk behind him, erased it completely.

Sick with dread, he wheeled blindly and ran dodging through the silent, dismal timber, wondering why Frank Rikker didn't call to him.

CHAPTER EIGHTEEN

WIND, RAIDING OUT of the southwest, came shouting and blustering against the thin frame building; gusts squeezed between the warped wall boarding and flung a freshness into the stale air.

Myles Pearce stirred and saw sunrise breaking new and dazzling over Two Sands and the forest of spaced derricks whose gas flares flickered steadily, the life-flame of these great rounded hills. He left the chair and flexed out his stiffness and rested his eyes upon the awakening world outside, upon this beginning of another day.

A smoothness spread to his stubbled face as he stepped to the window, humbled, loaded With a boundless gratitude. He let his attention wander again, at will, and it swept to the sunlight and the shining promise he read there somehow.

He thought, It's a sign—a good sign.

For he had prayed, to be sure with an awkwardness, but he had prayed from his depths and he had seen the hardwon answer.

Not long back, in that eramped room, he had watched Frank Rikker crawl away from the long shadows ... watched him falter, and then slowly, tenaciously fight into the light.

Bone-tired, Myles eased down to the chair and leaned back, dozing at once. He slept a considerable time, because when he opened his eyes the sun stood notches higher. He heard subdued voices and steps; these, he knew, had aroused him. He turned his head.

Dow and Sarah Rikker stood in the hall, just outside Frank's room. Suddenly to Myles they seemed much older than when he'd left the Flints, older in a manner that shocked and hurt.

He got up swiftly, with alarm. His mind froze to a single terrifying conclusion. He stared at them, afraid to speak—to ask.

Then Dow Rikker smiled and Myles relaxed, something like cool wind upon him.

Dow Rikker's body was wide, slung on a solid frame, barely heavy across the belt. His square face showed a weathered network of wrinkles, as so much hand-tooled leather worn over. His hawk's eyes, tilting up now, were direct and clear. They singled Myles out ... just as they had that day in the nester's yard.

"Long night," Dow sighed, though he seemed invincible to any weariness. "But we made it."

Myles turned to Sarah Rikker, noting the pleasant, sun-browned face. Maybe he just imagined it, but at this moment she made him think of the same day, when Dow had brought him home; when, with one look of her fine eyes, she'd given him complete acceptance and love and new backbone.

"We let you sleep," she said, softly humoring. "You could do with more, but Frank wants to see you now."

He stepped quietly inside the room. He glanced to the bed and was startled upon seeing Frank's eyes closed, till he saw the even rise and fall of Frank's breathing. He went across, one boot scuffing the floor despite his careful approach.

Frank's eyes opened instantly. His square, unshaven face made a pale wedge against the pillow, but his eyes told the story. They were bright and alert, intent with a mocking interest. This was the Frank Rikker of old, except the old discontent was missing. "You couldn't sneak up on a stump," he grinned weakly.

"Thought you were sleeping."

"Had all I want for a long time. Too much makes a man think." A grimace that wasn't physical pain passed across his face. "I told the folks everything. Pretty humble pie for me."

"Even the little act you pulled on Tyson, there in the timber?"

Frank's eyebrows lifted innocently. "Any fool can get shot."

"Not the way you did, deliberately. Tyson was coming up behind me. I didn't see him." Myles paused and drilled him with a severe look. "You took the bullet he meant for me, threw yourself in front. I realized it later."

"Man, if you ain't the smart one," Frank scoffed. "Guess I just happened to lean into it. He broke out of that smoke so fast I wasn't ready—he was. Anyhow, maybe that makes us even for Buck Hoyt. Guess he'd a-cut me up plenty."

"Forget Hoyt. I'd like to."

Frank's eyes, wandering a moment, turned soberly to Myles. "Dad says you got Sid Tyson."

Myles merely nodded.

"Sid framed me," Frank said, slow and bitter. "One night in Two Sands after he hired me...I got drunk...tangled with Ed Yancey in a card game." He stopped for breath.

"You're talking too much," Myles warned.

"Just started. This is long overdue. See, Sid'd had trouble with Yancey over a grass lease, so Yancey was on the prod. Well, he licked me good. You know me, I couldn't let a man get away with that. I took on some more drinks an' hunted him up. We met in an alley, I remember that. I whipped him, knocked him out. Rest of it's pretty hazy. But when I sobered up in a boarding house, Sid and Kutch were in the room. Sid claimed I'd knifed Yancey—murdered him!" Frank's mouth twisted. "Of course, they hadn't told anybody, bein' my friends. I said I never fought that way. But Sid said look at my knife...I did—it had blood on it. So...we made a deal."

"Bowdre says Kutch killed Yancey."

"That's right. He told us on the ridge, before he died. Kept ravin' about Sid. How Sid ran out on him. Kutch murdered Yancey with my knife! See, this whole business was planned, Myles....Sid had Wiley fire the pasture to draw Jeannette and the hired man away from the house. Sid, knowin' Charlie, figured he'd head for home first chance he got."

"Jeannette almost fooled them," Myles reminded. "She took Charlie to the pasture. But he walked home and got a horse." He looked at Frank and asked suddenly, "You mean you didn't know Charlie's number was up?"

"Not right then. Sid never let me in on the inside. But I realized something was up that day. I followed Kutch. Lost him in the timber. Then I met Bowdre along the road. After we found Charlie, I knew I had to lie you into jail somehow, because you were in the way."

"How's that?"

"You upset the cart. Sid didn't want Jeannette to marry. A husband would tangle up her estate. Sid thought you were gettin' serious about Jeannette. That's why he was hell-bent after you. And why I tried to get you away from it."

A gratefulness spread over Myles. "You just about did."

"Had to. I knew Kutch was going to bushwhack you. On the ridge he said—"

Myles waved him to silence. "Take it easy. Bowdre told me 'most everything. How Tyson killed Louis Garreau. Knocked him in the head—tossed him in the creek. Made it look like he'd drowned in that storm."

"You see the pattern, don't you?" Frank persisted. "Charlie was next after Jeannette's father. Charlie had willed his land to Jeanette, his headright to Nellie. See, Kutch said Sid drew up Charlie's will for him and knew all the provisions. Once Charlie and Jeanette were taken care of, Sid would get his hands on everything through Nellie." He rolled his head regretfully. "Poor Nellie ... she never knew."

"Frank, we'll never know what Nellie thought, but Tyson tipped his hand when he forced her into the car. Happy saw that. She wrecked the car. Guess that was when Tyson shot her."

Frank nodded miserably.

"There's a lot of loose ends. Caldwell, for one, Jeannette's hired hand. What happened to him? That's one thing I failed to ask Bowdre about."

"Kutch said Sid bought him off. With you in jail and Caldwell gone, that left Jeannette alone, set her up for Wiley to handle. But she ran off, thank God. According to Kutch, Wiley tried to murder her once before."

"Makes sense now," Myles said. "He worked me over in the barn the first day I went out to Jeannette's. He was waiting for her."

"Kutch said so. You messed that up, too."

"Walked into it, you mean."

Frank Rikker fell silent, his breathing short.

"You said there was a deal between you and Tyson," Myles went on, and wondered at his own uneasiness. "What was his price to keep his mouth shut about Yancey?"

For the first time, he thought, Frank seemed reluctant to talk.

"Well—" Frank began, and Myles saw his unwillingness, his inward struggle. "My job ... was to court Jeannette. Keep her busy, so nobody else would horn in. Worked all right at first. Kind of a game. Till things got out of hand. Guess both of us were lonesome." He paused and Myles heard his uneven breathing. "I went all the way, Myles. I—I told her I loved her. She—"

'Say it," Myles said, fighting an old feeling, old and futile.

Frank forced out the words. "Might as well. ... She said—well—she said she loved me. Only ... "

Frank broke off, suddenly relieved. He stared at the door, and Myles turned to see Tom Bowdre and Happy Adcock coming in. They tiptoed forward, hats held awkwardly.

Frank grinned. "Come on in here," he invited in a surprisingly strong voice. "Let me hear those spurs jingle, Tom."

They relaxed at that and rawhided Frank with remarks about the spoiling influence of lazy hospital life on a riding man.

"Doc says I'll carry this lead from here on," Frank told them.

"Just one bullet?" Bowdre mocked, "Hell, son, I pack three chunks myself. One won't bother you. Only time this lead mine I got ever acts up is when it turns off cold or right damp. Then I just stick by the fire an' add to my pitch winnin's."

Happy Adcock cleared his throat. "Can't make no such he-man claims to fame myself," he joined in, "but I've flipped a fliv-ver or two."

Thus the joshing ran. When Bowdre and Adcock broke it up after some moments and started drifting toward the door, Myles decided Frank had talked enough. As he moved to fol-low, Frank stirred. He reached upward suddenly, an instinctive act.

Myles gripped his hand and the past dropped away. It became tenuous, insignificant, nothing, and an inexpressible feeling filled the room. Myles tried to swallow, but his throat stuck. He went to the door and managed to grin back, "See you later, Leadville," and turned to go out.

Frank's voice stopped him. "One more thing . . ".

"You're mighty windy," Myles said.

Frank ignored him. "Remember when you got jumped in Two Sands? The night I was supposed to meet you?"

"I'm not likely to forget it."

"That"—Frank colored—"was me. I climbed you."

"You!" Myles felt a jolt of surprise. "I thought Kutch . . . " He pinned Frank with a swift, knowing glance. "But you always fought in a crouch, like Jack Dempsey. I should have guessed."

"Just another one of my crock-headed notions—"

"Don't apologize. I know—you did it to keep me out of trou-ble. I don't feel so bad about that punch at the creek now. You had it coming. Shut up," he said gruffly, "and get some sleep." He stepped to the door.

Again, Frank's voice caught him, "Say, Myles!"

"Now what?"

"Think I'll stay in the Osage. What do you think?"

FRED GROVE

Not long ago, Myles realized, he'd have spoken for the Flints.
Now he said, "Up to you. ... You'd be a fool not to stay."

"Thanks." Frank grinned. "Believe I will."

"You lucky cuss," Myles told him. "Which reminds me. Dow
tells me Laura Bailey married Buck Hoyt the other day."

He turned suddenly through the doorway, not looking back.
He'd spoken without revealing himself; that was the thing.

Bowdre waited with Adcock. "There's one boy what'll do to
ride the ridges with," the agency man said, nodding back. He
seemed overly thoughtful as he paced toward the vacant end of
the hall. "Poor time for business."

"Good time as any," said Myles, following curiously. "What
is it? Do I have to stand trial?"

"No. That bunch is paid for."

Myles shrugged.

Bowdre spoke with a certain hesitation, "Before long I'm
retiring to a little ranch down in the Hominy country. Nobody in
mind yet for my job, 'less you'd be interested." A shrewd respect
changed his habitually dogged look. "You've got a lawman's name
now, whether you know it or not."

Myles sobered, feeling his momentary elation go. "I'm not
proud of it—three men." Although meaning well, Bowdre had
hit center one of the sore spots within him. Till Bowdre spoke,
he hadn't realized how it had spread and ached to all corners of
him, influencing his thinking and outlook. He said, half musing,
"Wonder if I'll ever sleep easy again?"

"You did it the hard way," Bowdre acknowledged in understanding. "But you did it—you had to. That's what counts. Takes a
man. Sometimes that's the only way. Don't ever look back on the
cold tracks you've made. ... Well—how about it?"

Myles took two steps before he answered. "Thanks. But it
wouldn't work for me. I'm just a brush hand. My game is cows.
Whitefaces. I like to watch the tallow grow."

"You don't have to decide now."

"No, but I have. Besides, I'll be pulling out in a few days, now that Frank's on the road. My folks just closed the door and rushed down here. I'll have to go home, see about things, while they stay with Frank."

"You'll be back?"

"To see Frank, yes."

"Reckon you will," Bowdre said oddly, cocking an eye. "Sooner than you think." Something edged into his face; it passed quickly at Myles' blank look. "Frank gonna stay?"

"Looks that way."

"Don't blame him. Guess he'll be a family man before he knows it."

A silence settled, broken by Happy Adcock. "Myles, you don't leave Two Sands 'less'n I drive you to the depot."

"That's a promise, Happy."

High-heeled steps, light and quick, sounded in the hall. There was a familiar rhythm to the walk.

Steady tremors began beating through Myles. Glancing up, he saw Jeannette Garreau and Savannah Tyson enter the hall and pause before Frank's closed door. They turned questioningly to Dow Rikker, who waved them inside.

Jeannette hesitated, then slowly opened the door. Light fell across her in a rich glow. It caught the shading of her drawn face, her high, rounded cheekbones and her full, softly turned mouth, the shadowed pools of her dark eyes. She carried herself straight, self-possessed, as if steeled against grief.

Like yesterday, he thought, at the services.

At the last minute he'd driven the high-heeled road to Nellie Tyson's great house under the guarding cottonwoods. In time, he learned, to follow the long procession of cars across the ocean of prairie, to the grassy knoll where the tattered American flag snapped in the wind. Always the wind, he thought. And there he saw a blanketed full-blood woman, ancient and scarred, turn her despairing face to the clear sky. A wail tore from her throat, primitive and desolate.

Shaken, Myles couldn't help thinking of the violence that seemed to dog these peaceful people.

Soon everything was finished and he drove toward Two Sands, hurried by the gnawing fear for Frank. But as he passed the house, something told him that he also belonged with Jeannette. Earlier, when she first came to the hospital with Savannah, he had spoken the clumsy, futile words you always said and he'd held her briefly, her body numb as putty.

Stepping back, he was struck by what he discovered in her haggard face, a mingling of withdrawal with grief. The look slid away almost as he noted it, but he had seen it—undeniable, clear as noon sunlight.

Just now, the voices of Bowdre and Adcock registered, and he realized he'd all but forgotten them.

The three of them were standing there a short time later, when Jeannette and Savannah left Frank's room and spoke to the Rikkers. Bowdre and Happy moved over. Myles started to follow, then halted as Savannah, slim and grayeyed, came gracefully across to him.

He faced her with a stab of reluctance and considerable sympathy. Strange, in the light of events, that she should be closest now to Jeannette. They seemed like sisters, drawn together by a common tragedy.

"Savannah," he said earnestly, "I'm sorry it has to be this hard for you."

"You needn't be." A bitterness—it seemed long-standing—flashed in her eyes. "Sid was no father to me and I was never a daughter to him. My mother died of a broken heart. He used her as a stepping stone—just that—because she had respect" Quickly, as if sensing a question, she said, "I'm sure people are wondering now why I stayed at Nellie's."

"Your business."

"Not entirely. I wish people could know. Nellie was very good to me and I liked her. She needed someone, with Jeannette gone. I tried ... " She bit her lip. "I hope I helped her just a little. But I'm afraid I didn't, much. Looking back at things, I suppose no one could. Not really ... That's one reason why I stayed."

"You helped her in ways you'll never know," he insisted. "Now you're giving Jeannette a big lift." He stopped on a surge of regret. "Something I haven't done."

"How could you," she said quietly, "low as Frank's been?"

He thanked her with his eyes. Yet he couldn't understand the obscure expression she threw him.

He stood in silence, aware that Jeannette had left the others and stood near. Savannah excused herself somewhat hurriedly. "See you at the car," she said and was gone before Jeannette could speak.

They were alone. Voices made a distant murmur.

"Frank's out of the woods now," he told her. "He's going to be all right."

She returned him a smile and the shadows around her eyes seemed to lessen. "I'm thankful. For a while we didn't know, did we?"

"Touch and go. And did you hear what he did, Jeannette? There at the last, in the timber?"

"Tom Bowdre told me."

"Frank wouldn't say a word. I owe him everything."

She looked up, a slow smile forming upon her lips. "I know we all owe you something, too." The smile hovered just momentarily, replaced by an inscrutable expression. "I haven't yet thanked you for what you did."

"It's over," he said and this was as close as he could come to telling her how it had ended between him and Sid Tyson, there in the smoke-shrouded woods. He longed to forget. He had no high notions, no feeling of triumph. He felt a slackness inside, his temper burned out. Watching her, he recognized the shadow of something again, the turning away from him. Of a sudden he thought he understood.

"Jeannette," he said, "you're not worried about what happened that morning when we saw the posse, are you?"

"I'm sorry and ashamed. I showed I didn't trust you."

"Hard to think otherwise, wasn't it? Forget it! You did what seemed right at the time. That's all any of us can do. Believe me, I know."

Her face softened, quickly grateful. She spoke in a voice that affected him deeply. "You look tired, worn out. Why... why not come out to the ranch next day or two?"

He stared at her, powerfully tempted. His breathing locked. Wind shook the building, not roughly, just playfully pushing and capering on to the next row of hills. In these few days, he thought, I've come to know this country and the people in it and now I'm leaving it behind.

Everything in him felt empty and meaningless.

"Thanks. But I'm going back pretty quick. Maybe tomorrow." He told her why. His reasons sounded lame, like an excuse. He ended up wondering why he'd even bothered to explain, when he knew he was running. "I'm sure Frank will stay," he concluded.

"Yes, I expect he will." Her face revealed nothing.

"So long, Jeannette." He had spoken before he realized his intention.

She held out a slim hand, and he looked down into an expressionless face. He wished she hadn't done that, because, when he took it, the demanding desire to pull her to him became a mighty struggle. She stood only a step away, yet he got the stirring scent of her all over again. Her eyes mirrored a quietness, neither rejecting for asking.

His grip tightened. The deep pools altered swiftly, no longer unreadable. Except for that night by the abandoned rig, he'd never really slipped inside her guard. And although she had reason for coming into his arms, for wanting to fool him later, he had looked beyond the barrier. He had experienced briefly her overpowering sweetness, her strength and gentleness, and understood how fiercely giving her spirit could burn. He glimpsed these secret gifts again, for an instant, and he knew then that he saw them for the last time.

But even as he discovered all this once more, her expression shifted. She released her hand and stood back, cool and self-possessed again, and lovely in a way that rocked him.

"You mean good-bye, don't you?" she asked. There was nothing whatever for him in her tone, nothing.

"Guess that's it. Hard to say."

Then she left him, her passage light and rapid. He heard the hall door close behind her, between them. He heard the car roar and leave. Still, he stayed fixed.

The finest part of his life had gone. He knew that, knew it with the piercing clearness of loss. In the next moment, in his mind's eye, he saw himself as a wanderer across infinite distance who, having once sighted the wonderful green promise of a longed for destination, had now lost it. For the rest of his time he would search for it, but always it would elude him.

Seeing Happy Adcock drive up outside the Osage Hotel, Myles Pearce walked from the lobby and hoisted his grip to the back seat. "Let's go," he said and climbed in. Within the hour he had said his good-byes to the Rikkers and left with the satisfaction that soon Frank would be a difficult man to keep abed.

"Where's the stampede?" Adcock complained. "Twenty minutes till train time."

"Way you drive we'll need it."

Adcock grinned and worked the pedals. The flivver jumped along the street, the traffic scattered at this hour. He swung around a string of plodding teams and waved to the drivers.

The dull sandstone buildings gave ground to frame shacks, new yellow in the sun. As the glistening tracks and squat depot appeared ahead, Adcock said in a conversational tone, "Got your ticket?"

"Not yet. Why?"

"Oh. Just wondered."

When they parked by the empty, wind-swept platform, Myles stepped out and reached into his pocket for the fare.

"Your money's no good today," Adcock stopped him, his voice sharp.

"How you expect to buy that big car if you haul folks free?"

"Got it all fixed up." Adcock winked broadly. "The Osages are gonna adopt me into the tribe."

Myles laughed. "Well, much obliged, Happy. Thanks—thanks for everything." They shook hands and Myles waited a moment, expecting Adcock to drive off.

"Any idea when you'll be back?" Adcock asked, still lingering.

"Can't say for sure."

"Uh-huh. Well, don't forget your ticket."

Myles shot him a faint scowl of exasperation. "You're mighty anxious to get rid of me. Wet-nurse all your passengers this way?"

"Now don't hurt my feelin's," Adcock replied with mock injury. "You know how sensitive I am. But I've seen fellers get lost between the depot an' train—in broad daylight."

With that, he backed the flivver to a spraddled halt and, waving, rattled off toward town.

Afterward, it seemed unusually quiet and empty around Myles. His depression returned, and he took up the grip and walked slowly to the protruding telegraph window. Just the chatter of the sending key made him restless, uncertain. He swung inside and over to the grilled window.

A pale, white-haired man glanced up. He worked the lever a while longer, finally shuffled to the window.

Moments after, his ticket purchased, Myles was turning to go when the station agent's eyes seemed to bulge and hang.

He blurted on a note of excitement, "Say! Ain't you that fella Pearce—Myles Pearce?"

Myles grew rigid, pinned motionless by the terrible awe he saw. It was almost fear.

Without a word, he wheeled and shouldered through the door, outside to the platform. Dropping his grip, he put his back to the wind and rolled a cigarette with trembling fingers, all at once apalled by an oppressive knowledge. This would follow him over the years, wherever he went. He could not avoid it by running, and he was running now.

He glanced to the bold hills, but somehow they lacked promise today. Then he realized it wasn't the hills at all, for they were the same. The change had occurred within himself this past handful of days. He thought of Wiley and Kutch and Tyson, and saw them as blurred, agonized faces, and he even pitied them a little. What was it Bowdre had said about having a name? He felt utterly alone and weary.

Somebody drove a car over the crossing and pulled in at the platform. He scarcely noticed.

A car door slammed. Steps began on the platform, moving slowly across it.

"Myles."

He jerked and found her behind him. His eyes ran over her.

Jeannette Garreau wore a rose-colored dress and a closefitting hat. He remembered that she'd had on a dark dress at the hospital. Still, the transformation from riding breeches, work shirt and boots to traveling clothes startled him.

"Well—" he said and glanced around. "Anybody with you?"

"No."

"You're ... taking the train?"

"Depends ... " A sliver of feeling passed across her face. "After we talked at the hospital, I thought I'd gone as far as any woman could. I wanted you to stay. I tried to show you. But you couldn't

see it. And later I waited for you to come—and you never did."
Her shoulders moved expressively. "So ... here I am."

"It wasn't that. You and Frank—"

"I don't love Frank. I never did."

"You said you loved him. You told him."

Jeannette breathed deeply. "I know ... I thought I did—once.
But it just wasn't in me or in him." Impatience touched her.
"Frank wants Savannah. Has from the start—except they didn't
really know it. Not till all this happened."

"Frank never said—"

"But he did! A little while ago. I just left them." She waited
and he saw a flash of her will, of her self-possession. Then something mounted in her eyes. It stayed there, growing, warm and
immensely wonderful. Suddenly, he was no longer alone. A flaring excitement gripped him, as if he'd been born again.

In one motion he stepped forward ... felt the instant pressure
of her hands. "You got ready mighty quick," he said, humbled.

"I was coming, anyhow," she answered, still waiting.

"And I know now I'd never let you come back alone," he said.
"That's the way it's going to be."

His arms swept up. Then, only then, did she move into them
completely.

THE END

www.ingramcontent.com/pod-product-compliance
Lightning Source LLC
Chambersburg PA
CBHW030810020726
47499CB00006B/1851